# OUT OF THE DAWN LIGHT

*A brand new medieval mystery from the
author of the 'Hawkenlye' series*

England, 1087. On her sister's wedding day,
Lassair meets an attractive and enigmatic
stranger who brings a breath of the fascinating outside world to her backwater Fenland
village. When he asks Lassair to use her
unique talents to help locate a mysterious
treasure she accepts, despite the dangers. But
this is no ordinary treasure hunt; the object of
the perilous search is five hundred years old
and has a terrifying power of its own...

*Alys Clare titles available from
Severn House Large Print*

THE PATHS OF THE AIR
THE JOYS OF MY LIFE

# OUT OF THE DAWN LIGHT

Alys Clare

**Severn House Large Print**
London & New York

This first large print edition published 2010
in Great Britain and the USA by
SEVERN HOUSE PUBLISHERS LTD of
9-15 High Street, Sutton, Surrey, SM1 1DF.
First world regular print edition published 2009 by
Severn House Publishers Ltd., London and New York.

British Library Cataloguing in Publication Data

Clare, Alys.
    Out of the dawn light.
    1. Great Britain--History--William II, Rufus, 1087-1100--
    Fiction. 2. East Anglia (England)--History--Fiction.
    3. Detective and mystery stories. 4. Large type books
    I. Title
    823.9'2-dc22

                                                          LP

    ISBN-13: 978-0-7278-7878-6

Severn House Publishers support The Forest Stewardship Council
[FSC], the leading international forest certification organisation. All
our titles that are printed on Greenpeace-approved FSC-certified paper
carry the FSC logo.

 **Mixed Sources**
Product group from well-managed
forests and other controlled sources
www.fsc.org Cert no. SA-COC-1565
© 1996 Forest Stewardship Council
FSC

Printed and bound in Great Britain by the
MPG Books Group, Bodmin, Cornwall.

For my niece and goddaughter
Ellie Harris
with much love

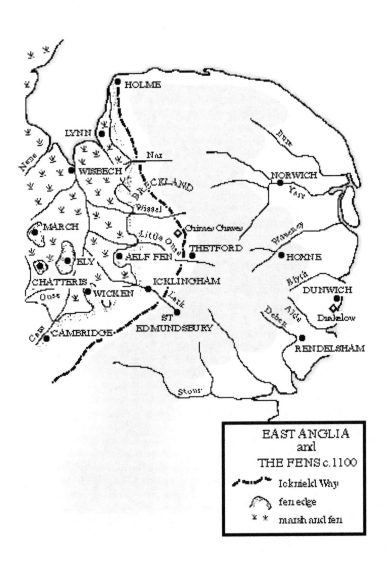

HOLME

LYNN

Nene

WISBECH

Nar

BRECKLAND

Wissel

NORWICH

Bure

Yare

MARCH

Little Ouse

Chimes Chimes

THETFORD

Waveney

ELY

AELF FEN

HOXNE

CHATTERIS

Ouse

WICKEN

ICKLINGHAM

Lark

Blyth

DUNWICH

Drakelow

Alde

Deben

Cam

CAMBRIDGE

ST
EDMUNDSBURY

RENDELSHAM

Stour

EAST ANGLIA
and
THE FENS c.1100

Icknield Way

fen edge

marsh and fen

# ONE

The news of William the Conqueror's death reached us when we were celebrating my sister's wedding. My mother sniffed, drew in her lips and remarked that it was scarcely likely to affect us in our lonely corner of England, one ruthless Norman king undoubtedly being very much like another.

My mother was wrong.

When I said we celebrated Goda's wedding, what I meant was we were rejoicing because we would no longer have to share a home with her. For all of us – my mother, my father, my granny, my dreamy sister Elfritha who wants to be a nun, my brother Haward who has a terrible stammer but the kindest eyes in the Fens, my little brother Squeak the trickster, the baby in his cradle and me – this long-awaited day was just too good to let anything spoil it, even the news that the mighty King William, called the Conqueror, had died far away somewhere in France.

Squeak had prepared a sackful of tricks to play on the bride but for once my parents were in agreement and they strictly forbade him to perform any sort of a tease until Goda was safely wed. Squeak pleaded and wheedled – he is very good at both – and begged to be allowed just one little jest. The grass snake slipped into the foot of Goda's bed, he suggested craftily, would be good because it would make sure she did not snore away half the morning and then get into a state because she did not have enough time to get herself ready. My mother heard him out impassively. Then she said, 'Do the trick if you must. But if you do, you will stay here in the house while the rest of us enjoy ourselves and I shall pack you off to bed early in the lean-to. You will miss not only the food and the drink but also the storytelling.'

You could see Squeak weighing up the options. Teasing Goda has been the mainstay of his existence for most of his eight years and he was clearly loath to give up this one last chance to make her lose her fearsome temper. But Squeak loves stories even more than he loves playing tricks. With a fierce scowl, he grabbed the grass snake – already slithering enquiringly towards the cot where Goda still slept and snored – and stuffed it back in the sack.

I felt sorry for Squeak. But as my mother pointed out, nobody wanted Goda throwing a tantrum, holding her breath till her lips went blue and then announcing that she'd changed her mind and wasn't going to get married after all. She had worked her way through this familiar sequence of events all too often in the preceding months. Now her wedding day had come and her family were united in their determination that nothing should prevent the marriage going ahead.

Goda has been a burden to me all the thirteen years of my life. Her only natural gift – a pair of breasts the size and shape of cabbages – never made up, in my mind, for her bad-tempered expression, her constant, grumbling self-pity, her laziness, her cruelty and her long tongue that could scold without ceasing for days on end. She has always disliked me. Once when we were playing in the water meadow she slipped and sat down in a cow-flop and I laughed and laughed, until she struggled up to display a large shit-brown stain on the back of her new tunic and boxed my ears so hard that, for all it was five years ago and more, I am still a little deaf in the left one.

Outsiders are wary of the Fens and tell fearsome tales of wicked spirits who infest our crude hovels, squeezing huge heads on skinny little necks through gaps in the walls, their fiery eyes glaring and their wide mouths full of horses' teeth gnashing and gaping at us. They are sarcastic about the people of the Fens, saying that we are primitive, scarcely above the animals in our squalid, desolate marshy homeland. However, not being the backward simpletons they take us for, we know better than to permit inbreeding. We do not need the Church's list of proscribed pairings. We know without being told that close relatives produce damaged

11

offspring. So, several times a year when we take our animals to and from the summer pastures in the water meadows that flood from autumn to spring, we take our young adults along to the markets that draw folk from all around and usually one thing leads to another and betrothals are soon announced.

Goda was now eighteen and, maturing early as she did, she had been on the marriage market for four years and went to twelve markets before someone asked for her. Cerdic had come with his father and his uncle from their home down in Icklingham and one look at Goda was enough. She was wearing her gown low-cut that day and had somehow contrived to push up her breasts so that their upper curves all but spilt out. Cerdic drooled as he stared at her, open-mouthed and wide-eyed, and he set about winning her hand there and then. Poor man, he thought he had to fight off competition from others – no doubt Goda told him so – and in a way I hoped he never found out that every man but him might have appreciated Goda's two unmistakable assets but soon discovered that they were vastly outweighed by everything else about her.

Well, it was too late now for him to turn back, or so we all fervently hoped. The morning went by in a flash – Goda reminded us constantly that this was her day and we all had to help her, so we were kept busy – and at last she was ready. There was no money for a new gown but she had restored last year's, carefully unpicking the seams and turning it so that the faded outside was now inside and the outside was so bright that it almost looked new. She was clever with her needle and she had done a good job, although all the time she stitched my poor father had to endure her constant whining voice complaining that it was so unfair that nobody – by which she meant my father – had managed to stump up for her and here she was, reduced to turning a worn old gown, and wasn't it just so sad for her? Then she would sniff and pretend to mop at her eyes. Father would usually get up from his place by the hearth and quietly leave the house.

Haward and Elfritha made a garland of flowers for Goda to wear in her freshly washed hair. Like me she has red hair, although hers is like carrots whereas mine, according to my father, is like new, untarnished copper. The garland was so pretty – Elfritha is very artistic – but, of course, it wasn't good enough for Goda, who complained that the pink bindweed flowers clashed with her hair, and made Haward unwind every one.

At last we got her to the church door, where Cerdic was waiting. The priest prompted their vows and with our own ears we heard Goda state that she took Cerdic there present to be her husband. We all gave quiet but heartfelt sighs of relief.

When the vows and the praying were finished, we trooped back to our house and everyone milled about in the yard outside waiting to see what they were going to be offered by way of refreshment. Their feet made clouds of dust, only nobody seemed to mind. It was September, quite late in the month, but the weather was warm and sunny. Helped by my sister and my little brother, I had done my best to make the house look festive – it's surprising what you can do with wild flowers, bunches of leaves and ears of dry corn – and there were several appreciative glances. At least, that's what I told myself.

The one person whom I had really hoped to impress with my artistry, however, did not notice the decorations at all. He had found a place on one end of a straw bale and there he sat down, hunched his shoulders and then gave every appearance of someone trying to pretend they're not there at all. Presently he was joined on his bale by a very old man whose spreading rump and widely splayed legs took up far more than his share. Serve you right! I said with silent venom to the youth beside him. Serve you right for sitting there looking as miserable as a wet summer and ignoring me all day!

The youth was called Sibert. He is quite a close neighbour of ours which, in a settlement as small as Aelf Fen, means that we see quite a lot of each other. He is fifteen, tall and slim, with fair hair that bleaches to white under the sun and light, bright eyes which sometimes look blue and sometimes green. I like him a lot and sometimes he likes me too.

Not today, though.

I tried one last time to catch his attention. By now my mother was sending out food and drink and I grabbed a mug of beer from the four that my father was holding in his large hands and, before he could protest and insist that elders must be served first, I dashed over and offered it to Sibert. Unfortunately, in my haste I tripped over my own feet and spilt most of the beer down my gown.

Sibert looked up and stared at me. If you laugh, I thought, feeling the hot blood flush up into my cheeks, I'll ... I'll...

He didn't laugh. With a faint sigh, as if I were nothing but a nuisance, he took the half-full mug and gave it to the old man beside him. Then he turned away.

I felt as if I'd been slapped. I would not let him see; I spun round and hurried away.

Why was he being like this? Had I offended him, or was it some private concern of his own that was making him so offhand with me? He had his troubles, I well knew. We all knew, in fact; as I said, it's a small village. Sibert lives with his widowed mother, Froya, and his uncle Hrype, who is Froya's brother. Hrype is a strange man – they whisper that he's a sorcerer, a spell-weaver, a cunning man even, although nobody dares say so to his face – and Froya is one of those women who looks as if she carries the weight of the world on her shoulders. Admittedly, she's had bad luck. Sibert's father Edmer, who must have been considerably older than his wife, fought against William the

15

Bastard (as he then was known) at Battle and later he joined the Ely uprising of 1071, where he took the wound that killed him. There was a price on his head, as was the case with all the rebels, and Froya brought him secretly to Aelf Fen to die. Sibert was a posthumous child and he never knew his father. I often give myself shudders of dread, trying to imagine Froya with Sibert swelling in her belly half-carrying and half-dragging a dying man through the lonely and treacherous terrain of the Fens...

So, Sibert has a hard life, but then so do we all. He's not the only one to have lost close kin in the vicious, desperate and terrible fighting against the Normans, nor to have suffered in the new and very different life that followed. People of our lowly status have no choice but to accept our lot and most of the time that amounts to being hungry, cold, worried about the health of our loved ones and our livestock and racked with uncertainty as to whether the food will last through the winter. We don't all go around with long faces, though.

As I hurried away from where Sibert sat sulking, I felt eyes on me and, turning, saw a sight that drove my unapproachable neighbour right out of my mind.

A man stood watching me. He was dark, the glossy hair cut in the new style, and his brown eyes were sort of crinkled round the corners, as if he laughed a lot. Although not tall like Sibert, he was broad-shouldered and had, as Goda might say, a manly figure. He was perhaps five

16

or six years older than me, clad in a flowing cloak of rich chestnut brown over a tunic of dark red and his boots shone as if he'd spent all morning buffing them up.

None of that would have impressed me, thought, except for two things: he was extremely handsome and he was smiling at me.

Boldly and unhesitatingly – I was still hurt by Sibert's rebuff – I went over to him. 'I'm Lassair,' I said. 'I'm the bride's sister. Have you had enough to eat?'

His smile widened. 'I haven't had anything yet.'

'Wait there!'

I hurried inside, elbowed about a dozen people out of the way – our little house seemed to be bursting at the seams – and found my mother with her sleeves rolled up and her forehead damp with sweat. The day was warm anyway but she'd been stoking the fire all morning and the hot coals were crammed with clay pots, many borrowed from our neighbours, in which the bread was baking. Now my mother was busy setting out bread, cheese, tartlets and spiced cakes. I grabbed what I could reach and before she could issue any orders – she'd had me in mind as serving lass for the elders – dashed out again.

I heard her yell, *'Lassair!'*

I ignored her.

My handsome man accepted my offering – a chunk of rather sweaty cheese and a piece of gingerbread – with what I thought was a pleasing grace. He chewed thoughtfully for some time – I realized I ought to have brought something to drink to help the food down – and then he said, 'Lassair. What a pretty name.'

Again I felt myself blush, although this time for a different reason. 'Thank you,' I mumbled.

'I am called Romain.'

Romain. Oh, it suited him, I thought wildly, although I had no idea why I should think so. I risked a quick glance up at his face; he might not have been all that tall but he was head and shoulders over me. He was smiling again.

The day had just improved and it was about to get even better. He was full of charm and soon I was chatting away about my life, my village and my neighbours, as easy with him as if I'd known him for years. He seemed to be fascinated by all that I said, glancing around at the company as I spoke of this person or that as if making sure he identified the right subject. Of course it couldn't last; my mother's voice called again, urgently this time – *LASSAIR!* – and I had to go.

He was kind enough to look regretful as I reluctantly left him and went inside the house.

Apart from getting rid of my elder sister and meeting *and talking to* a handsome man, the other wonderful thing about Goda's wedding day was that my granny came home. She can't stand Goda – she has quite a penetrating voice and could frequently be overheard commenting that Goda needed a good spanking – and, since

18

wedding nerves caused my sister's temper to go from bad to unendurable in the weeks leading up to her wedding, my granny moved out and went to live with her widowed daughter over in the Breckland. I was afraid she wouldn't come back. My aunt Alvela is my father's younger sister and she's a real sweetheart. She lost her equally nice husband about five years ago – I hate it that so often the good people die when, if the rest of us were given the choice, we'd rather it had been someone nobody liked – and she lives in a tiny cottage with her son, Morcar, who is a man of few words and also a flint-knapper. It must have been so peaceful there for my granny after the noisy, over-crowded conditions in our house and for some time I waited anxiously for the inevitable news that my grandmother had decided to stay with Alvela. It was a deeply depressing thought, for I love her dearly and would miss her so much.

My paternal grandmother's name is Cordeilla and she can trace her – our – ancestry right back to the ancient gods of Britain. She can reel off a vast list of names and if she is allowed to do so uninterrupted, it takes from noon to midwinter sunset. But she never is uninterrupted, for as soon as she gets to the most interesting names people always clamour to be told the old legends and tales of their miraculous deeds. There's Lir the Magical, Ordic the Blessed Child (the only son out of seven children to grow to adulthood), Alaimna the Lovely who married, bore a child and died all in a year,

Livilda the One-Legged Heiress, Sigbehrt the Mighty Oak who fell at Battle and – my favourites – Luanmaisi and her strange, sorceress daughter Lassair (my namesake), long ago lost in the wilderness to some unknown fate.

Cordeilla is a bard. One of the very best, and she is my grandmother!

I did not see my handsome man again and Sibert too seemed to have slunk away, although I was kept so busy that I did not get much of a chance to look for either of them. When everyone had had something to eat and drink – my father, well into his cups by now, kept muttering that we had to show Cerdic's kin that his new wife came from substantial people, whatever that meant – Goda and Cerdic were escorted by a very rowdy, bawdy crowd off to Cerdic's village, where their wedding bed was no doubt waiting for them. I didn't want to think about that and I got acutely embarrassed over the jokes, many of which made very rude references to Goda's breasts. Some of them went so far as to speak of her hips and belly and hint at the deep, dark cavern between her legs, which I thought was going much too far. I was actually very relieved that neither Romain nor Sibert could see me since I could feel that my face had gone red-hot and I had to keep making excuses to run round to the bucket by the well and splash my cheeks with cold water. Anyway, off went the newly-weds at last, and as the crowd ran off down the track after them, I ducked back into the yard and set about tidying up the mess. I had almost finished when I heard a voice say, 'Not gone with the revellers then, young Lassair?'

I knew that voice. I spun round and there was Granny, leaning on the gatepost with a smile like the midday sun on her round face. I was so pleased to see her, so relieved that she had come back to us, that I did not stop to think but rushed at her and wrapped my arms around her. Too forcefully – she gasped and instantly I loosened my hold.

'That's better!' she said with a grin. 'You may be only thirteen, child, but you're growing fast, you're well-made and strong as a boy.'

I basked in her praise. I like it when people say I'm like a boy. I wish I had been born a boy and I dread the day when my courses start and I have to start prinking and fussing and *behaving like a woman*, as my mother says. I suppose I'll grow great big breasts like Goda's too, although Elfritha is still quite flat-chested and she's more than a year older than me.

I was still hugging my granny. 'I thought you might not come back,' I whispered.

She patted my cheek. 'Well, I do like it over at Alvela's,' she said thoughtfully. 'Morcar's making good money now and they have meat at least once a week. They provided me with a feather pillow, too.'

'Oh.'

She must have picked up my dejection and she stopped teasing me. 'But this is my home, child,' she added softly. 'How many times must I tell you? I was born here in Aelf Fen and so were all my ancestors, right back into the ancient times. This is where I belong and I won't leave till I make my final journey.'

I did not want to think about that. 'We're having a feast tonight,' I said, taking her hand and leading her inside the house. 'Mother got together a bit of a bite for Cerdic's kin after the wedding but she's saving the best for later.' I looked at her out of the corner of my eye. 'We were hoping that you might accept the best place by the fire and tell us a story.'

She sighed. 'Oh, Lassair, child, I really don't think I'm up to it,' she said mournfully. 'I'm very tired – it's a long way from Breckland and the carter dropped me off at the fen edge, so I had to walk the last few miles – and I think I might turn in early.'

'But—' I began. But she was my grand-mother, my revered elder, and out of the respect that was her due I knew I was not allowed to protest at anything she decided. 'Very well,' I said meekly.

There was a moment's silence. Then Granny chuckled. 'Silly girl. Don't you know your old Granny at all? What, miss a feast, with my daughter-in-law's excellent grub and my son's mead? Oh, no. Dear Lassair, child, I'll be telling stories all night.'

Although I was sorry that Romain did not return and almost but not quite as sorry that

Sibert had evidently slumped off home, I had to admit that the evening was wonderful and it was lovely to be just the family. We had all held such high hopes of what life in our little house would be like after Goda had gone and if that first night were to prove typical, then not one of us was going to be disappointed.

Granny sat by the fire in the traditional story-teller's place. Even had she not been so uniquely gifted, the seat was hers because she was the eldest, although that had never stopped Goda from trying to usurp her. Not that Granny had let her. My father sat opposite, my mother beside him on the bench. He reached out and took her hand and she gave him a loving glance. He nodded and raised his bushy eyebrows, as if to say, this is good, isn't it, and she put up her free hand and gently touched his cheek. It looked as if my siblings and I were going to have to do our we've-all-suddenly-gone-deaf act later on.

Haward, Elfritha, Squeak and I sat on the floor in a semicircle round the hearth and Leir lay asleep in his cradle. Then Granny began.

She did not go on all night but, all the same, nobody could have complained. She recounted some of the favourite tales – Lassair the Sorceress, child of the Fire and the Air, had her moment, as she so often does when I am there to listen – and so did Sigbehrt the Mighty Oak. Granny's voice always breaks when she speaks of him and his great valour, how he risked and lost his own life defending his king and trying to save his kindred, but then he was her best-loved brother so she is entitled to a tear or two.

She finished with a tale that I had not heard before and at the time I did not know what had prompted her. 'Now it was our ancestor Aelfbryga who first led her people here to Aelf Fen,' she began in a sing-song, chanting tone that for some reason sent a delicious shiver through me. 'Her daughter Aelfburga took as her husband Aedelac the Spearsman, and they had many children. Their two eldest sons were Berie and Beofor, who were very close in age and fierce rivals from their cradle days. As they grew through boyhood to manhood, their violent quarrels reached such a pitch that the Elders drew together in council and, with the blessing of the boys' parents, made the difficult decision to send one of the young men away. A series of five tests of strength was devised and the victor was to be allowed to choose whether to stay at Aelf Fen or, with a bag of gold in his hand, be sent to make his fortune elsewhere. The boys were similar in strength and stature but Berie, the elder son, was cunning and clever and not above subterfuge. He it was who bested his brother by three challenges to two and he elected to remain at Aelf Fen, and out of his loins sprang a great line of wise women and cunning men, as well as herbalists, healers, and rune casters. The brothers and sisters of these rarefied beings, content with a more earthly lot, were farmers, fishermen, fowlers and shepherds, who husbanded the land in much the

24

same way as we their descendants still do today.'

'What happened to Beofor?' Haward demanded, eyes wide in the firelight and his stammer quite forgotten as he sat entranced.

Granny smiled down at him. 'He wandered for many moons and had many adventures, and finally he settled on the coast, in a very special place that called out to him in a magical voice that sounded like the deep murmuring roar of a dragon. There he took two wives and fathered many children and' – the transition was so smooth and so unexpected that I for one did not suspect a thing – 'that is quite enough for one night and now I am going to bed.'

We all went about our little rituals for the end of the day. Just before I lay down on my cot, I slipped outside to sniff the night air and look at the stars. I could not resist a quick glance up the track – it was just possible that Romain, perhaps unable to find a bed for the night, might return and beg our hospitality. But the path was empty, the settlement silent and still.

I sensed someone beside me.

'He won't come back here,' Granny said softly.

I was about to pretend I didn't know who she was talking about but there really was no point. 'Oh.' Then: 'How did you know?'

She took my hand and gave it a little shake. 'I saw you earlier. I was just coming back to the village and I stood watching you from over there.' She nodded towards where the path went through a stand of willows.

'Oh,' I said again.

She hesitated, then said, 'Don't waste your hopes on him, Lassair child.'

'But he's so handsome!' The foolish words had burst out of me before I could check them.

Granny sighed. 'Handsome he may be, but he is not a man to whom my beloved granddaughter should go giving her heart.'

'But—' I began.

She did not register my interruption. Dreamily, as if she spoke out of a trance, she murmured, 'Nor indeed should any young woman, for he walks in shadow.'

'In shadow?' I repeated, my words a terrified whisper. 'Wh–what sort of shadow, Granny?'

At last she turned to meet my eyes. 'The shadow of death.'

# TWO

The autumn went on and the days got steadily colder and shorter. We all worked hard, none more so than my poor father. The demands of our ruthless Norman overlord were diluted down through several tiers before they reached our lowly level, and indeed our local master,

Lord Gilbert de Caudebec, was not too hard on us, being a chubby, indolent man who relied heavily on his reeve – who was chilly, self-contained but basically fair – and tended to leave us alone. Nevertheless we were left in no doubt as to what our fate would be if the rigid rules were not obeyed. The few elders who could remember what life had been like before the Conquest spoke wistfully (and very quietly) of the good old days. Most of us had known nothing but the Norman rule and could only take their word for it.

My parents, however, succeeded in shutting out the cruel world every evening when my father closed and fastened the door. The seven of us (eight if you counted the baby) settled down to life without Goda as contentedly and as cheerfully as we had anticipated and, in due course, I forgot Granny's awful warning about my handsome man.

I did not, however, forget about *him*.

He had come to Goda and Cerdic's wedding, I reasoned, and so surely he must be acquainted with one or other family. He didn't know us, so therefore his attendance must have been on Cerdic's behalf. There was little point in asking around in the village to see if anyone knew more about him than I did, although this didn't stop me. The only person who even appeared to know who I was talking about was the old man who had shared Sibert's straw bale – he's my mother's friend Ella's father-in-law's brother – who muttered something to the effect that the 'shiny well-dressed little cockerel' had talked with him and Sibert for some time.

I found his attitude disrespectful so I went off in a huff and didn't ask him any more.

I saw little of Sibert. For some reason he seemed to be keeping himself to himself and when we did happen to meet, he did his best to pretend I wasn't there. *Well, I don't care,* I wanted to shout into his frowning face with its preoccupied expression, *these days it's a better man than you that I see when I close my eyes at night!*

In any case, life was becoming too full and too exciting for me to spare either man all that many moments. I was newly apprenticed to my fascinating aunt Edild, and Edild is a herbalist and a healer.

She lives in a little house on the fringes of Aelf Fen, by herself apart from a cat, some hens and a nanny goat and quite content with life. Her living space is even smaller than ours but, despite the lack of space, I really love it because Edild has a talent for making a place seem welcoming, homely and secure. Her low door opens into a little room whose beaten-earth floor is always immaculately swept, and the central hearth in its ring of evenly sized stones either contains a fire, burning merrily, or else is laid with logs and kindling and all ready to be lit. Edild sets bunches of herbs to smoulder in among the firewood and I would know her little house blindfold for its sweet scent; in addition to the burning bunches of herbs, the shelves in her house are laden with her remedies and she stores the ingredients in sacks kept in a special wooden box. She has fashioned a narrow platform to the rear of her house and up there, reached by a little ladder, she sleeps in a nest of regularly washed linen and soft woollen covers.

Her garden was always tidily kept and even now, as October gave way to November, you just knew there were bulbs and seeds safely tucked up beneath the smooth brown soil just waiting for spring to bring them back to life. Her reputation had spread beyond the settlement and not many days passed without someone tapping on her door to ask advice, on anything from piles to the suspicion that a neighbour was doing some ill-wishing. Strictly speaking, I was not meant to be privy to Edild's consultations with her visitors but the cottage was small and sometimes I just couldn't help overhearing.

It was Granny who had suggested my apprenticeship with my aunt. Granny, as well as knowing all about the ancestors, is very knowledgeable about the living, in particular her three sons (Ordic and Alwyn, fishermen and fowlers, and my father, whose name is Wymond and who is an eel catcher) and her two daughters Alvela (the one who's the widow of nice Matthew and mother to my taciturn cousin Morcar) and Edild. She knows their strengths and their weaknesses; she also has an uncanny way of appreciating who is likely to get on with whom. She knows, for example, that my uncle Ordic puts a deep, dark fear into my brother Haward so that his stutter gags him to silence when Ordic is about.

I often wonder if Granny suggested my vocation because she knows about the dowsing. Not that I knew it was called that, not till she spoke of it to me. As far as I was concerned, it was just something I could do, in the way other children could wiggle their ears, raise one eyebrow or turn a line of handsprings. My talent is being able to find things. I knew where my mother's pewter brooch was when it fell off her tunic into the woodpile. Out in the pasture I found a coin with a woman's face on it. I know where water is, not that there's any great skill in that when you live in the Fens, but actually I can find water sources that are hidden deep in the earth. All I have to do is focus my mind, hold out my hands and sort of feel the ground before me. When I approach the object of the search, whether it's water or a lost object, my palms begin to tingle and after that it's easy. Granny saw me mucking about with my friends one day and asked me quite sharply what I thought I was doing. When I told her, there was a sudden bright light in her eyes and she gave me a wide smile. Then she grabbed my hand and hurried me away to the hazel grove, where, after a bit of muttering to the tree and some funny movements with her hand, she broke off a little branch, stripped off the twigs and the leaves and then split one end. She pushed the split ends in my hands, turned me round, gave me a shove and said, 'Now, walk. Tell me if anything happens.'

Excited, strangely fearful, I walked. After a few moments the hazel rod started trembling. Then it bucked and spun in my hands, so violently that I dropped it. I turned to Granny, aghast.

I didn't know it, but she had made me walk across the line of a stream that runs deep underground beneath the path that leads out of the village.

I hurried to pick up the stick, holding it out to her in the full expectation of a scolding. But instead she came to stand beside me, gave me a hard hug and said, 'Child, you're a dowser.'

Even apart from my peculiar skill, Granny knew that Edild and I would get on and we do. We have similar colouring and we look alike – sometimes people take us for mother and daughter – and we laugh at the same things, finding amusement in the incongruous and sometimes, it has to be said, in the vulgar and the frivolous. Not that Edild ever shows this light-hearted, laughing side to those who come seeking her help; it is an indication of how well we understand one another that she has never had occasion to tell *me* not to appear in the presence of a patient with anything but a serious face and a studious, intent manner.

Since the late summer Edild had been in-structing me in an overview of her craft. I have learned about the main healing herbs and how to prepare and use them, the making of amulets and talismans and the composition and reciting of charms. She also explained to me the workings of the human body, male as well as female, which I must admit caused me to blush more than once despite the fact that, like all country children who grow up cheek by jowl with their family's animals, I first witnessed the mystery of procreation when I was still learning to walk. Still, animals mating is one thing; people, quite another. Now, as the winter days grew short and the darkness waxed, Edild began teaching me about the stars and their influence on everything – people, animals, plants – that lives under the great bowl of the sky.

'I have cast your web of destiny, Lassair,' she said to me one bright morning. 'We shall use the knowledge that it provides as a basis for our discussion on how the planets guard us, guide us and, indeed, make us what we are.' I like that about Edild; even when the lesson consisted of her talking and me silently listening, she still calls it a discussion. 'You are air and fire,' she went on, 'and you live in your mind and not your body. You are restless, drawing on a great well of energy, and in time you will perceive and penetrate the web that connects all of life. You will brim over with creativity and new ideas and you will be brave, uncompromising and direct, yet possess the ability to conceal your true self with a plausible false skin.' Yes, that bit sounded like me; I had always been a good liar. 'You are essentially a private person, and your friends and your lovers' – I blushed violently – 'will sense that they are never truly close to you. You must learn to distinguish between independence, which is admirable, especially in a woman, and its darker face, isolation.'

'But I'm not isolated!' I protested. I felt the urgent need to lighten the mood. 'I live in a tiny cottage with seven other people!'

Edild regarded me, her green eyes solemn. Then, ignoring my foolish comment and my nervous little laugh, she went on, 'At the time of your birth, the Sun, the Moon and the planets were all in signs of air and fire. You are water-lacking, so that the turmoil of emotions experienced by others will be incomprehensible to you, and you are also earth-lacking, and will thus have little sense of being grounded firmly in the good Earth.'

I was never going to achieve closeness with people, even my lovers. I would never understand emotion, presumably not even my own. Oh, it sounded bitter. My dismay must have shown in my face for Edild reached out and took my hand, squeezing it in her own.

'Look,' she said brightly after a moment. 'Look at your chart, Lassair.' She spread out a large square of vellum, beautifully marked with a big circle divided into segments and dotted with intriguing little signs and symbols. 'This is the moment of your birth, in the early pre-dawn light of the twentieth of June, in the year 1074, and this is where the planets were positioned.' I followed the long finger with its short, clean nail as she pointed. There were the Sun, the Moon, Mercury, Venus, Mars, Jupiter and Saturn, marked on my web of destiny as if for that instant of my birth, their sole purpose had been to make me what I was. It was an awesome thought.

Something struck me; I heard Granny's voice, speaking of another Lassair. 'My namesake was a child of the fire and the air,' I said cautiously. 'It's in Granny's story.'

Edild smiled. 'I thought you would remember. Yes, Lassair's web was very similar to yours – she too had Mercury placed in his own house of Gemini, the planet of love in the same air sign and the warrior god in Aries, most warlike sign of all.'

She fell silent, frowning as if in thought. Perhaps she was thinking, as I was, of the mysterious ancestress who had borne my name before me and I knew enough about her to understand that she cannot have had an easy life, to say the least. I hesitated, and then said in a small voice, 'Will I be a mystery too? Will I disappear into the mist one day and nobody will know what's happened to me?'

Edild have me a hug. 'I doubt it,' she said robustly. 'You usually chatter so much that we're left in no doubt whatsoever where you are and what you're up to. Now, come and look at my model of the planets and I'll tell you which of them influence which healing herbs and show you how to work out the best time for planting and harvesting.'

34

* * *

Later that day, while Edild was closeted with a young woman suffering from something that necessitated privacy while she removed her undergarments, I crept back to have another look at my fascinating but alarming web of destiny. My head was full of the morning's lesson and I now knew what some of the symbols meant. There was the Sun, as Edild had said, in the sign of Gemini at the moment of my birth; there was the Moon, in distant, mysterious Aquarius; I had believed Aquarius the Water-Carrier to be a water sign (it seemed logical) until Edild put me right and said he was an air sign. There were Mercury and Venus, both also in Gemini; there were Mars, Jupiter and Saturn, in the fire signs of Aries and Sagittarius. All placed just as Edild had said.

And, apparently, very similar to their positions in the chart of Lassair the Sorceress, whose fate we do not know but who was strongly believed to be half elfish...

*Oh!*

I rolled up the chart and retied its ribbon. I did not want to know any more.

The Winter Solstice was upon us and, as my family has always done, we celebrated with a meal eaten as the light faded. As well as my immediate family, my uncle Alwyn, my aunts Edild and Alvela and my cousin Morcar were also there, which meant it was a crush but nobody minded. When we were all seated, my father blew out the lamp and we all sat in the darkness. Out of the silence came Granny's voice, intoning that tonight was the longest night of the year and that tomorrow the dark began to give way to the light. This was the signal; my father struck a spark with his flint and lit a precious stump of candle, saved for this purpose, and from that one light we each lit little tallow lamps of our own until the flames shone out in a circle that illuminated our faces and showed that all of us were smiling.

It might be midwinter still, with many cold, hard days of frozen ground and driving rain ahead, but now that the Solstice was here, we knew that the year had turned and the Sun was coming back. On that frosty night, with the stars shining brilliantly in the sky, that was something to smile about.

A couple of months after Christmas, Goda sent word. She was pregnant, she was perpetually sick, her entire body had swollen up so that she could barely move and she needed me to go and look after her.

I protested as violently as I could, bringing to bear every argument from the necessity to continue my instruction with Edild to the well-known fact that Goda didn't like me and it couldn't possibly be good for a pregnant woman to be in the perpetual company of someone who was so far from being a kindred spirit. Nothing made a jot of difference. Goda had sent for me and I must do as my parents commanded and go to her.

In desperation I turned to Granny. Whatever anyone else said, if Granny decreed I did not have to go – if, for instance, she insisted that it was far more important for me to get on with my studies than to tend my ingrate of a sister – then I would be saved.

But Granny took me aside, put her thin arms round me in a sudden intense hug and said quietly, 'It'll be a sore trial and you'll hate it. But you must go, child.'

I had tears in my eyes and angrily I brushed them away. I made it a rule never to let anything Goda did make me cry, or at least not when anyone was watching. *'Why?'* I wailed. To my shame I sounded like a three-year-old whining against sense and reason for its own way.

Granny had broken away and now she gave me a little shake. She muttered something – it sounded like *wait and see*, but that did not seem to make any sense – and then she said brusquely, 'We all have to do things we don't like and it won't be for ever.'

Then she turned aside and hurried away.

Even in the extremity of my despair, I did not suggest that Elfritha go in my place. Elfritha is a year and four months older than I am, as I have already said, and she wants to be a nun. She is also gentle, impractical – when she's in the convent they'll have to watch her to make sure she doesn't spill swill buckets and absent-mindedly tear her clothing on brambles like she's always doing with us because I'm sure people vowed to poverty aren't allowed to be wasteful – and inclined to daydream. All of which qualities drive Goda to distraction so that she has always been even rougher with poor Elfritha than with me. Besides the fact that nobody in their right mind would ask Elfritha to look after a tetchy and uncomfortable pregnant woman, I love my second-eldest sister far too much to make her suffer as she undoubtedly would in Goda's household.

Elfritha may be dreamy and unworldly but she is not lacking in intelligence. She must have realized that I was being forced to take on an unpleasant task because she wasn't suited to it, and just before I left for Icklingham and my new (and I hoped purely temporary) abode, she sought me out and gave me a present.

'What is it?' I asked. She had wrapped it in a piece of old linen and bound it with twine so I couldn't tell, although whatever it was felt soft and squidgy.

She smiled shyly. 'It's something to remind you of home and a sister who loves you.' No possibility that I would have one of *those* where I was going, I thought. 'Open it when you get there,' Elfritha added quickly as I went to pull at the twine. 'And' – she leant in very close and spoke right into my ear – '*thank you.*'

I looked at her quickly and I saw that she had tears in her eyes.

Would they miss me? I wondered as I trudged

the six miles from Aelf Fen to Icklingham on a sharp, cold morning a week later. My parents would, I supposed, even if only as another pair of hands to get through the extraordinary amount of work there was to do each day. I was sure my brothers and sister would too, since, with Goda gone and no longer a selfish, bossy and malicious presence in our lives, we seemed to appreciate each other all the more. Granny and Edild would miss me, of course.

Anyone else?

I was thinking, naturally, of Sibert. Since the wedding, my memories of and crush on Romain had faded considerably and once again it was Sibert whom I imagined walking, talking and sometimes fighting by my side as I slid into sleep at night. Well, it was understandable, Sibert being on hand, as it were, and Romain long gone. Not that I had in truth seen very much of Sibert during the autumn and winter. Once I had come across him in earnest conversation with Granny, although what they were talking about I never discovered since they clammed up as soon as they saw me and neither would say a word. Once he had fallen into step with me as I returned from checking on the sheep in their outhouse and we exchanged a few rather stiff comments. That was about it but all the same I wished, as I hunched up my pack and tried to blow warmth into my cold hands, that there had been the occasion to say goodbye.

Perhaps he would not even realize that I

had gone.

Depressed, I put my head down, struggled against the wind – just to add to my misery, it was blowing hard out of the east, almost exactly the direction in which I was walking – and plodded on. All too soon, the huddle of small cottages, pens and outbuildings that was Icklingham came into sight.

I strode up to Goda's door – they had made quite sure I knew where to go – knocked and waited. As if she were deliberately making me stand out there in the cold, perhaps to indicate right from the outset just who was in charge around here, it was some moments before she answered. Then I heard her voice, its timbre rasping, its tone discontented and complaining.

'Don't loiter out there all day!' called my sister. 'I've just been sick, I'm shivering and I need a hot drink, oh, and you'd better clear up the mess. I missed the pot.'

My first two orders, before I'd even got through the door. It was without doubt a taste of things to come. With a secret sigh, I went in.

You could be forgiven for thinking that a woman not quite six months married to the man of her choice, in a decent enough little house and with a baby on the way, might have been happy; ecstatic, even. You don't know my sister. It was hard to imagine why on earth she'd wanted to marry Cerdic, since now that she was his wife she spent all her time telling him how useless he was and how she'd been far better off at home. I couldn't see how she reasoned that out. At home she had been made to do at least some of her share of the work (my mother can be a tough woman) and she had shared her cot and her tiny amount of privacy with Elfritha. Cerdic's house might have consisted of just one small room (I slept in the lean-to with the placid and gentle-mannered family cow, an arrangement I would have chosen even had there been room for me in the house), but he was a skilled carpenter and had made it soundly so that it was wind-proof and, when the fire in the central hearth was well alight, really quite snug. He had built a low cot up against one wall and on it he and Goda had the luxury of two wool blankets, made for them by Cerdic's mother, as well as a mattress stuffed with new straw. There was even a curtain fixed up to draw across in front of the bed if Goda so wished. Cerdic was not a poor man; a good carpenter always finds work. Like everyone else, he had to spend a part of each week working for the lord but he was eager and had an honest face, two qualities that ensured a regular stream of requests for his services.

Whatever he did, he was never going to be good enough for my sister and, poor man, he must have realized it. I wondered, with pity in my heart, just how soon after the wedding she had revealed her true self; how soon the now even more massive breasts had begun to pale in significance in the face of the bad temper, the selfishness, the foul mouth and the unerring

41

aim with a wooden spoon or, in really bad moments, a clog. When I arrived, I noticed that Cerdic had a bruise on his left temple and I had a pretty good idea how he'd come by it.

When out in my lean-to I had unwrapped Elfritha's present, I discovered that she'd woven for me a beautifully soft shawl of lamb's wool, dyed in the lovely, subtle shades of green that she knows are my favourites. I was very glad that I had opened it in private, for Goda would have taken one look and demanded to be given it since, as she so often repeated, she was the pregnant one, she was the one suffering all this discomfort and misery and she was the one who needed spoiling. I vowed to make sure she never found out about my shawl. If this meant I could only snuggle into it in the lean-to, with no one but the friendly cow to appreciate how its colours made my eyes bright, it was a price worth paying.

I studied Goda subtly, trying to work out how far along she was in her pregnancy. When I had asked when the baby was due she was at first vague and then, when I protested that surely she must have some idea, violent. 'Mind your own business!' she screamed, only there was another word between *own* and *business*, one that I would have been thrashed for using. I could have pointed out that, since I had to look after her during her pregnancy, it was my business, but the bruise on Cerdic's temple was still in evidence and I kept my mouth shut.

But I reckoned that, armed as I was with

Edild's instruction in the mystery of how women have babies, I could work it out for myself. The vastly swollen breasts and the sickness were, I believed, symptoms of the first three months, but I thought Goda was further along than that. Edild had demonstrated, using little drawings, how the baby in the womb gradually pushes upwards, so that a good midwife could judge from the height of the bulge how many months had passed since conception. I had to help my sister with her weekly wash – she complained, among many other things, that her condition caused her to sweat copiously – and, since she appeared to have left all modesty far behind her, she was in the habit of flinging off her clothes, lying back and ordering me to sponge her all over. Thus I was able not only to look at the big bump of baby but also run my hand over it and I calculated that she could be as much as six months pregnant.

It was now the end of March and she had wed Cerdic in late September. This baby must have been conceived virtually on their wedding night.

If not before.

I did not waste much time on the fact that my sister might have anticipated her wedding vows. If she had, she was far from being the only one. Possibly she had feared a last-minute defection in her husband-to-be, and letting him make love to her – perhaps encouraging him to – had been a way of ensuring he made an honest woman of her. Who knew? Who cared? No –

what concerned me was when I might expect to be released from her household. If I was right and she was six months gone, my deliverance could come as early as June or the beginning of July. I could be home – and back at my lessons with Edild – soon after midsummer, with the rest of that bright, happy, outdoor season still ahead.

It was a lovely, heartening thought and it kept me going through the spring and early summer as inevitably, as Goda grew bigger, more cumbersome and more uncomfortable, matters went from bad to worse.

# THREE

Romain de la Flèche's well-dressed appearance, level gaze and ready smile gave the impression that he was an amiable young man with plenty of money and not a great deal to concern him beyond the cut of his cloak and keeping a shine on his boots. The impression, however, was, like much about Romain, carefully calculated. He maintained it because it was in his own best interests to disguise his true personality and the pressing concern that drove him, relentlessly now, and held him so tightly in its grasp.

As the days lengthened and it seemed that at long last spring was turning to summer, he watched in impotent rage and growing fear as the situation he most dreaded – and whose coming to pass he had at first only entertained in the most anxious of sleepless nights – unfolded before him. There was nothing he could do. His protests, had he dared to express them, would at best have been ignored and at worst earned him a hard cuff round the ear. He was eighteen now. It was not fair that he was still treated like a wayward child.

There *was* a way in which he might escape the potentially fateful consequences of what was inevitably going to happen. By pure chance he had learned something amazing. It was so amazing that, when as so often happened it slipped quietly into his mind, he found himself wondering if he was investing far too much hope on what must surely be no more than an old tale whispered in the dark. He forced himself to ignore his misgivings. There was, when all said and done, nothing else...

He had been so excited when he first heard about the amazing thing. To begin with, it had stirred his blood simply for its own sake and it was only later, when he realized that the bright future he had envisioned for himself was going to be blasted apart, that it had occurred to him how he might use his discovery to his own advantage.

He needed help, for if this thing in truth had substance and was not just a wonderful myth, he had to track it down. Disguising the growing urgency of his need with his usual charming smile and the mild, slightly puzzled manner which, as he well knew, made people believe he was slow-witted if not actually simple, he had asked some very careful questions. And, eventually, he found out where he must go and to whom he must speak.

He had made the journey – of some fifty miles across East Anglia, over farm land, scrubland and, on occasion, through the wild, desolate and dangerous parts of the region – the previous September. He had been at pains not to be observed, travelling under cover of darkness. For one thing, he had not sought permission for his pilgrimage. He could not have done, for when the inevitable questions as to the purpose of his journey had been asked he would have had no creditable answer other than the truthful one, and that was secret. For another thing, the Conqueror had just died and the whole country was uneasy. It was really no time to go off on a clandestine mission but, with the king's death, time was running out and he no longer had a choice.

As he trudged through the darkness, thankful that at least the weather appeared to be on his side, he tried to take his mind off his many anxieties by speculating on what sort of a king the Conqueror's son would be.

Normandy had gone to the eldest brother, Robert, and the second, Richard, was dead, killed while hunting in the New Forest. Henry, the fourth son, had, or so they said, been left a huge sum of money. With some difficulty, Romain turned his mind from the thrilling, tantalizing prospect of what he could have done with a huge sum of money. Life was so *unfair*...

England had been left to William, the third son.

So, William was to be king and not Robert. Well, it was what Romain had been led to expect. He moved in circles where such matters were a frequent topic of conversation and he was well aware that the Conqueror's relationship with his plump and lazy eldest son had been tempestuous. The king had used a variety of nicknames for the boy, his favourites being Short-Boots and Fat-Legs, and this disparaging attitude had, as Robert frequently complained, robbed him of the respect that he felt was his due. His resentment of his powerful parent broke out into open rebellion. On one occasion bitter fighting ensued, in the course of which Robert personally inflicted a wound on the great Conqueror's hand. Father and son were later reconciled but it seemed unlikely that, given his ruthless nature, the king either forgot or forgave. William the Conqueror had died from an injury sustained as he fought the French in the Vexin, that troubled and perpetually strife-torn area between Normandy and neighbouring France to the south-east. On his deathbed he dictated the necessary letter that nominated his namesake as his heir and, together with the royal seal, dispatched it to England.

The dying king had probably hoped that his carefully thought-out solution – Normandy to the first-born, England to the younger brother – would be appreciated as fair and therefore accepted meekly by all concerned. He ought to have known better. Apart from the main protagonists, every other Norman lord with a plot to call his own seemed to have a loud and forceful opinion. Particularly vociferous were that multitude of men whose fathers had fought with the Conqueror in 1066 and been awarded manors in the newly acquired kingdom as their reward. Since to a man they already possessed estates in Normandy, they now must decide whether to put their wealth and strength at the disposal of Duke Robert, their Norman overlord, or King William, their English one.

That the two sons of the Conqueror would sooner or later come to blows did not seem to be in any doubt at all.

Romain's musings on the perils that the brand-new reign would bring were brought to a halt; it was dawn, he had just rounded a bend in the track and a small settlement rose up out of the mists ahead of him. If he had remembered the directions correctly, it must be Aelf Fen.

He crept into a stand of willows, made himself a comfortable nest in the dry grass and, wrapping his cloak around him, settled down to sleep.

* * *

He was woken much later by the sound of laughter and excited chatter. Of all things, the village appeared to be celebrating a wedding. At first dismayed, he quickly realized that there could be no better cover for a stranger on a secret mission. Everyone would be too busy enjoying themselves to pay him much mind and if relatives from the bride's or the groom's family did not know who he was – which of course they wouldn't – they would simply assume that he was connected with the other side.

He spruced himself up, buffed up his boots and rubbed the mud from the hem of his cloak. He ran a nervous hand over his hair and then, waiting while a gaggle of laughing girls hurried past his hiding place, slipped out behind them and followed them into the village.

Then it was just a matter of listening carefully until he heard the name of the person he had come to find. People smiled at him. A skinny girl with copper-coloured hair brought him something to eat. The cheese was tasteless and rather acid, the sweet cake bland and dry. They were poor people here, he thought. The girl insisted on talking to him and, impatient to get away from her and set about running down his quarry, he barely listened, instead beaming at her and nodding, occasionally throwing in an 'Is that so?' and a 'How very interesting!' But then she began telling him about her fellow villagers and, disguising his sudden interest behind his wide, vacant smile, he gave her his full attention. Quite soon she identified the person he had come to find and, after that, it was easy.

April came and Easter was celebrated. Romain had at long last persuaded his reluctant accomplice to join him in the awesome task ahead, although he was well aware that he would have to work hard to prevent the younger man from changing his mind. But events in the wider world had already begun on their inevitable progress to the disaster he saw ahead. Now his fellow conspirator would surely have to admit that Romain's grim predictions had been accurate.

The rebellion broke out just after Easter. It was rumoured that the great lords who celebrated the feast with the king had put the final details to their plotting and planning while they were under his very roof. The king's half-brother Odo, Bishop of Bayeux, was the instigator; loyal adviser to Duke Robert of Normandy, he had hurried across the Channel on William's accession hoping to win the same influential position in England that he enjoyed with Duke Robert in Normandy. But William had already appointed his chief adviser. The ambitious and devious Odo, however, was ever power-hungry. He was once more Earl of Kent, the honour having been awarded and later withdrawn by the Conqueror and reinstated by the new king, but it seemed that was not enough. If his status in England were to improve, it was going to have to be at Duke

Robert's side, where his position was already assured. So the way ahead was clear: Odo would help Duke Robert add England to the sum of his possessions and he, as Robert's most trusted man, would thereby gain his reward.

Odo first appealed to the lords who held lands in both England and Normandy. Romain knew all about them. Hidden and forgotten in his corner of the great hall, he had listened avidly as Odo's representative set out on his master's behalf the situation that the lords now faced. If they supported King William and he lost, then Duke Robert would seize their Normandy estates. If King William defeated Duke Robert, their English lands would be forfeit. In summary, the man concluded after what seemed to Romain hours of talk, it amounted to a simple question: would you prefer to lose your Normandy estates or your English ones?

Another question rose urgently in Romain's mind, which was: who is going to win?

The men whose lengthy conversation he was listening to so carefully did not discuss that. Was this because Duke Robert's victory was certain? If so, Romain thought, then the assumption that Robert would easily overcome William was surely wishful thinking. The lords might well mutter that Robert was a preferable monarch to the fiery and obstinate William, but that must be because he was known to be easy-going and pliable. What important lord with his eyes set on advancement would not prefer a sociable, jovial, approachable and malleable king?

Persevering with his espionage, Romain managed to follow the progress of the rebellion. He had always had the sense that he knew very well what was going to happen; that he had foreseen the catastrophe that would overtake him and his kin. Experiencing the painfully diverse emotions of pride at having been right and terror at what he saw happening, he had just one tiny sliver of hope. His plan, his careful, deeply secret plan...

The rebellion raged on. Across the southern half of England the fighting flared up as, in Duke Robert's name, Odo's rebels attacked the estates of the king and those loyal to him. Bristol. Bath. Hereford. Shropshire. Leicester. The names of towns and counties of which Romain knew little or nothing cropped up in the anxious discussions that he overheard. Pevensey. Rochester, Odo's own stronghold. And then, all at once terrifyingly close, Norwich.

From his castle in the city, the great lord Roger Bigod and his followers had set out to loot and burn right across East Anglia, concentrating their might on the royal lands. Once destroyed, these lands could produce nothing to help the king's cause and, with the battle won, they would quietly pass into the rebels' hands. The moment of truth was upon them and Romain could do nothing but watch helplessly as the rebel lords of the region gathered up their forces, locked up their estates and marched off to join Lord Roger.

Romain made quite sure that he did not go with them.

The rebellion did not go on for long; by mid-summer it was all over. It had become clear that the focus of the fighting would be Kent, and King William led his army against Tonbridge Castle. He sent out an appeal to Englishmen, making rash and exciting promises to entice them into supporting him, and the force thus amassed won the day. The king then marched on Rochester where, rumour said, the garrison had been greatly strengthened by the arrival of a contingent of soldiers sent over by Duke Robert from Normandy. The rumours were wrong; the Englishmen guarding the coast had bravely faced up to the would-be invaders and the majority had been captured or drowned.

Nevertheless, Rochester held out. Desperate for news, the anxiety almost more than he could bear, Romain waited. Could he have been wrong? Would Odo prevail after all, ushering in a new monarch and a different order? *Please, please let it happen!* Romain prayed as hard as he knew how for a last-minute victory.

It did not come. As the June weather grew hotter, besieged and overcrowded Rochester succumbed to the heat, the rubbish, the dead and the swarms of eager flies. Clean water and wholesome food became mere memories and, inevitably, sickness spread. It was said that a man could not cram a morsel of meat into his hungry mouth unless someone else was on hand to swat the flies away.

Rochester surrendered. The rebellion had failed.

Without waiting to hear more, Romain swung into action.

# FOUR

I ought to have realized that Goda would become steadily more intolerable as her pregnancy went on. She was my sister after all and I'd known her my entire life. Had she ever shown the tiniest amount of courage in adversity? Had she just once endured discomfort of any kind with a saintly silence and a brave little smile on her lips? Of course she hadn't. She was Goda and she always found something or someone to blame for her own suffering, even when that suffering had been brought about by nobody other than herself.

Well, she was suffering now because, either before or immediately after she married Cerdic, on at least one occasion she had made love with him. Unless he had taken her by force – unlikely because she's a well-muscled woman with a fierce temper and a heavy right fist and he's a gentle sort of a man – then she must have wanted the lovemaking and, not being an idiot, known that it could lead to conception. So, she'd brought it on herself. Nevertheless, she had to blame someone and that someone was me.

She made a hell of my life such as I had never experienced before (and not since, either; I don't make mistakes like letting myself be used by people such as my sister anymore). The odd thing was that if just for a moment she'd stopped being so horrible to me, my sympathy would have come rushing back and I'd have looked after her willingly. You see, she really was in a bad way. As she entered the last couple of months of her pregnancy, she swelled up like a leather bag slowly and steadily being filled with water. The skin of her vast belly stretched and something in its structure must have broken, for long, dark-red lines began to snake across her white flesh as if there was something living in there. Well, of course there was – a baby, and a pretty large one at that – but that's not what I mean. Goda has always been lazy and now that she had got so big she barely left her seat by the hearth. As June came, often she would not even get out of bed.

She was pale and, despite my ministrations with the wash cloth and the bowl of water, she was dirty and she stank. Her filthy hair was tangled and I could not get the comb through it, or rather, I *could* but she pinched my arm so viciously when I pulled at the tangles that I stopped trying.

Her favourite punishment was to box my ears.

I usually tried to dodge so that she hit the left one, which she had already damaged. That way I might emerge from my time with her still with one good ear.

I don't know what poor Cerdic made of it, although I can make an accurate guess. He was, as I've said, a good worker and there was always plenty for him to do. Goda was demanding, forever wanting to be brought something new for her house or some little personal present, and in a way that made it easier for him because to acquire the things she wanted he had to earn more money. She was quite capable of working that out for herself and so could not complain if her husband was out far more often than he was in. As far as she knew, he was off on a job somewhere.

If I knew different – and I had my ways of keeping an eye on what was happening around me – then I kept it to myself. Goda did not really deserve a man like Cerdic and in her present state she offered no inducement whatsoever for him to come home in the evening until after she was in her bed and snoring (with advanced pregnancy she had to sleep on her back and made a noise like a boar being throttled). No, I didn't blame Cerdic for avoiding his wife. I only envied him from the bottom of my heart because that option was not available for me.

I fought self-pity all the time, and never more so than when Midsummer's Eve was approaching. I remembered how, earlier in the year, I had calculated that the baby could have been born round about now and I would be released from my servitude with my sister and sent home to Aelf Fen. But nothing happened, other than that Goda tried to punch my face when I asked if I might go out to join the people of Icklingham in their midsummer celebrations.

I skipped out of the way and her angry, frustrated fist swung on empty air. And I went out anyway. As part of my instruction with Edild she had shown me how to brew up a mild sedative and it was now summer, a time when the plants, fresh, green and vibrant with life, are at their most potent. Perhaps I ought to have taken this into account more than I did, for the drink that I carefully prepared and fed to my red-faced, sweaty and heaving sister knocked her out as if she'd been poleaxed. For quite a long time I stood there staring down at her, all sorts of questions running through my mind. I'd used cowslips as my main ingredient but I'd added dill and just a tiny amount of hemlock, which Edild had frequently warned me was poisonous. And what about the incantation I had murmured as I worked? I thought I'd remembered the words correctly and in the right order, but I could have made a mistake ... But it was all right, Goda was still breathing, and I muttered a prayer of gratitude. I might not like her but I've never actually wanted to *kill* her, especially when she carried an innocent new life inside her.

It was twilight on Midsummer's Eve. Goda

was sound asleep and I had sufficient faith in my skills to know that she was very unlikely to wake before morning. Cerdic had not yet returned; I guessed he had gone straight from his work to his regular retreat in his cousin's house on the other side of the village, where he'd probably stay till he thought it was safe to come home.

I slipped into the lean-to and hastily set about making myself as neat and tidy as time and circumstance allowed. I took off my gown and beat it hard with the flat of my hand until the dust came out of it in clouds. The woven fabric was soft and floppy with long wear and it had gone into holes in various places, but I was deft with a needle and the darns were all but invisible unless you looked really closely. My under-tunic was only two days on and still looked crisp and fresh where it showed in the neck of my gown. I fastened the laces down the sides of my gown, pulling them tight in an attempt to give myself some shape. I unwound my hair from its plait and brushed and brushed it till its smooth texture under my hand suggested it might be shining. Then I pinched my cheeks to put some colour in them, took Elfritha's beautiful shawl from its hiding place under my bed and, having arranged it decoratively around my shoulders, went out into the softly falling darkness.

Midsummer is my favourite festival of all. Granny says I'm a midsummer person, born on the eve of the solstice, and that's why I have an affinity with the season. I'm not entirely sure what she means but I think I agree. I wished, as I hurried through the gathering darkness, that I was home in Aelf Fen, because in our village we certainly know how to celebrate the Sun's position high above us in the sky and the presence of the light in all its glory. But I wasn't. I was in Icklingham, among people I hadn't even known four months ago.

I need not have worried. They might not know me very well either but they knew who I was and what I was doing in their village. From the kindness and sympathy I received in such full measure that lovely night, I gathered the impression that they didn't think much of my sister, and that was putting it mildly.

They had prepared a huge bonfire in a clearing on the edge of the village and they lit it as the first stars appeared in the sky. The clearing had been decorated with foliage, chiefly branches of oak since this was the supreme night of the Oak King and tomorrow he must begin to lose way before the coming of the dark and the Holly King, ruler of the winter solstice. For that reason, midsummer is always tinged with sadness for me, since from then on the light fades.

The sadness, however, was in abeyance for the moment. It was so wonderful to be out of Goda's house and away from the sight, smell and even the sound of her – if she was awake she was nagging and sniping at me; if asleep, she snored and farted – that I would have enjoyed even the most modest celebration. There was nothing modest about Icklingham's festivities, however. Soon I had a mug of ale in my hand, a garland of flowers on my head and a boy was shouting above the cheerful laughing, singing voices that the music would soon begin and who was going to dance with him?

I did. I danced with him, with several others – boys, girls, women, men – and then with the first boy again. He was spinning me round in a vigorous circle and I was just thinking that he wasn't bad looking if you ignored the pimples on his forehead and the distinct lack of a chin when someone broke us apart, said, 'My turn, I think,' and I looked up into the handsome, smiling face of Romain.

I stared at him with my mouth open. His hair shone just as I remembered and his expensive garments, tonight covered by a worn cloak of indeterminate colour, stood out in this company of the lowly like a ruby on a midden.

'You don't live here!' I gasped, totally lost for any more intelligent comment.

'No,' he agreed, dancing along with the rest, his hand tightly clutching mine and pumping it up and down as if he were drawing water. 'But I'm sure you're glad to see me, all the same!'

'I am, oh, I am!' I agreed fervently. 'I've been looking after my sister – you know, the one whose wedding you came to.'

'Oh – er, yes.'

Of course, I reminded myself, he didn't know Goda, he was from Cerdic's side. He was a friend of my brother-in-law, which, naturally, must be why he was here now. This put me in an awkward position. I hadn't seen Cerdic at the feast and, as I've said, I had a pretty good idea where he was. But if I told Romain, for one thing it might reveal more about the state of my sister's marriage than ought to be revealed to an outsider and for another, Romain might well go off to find Cerdic and therefore stop dancing with me.

I said nothing.

We danced on – he was very good, light on his feet and as practised in the steps of the old dances as any of the villagers – and presently I noticed that he had guided me to the edge of the clearing where the surrounding trees cast deep shadows.

Was this deliberate? Did he want to be alone with me in the darkness? Did he want to *kiss* me?

The thought was both thrilling and alarming. Nobody had kissed me *like that* before. I was young for my age – all my female relatives kept saying so – and my body was boyishly straight. The sensible part of my mind had already worked out that Romain must have something other than sex in mind when abruptly he stopped dancing, dragged me to a halt beside him and, ducking down beneath the trees, whispered, 'There's someone else here who wants to see you.'

My sweet and short-lived little fantasy of collapsing into Romain's strong and manly arms as his firm mouth found mine gave a wave of its flirtatious hand and melted away.

I followed Romain through the undergrowth. I had no choice, for he had hold of my wrist and I could not break away. He moved quickly and, afraid that my beautiful shawl would be snagged on a bramble and spoiled, I said quite sharply, 'Slow down!'

To my great surprise, for he seemed preoccupied and intent, he did. Then, after progressing more decorously through the thin woodland for perhaps another hundred paces, we emerged into an open space where a shallow stream ran over stones. Somebody was there, leaning against a tree. He stepped forward into the moonlight and I saw that it was Sibert.

We had not parted on good terms. I said rudely, 'What do *you* want?'

He gave a guilty smile, just like Squeak when he's been found out in some bit of mischief he thought he'd got away with. 'Now, Lassair, don't be unkind,' he began, holding out his hands palm down and patting at the air as if by so doing he would soothe me out of my anger. 'You—'

'I thought you were my friend,' I shouted, ignoring his protest, 'and did you come to see me when I was told I had to come and look after Goda? Did you sympathize and promise that you'd come to visit me in my exile, if you were allowed to? Did you even bother to say good-bye?'

'I—'

'*No you didn't!*' I answered for him, at a considerably higher volume than he would have done. 'You were barely speaking to me at Goda's wedding and afterwards you – you – *disappeared*, and I didn't know if I'd offended you or if it wasn't just me and you were cross with the whole world, and you never gave me the chance to find out because every time I saw you, you ran away!'

I stopped, listening to the echoes of my furious words on the still air. Goodness, I hadn't realized how much his defection had hurt me and now, *oh, no*, now I'd blurted it out and neither of us could be in any doubt at all.

I felt deeply embarrassed. I felt the hot blood flush up into my face and was very glad of the darkness. All cats are grey in the dark, they say, and hopefully, by the same token, all faces too.

After a moment Romain cleared his throat and said diplomatically, 'Er, actually, Lassair, I'm afraid it's all my fault.'

I spun round to face him. 'All what?' I demanded.

'Um – Sibert's preoccupation. His disappearance.'

Disappearance? I was puzzled. 'You mean he left the village? He left Aelf Fen, with you, and that's why I didn't see him?' No, that couldn't be right, because I had seen Sibert once or twice, but he had refused to meet my eyes or speak to me.

'No,' Romain said. He took a deep breath and then went on, 'I have asked Sibert to do something for – I should say, *with* me. We are' – he paused and shot a glance at Sibert – 'conspirators. Accomplices.'

'*Oh,*' I breathed. It sounded alarming. Intriguing. Exciting. I thought they had better explain. 'What exactly do you mean?'

Again, Romain sent that quick glance at Sibert. I could have been mistaken – the only light, after all, was from the moon and the stars – but I thought I saw Romain give a tiny nod. Probably I did, because it was Sibert who spoke.

'Romain and I have much in common,' he began pompously, and I almost laughed because, as far as I was concerned, they could not have been more different and all that united them was their age, although Romain was maybe two or three years older. 'You don't understand,' Sibert was hurrying on huffily, as if he'd sensed my reaction, 'but it is the truth. We have decided to combine our efforts to achieve a certain clandestine purpose, and it is profoundly in both our interests to do so.'

He was speaking, but the words did not make much sense. Furthermore, they did not sound like Sibert's natural speech. I'd never heard him use words like *clandestine* and *profoundly* and I was almost sure that, although Sibert was doing the talking, Romain had told him what to say.

'So what is this great purpose?' I asked, not disguising the sarcasm. 'What is it going to gain and why' – I really ought to have asked this first – 'are you telling me?'

'The purpose involves a search,' Romain said smoothly. 'I know the rough location where the search must be carried out and Sibert knows about the – er, the object of the search. It is quite possible, indeed likely, that we will find what we seek ourselves. However, Sibert has told me that you have a very particular talent, and so we thought it was worthwhile approaching you to see if you would care to help us.'

'I'm a dowser,' I said shortly. I was becoming tired of his flowery way of speaking.

'Yes, I know.' He gave me a beaming smile. 'So, would you like to help us?'

My suspicions were growing. He was making it sound as if it would be quite useful to have me along, although far from essential. Yet he had started to sweat and the muscles of his jaw were working and I knew that a great deal depended on my answer.

I knew I was going to say yes. Whatever this business was all about, it was just too enticing to refuse. But I decided to make them wait.

'What sort of help would you want?' I asked, making my voice feeble and scared. 'Finding something, I realize that, but where would I have to look? Here?' I looked around me. 'In Aelf Fen?'

'Neither, exactly,' Romain said cautiously. 'You – in fact, Lassair, our purpose would necessitate a journey.'

'A long journey?' I was finding it hard to keep up the pretence of nervous little ninny, but I did my best. 'Oh, I don't know if I'd be brave enough for that.'

Sibert, I noticed, was eyeing me closely. I had better be careful.

'Oh, not that long!' Romain gave a very false-sounding laugh. 'We have to go – er – to the coast.'

The nearest sea to where we stood was about thirty miles north. Eastwards, it was maybe forty-five or fifty miles. 'Oh dear,' I whispered, 'that sounds a very great distance.' I was thinking hard, for I urgently needed to know more about this business than they seemed prepared to tell me. 'How long would I be away? I'm looking after Goda, you know, and I don't think she would want me to leave her, especially now when the baby's birth will surely be quite soon.'

'She must not know where you're going!' Sibert said quickly. 'You can't tell *anyone*, Lassair!'

I certainly can't unless you first tell me, I almost said. I stopped myself. 'Then I suppose I would have to think of an excuse,' I said, frowning as if this was going to be difficult.

'Can you do that?' Romain asked, unable to keep the anxiety out of his voice. 'Can you tell a convincing lie?' He didn't know me very well.

'Oh, I expect so,' I replied innocently. I felt Sibert's quick, suspicious glance. He, on the other hand, knew me much better.

'Do you mean you'll come with us?' Romain said. He was standing right beside me now, almost breathless as he waited to hear what I would say.

I pretended to think. 'If we must travel for as much as fifty miles, do this search for whatever it is and then come back again, we must surely be away for several days and—'

'We shall travel fast,' Romain interrupted eagerly. 'The weather is fine, the roads and tracks are dry. We may be able to cover as much as twenty miles in each march.'

'There's plenty of daylight at this time of year,' I added.

The two of them exchanged a look. 'I'm afraid we'll have to travel after dark,' Romain said.

I had a feeling he would say that. 'Because all of this is so secret?' I asked.

He nodded. 'Yes. So secret that you won't be able to seek permission to make the journey. In fact, Sibert shouldn't even be here now, which is why you had to meet him out here in the woods.'

Oh. Not only did I seem to have agreed to act as treasure-seeker for these two conspirators, but I was about to compound my potential misdemeanours by setting out on a considerable journey – to the sea! Oh, it was exciting! I'd never in my life seen the sea! – without the knowledge or agreement of the lord.

This should have made me come to my senses and say a courteous but very firm no. I was not quite sure what sort of trouble a girl of my age would land in if caught absconding from the manor without permission but I knew it would be grave. Very grave, and probably not only for me. But then I thought of Goda, moaning and sweating in her smelly bed. I thought of how furious she would be if – probably when – she discovered that I'd drugged her so that I could disobey her explicit command and go out to join in the Midsummer's Eve celebrations. Life in her house was already miserably hard. How much more would I have to suffer when she heard how I'd tricked her?

As I prepared to give them my answer, I was already planning what I would say to my sister to justify the sudden urgent need to be away from her for perhaps as long as a week.

That was going to be the easy part.

# FIVE

I was good at making up creditable fictions but, although I say it myself, the tale I wove for Goda was convincing even by my standards. I knew that if I were to cite anybody who might at some point be asked to verify my story, then it had better be someone I trusted not to let me down. The obvious person, since we already shared quite a lot of secrets, was my aunt Edild.

She is, as I have said, a herbalist and a healer. She is honest and good and always does her best to help people. If they are very poor and in desperate need, sometimes she does not charge them, merely saying that one day when she was in need, they can do something for her. Those days never seem to come.

Times, however, were changing. Churches, abbeys and monasteries were springing up all over the place and the black-clad priests seemed to be multiplying fast. Not that I had any complaints about that. The vast majority of the people were poor and the men of the Church gave them much-needed support when they were desperate. Most of them did, that is; there were exceptions. However, the problem was that some of the priests apparently believed that sickness and injury happened to people who had in some way offended God and therefore they should be made to suffer, or at least have their pain helped only by God's own men. Edild and I did not see it quite like that and we helped all who came asking, without first enquiring whether we should let them suffer a while for the good of their soul before we did so. Furthermore, women like my aunt always aroused suspicion because they were different. Edild, typical of her kind, was unmarried, dependent on no man for the food on her table or the roof over her head. She was clever and could read and write (I once heard a priest say that a literate woman was an abomination in the eyes of God, although he was talking in general and not about Edild). And people – particularly priests – were deeply suspicious of the old ways. The

God whom they worshipped, to the ruthless exclusion of any other, did not allow people to believe in the old deities or the spirits that inhabited the streams, the trees and the very stones of the earth. Edild's methods, in their eyes, were very close to sorcery.

It had always seemed quite natural and logical, therefore, that much of what I learned from my aunt must not be spoken of outside the four walls of her snug little house. She could depend on me to be diplomatic and she knew, I hoped, that I would lie to protect her if I had to. I was as sure as I could be that she would do the same for me.

On the morning after my night-time meeting with Romain and Sibert, Goda woke from a long and profound sleep – so profound that she did not appear to have moved at all throughout the night – in a surprisingly good mood. All things are relative, and for my sister a good mood meant that she didn't shout at me because a refreshing drink wasn't ready for her the instant she awoke or hurl the mug at me if the drink wasn't precisely to her liking. Still, to have her glare at me in silence was an improvement on her usual torrent of abuse.

I took advantage of the fact that she had slept so late and told her that first thing that morning, just after Cerdic had left for work, a messenger had come from Aelf Fen to summon me because Edild needed me urgently.

'What does she want *you* for?' demanded Goda.

Modestly I cast down my eyes. 'Several people have been injured in an accident and she needs another pair of hands to treat them all.'

Goda looked at me with her mouth turned down in a sarcastic scowl. 'She must be desperate if she wants a clumsy, ham-fisted oaf like you to tend the wounded,' she observed. Then, prurient curiosity getting the better of her as I had known it would: 'What sort of accident?'

'There was a heavily loaded hay cart being drawn back to the lord's yard and lots of people were riding on it,' I said in a hushed tone. 'Many more were walking along beside it and then something startled the horse – they think it may have been stung by a hornet – and somehow it put its offside feet over the edge of the ditch and before anyone could do anything the cart went over.'

'Were many people hurt?' Goda asked.

'Oh, yes. Broken arms, collarbones, concussion, bad bruising. Some of the injured,' I added, 'were small children.'

Even Goda could not ignore the necessity to offer all possible aid to a hurt child, could she?

'It sounds bad,' she muttered, frowning.

It *was* bad. It happened just as I had described it, but it had happened more than a week ago and Edild had managed perfectly well on her own. I was told the news by the tinker who visited Icklingham. He usually went to Aelf Fen as his previous call and, knowing I came from there, often brought titbits of gossip.

One of my cardinal rules is if you're going to

71

lie, make it as close to the truth as you can. In this instance, all I was altering was the timing.

'Yes, awful,' I agreed. 'I don't really want to go but I think I should,' I added, frowning to express my pretended reluctance. 'Apparently a man's got a bone actually sticking through the flesh of his leg and Edild needs me to help her push and pull till the bones go back into their proper position, which means we'll have to—'

Goda had gone quite pale. 'Yes, yes, enough!' she said abruptly. Then, after a moment, 'How long will you be gone?'

'Oh, quite some time, I'm afraid,' I said, my frown deepening as if I hated the very thought. 'Perhaps as long as a week? There will be such a lot to do. You have to be so careful to keep flesh wounds clean, you see, especially in summer, what with the flies and—'

'*All right!*' bellowed my sister. She shifted in the bed and a smell of stale sweat wafted out, accompanied by the sharper stench of urine. 'You'd better get me cleaned up if you're going away. Then you can fetch the midwife for me – she'll have to look after me till you get back.'

For a moment I stood unmoving, quite taken aback at how easy it had been. Then I saw Goda flap her hand about and I realized she was searching for something to throw at me. I spun on my heel and hurried away to heat up the water and find the wash cloth.

The sooner I was out of the house, the better. Goda clearly didn't know yet about my forbidden excursion last night. If she had noticed my pallor and the dark circles that must surely be under my eyes – very unlikely, as the only person whose well-being concerned her was herself – she did not comment. By the time she found out what I'd been up to, I wanted to be well away from Icklingham. That morning, my sister received the swiftest, most obliging attention I had ever given her.

Even that failed to make her smile.

I had arranged to meet Romain and Sibert as dusk fell, under a spinney of beech trees that stood beside the road that led east out of Icklingham. I hurried through the rest of my appointed tasks for Goda and then, as befitted someone on an urgent healing mission, I set off north-westwards on the road to Aelf Fen.

I walked through the neat strips of land for a couple of miles or more. Many people were out that fine morning tending their land and several of them straightened up as I passed to smile and nod a greeting. One of Goda's neighbours was trying to turn his plough at the end of a field, cursing and swearing because the shoe was deep in a rut. He looked up, saw me and, smiling wryly, apologized for his language. Returning his smile, I hurried on. I crossed a stream and passed through a narrow belt of woodland where, I noticed, several of the villagers had left wrapped bundles of food for the midday meal in the shade of the trees. On the other side of the copse there was a patch of rough ground where a few goats were tethered. I looked around carefully but could see nobody watching me. I walked quickly across the wiry grass. Then, sure that at last I was out of sight of interested eyes, I doubled back and, keeping to the cover of trees and hedgerows, made my way to the meeting point. It was just after noon; I had several hours to wait.

Crouching there deep in my hiding place with nothing to do but think was the last thing I wanted as it gave me the chance to reflect on my decision. With hindsight, it seemed to me that I had been incredibly reckless. Romain and Sibert had told me next to nothing about this extraordinary mission and I had no idea where we were going, other than to the coast, or why, except that I was to help them search for something. Did this thing belong to one of them and was it something they had carelessly lost? Or – and this seemed far more likely – was it someone else's property that they were plotting to steal? Surely that was right, or why else was this whole business shadowed so deeply in secrecy? Why else were we forced to travel by night?

Yet again I reminded myself that if we were caught we would find ourselves in very serious trouble. For one thing, people just didn't set off across the country unless they really had to and even then, as Romain had implied and I very well knew, people of our lowly status could not go anywhere unless the lord of the manor said they could. There was also the ticklish question of theft, a crime which carried the most severe penalty of death by hanging if you were lucky or by some longer drawn-out and, invariably, extremely painful alternative process if you were not.

I forced my mind away from that dreadful thought and made myself try to be more positive. We might not be caught. And how often did a girl like me get the chance to do something risky and exciting?

Then, my spirits rising as excitement once again coursed through me, I reflected that I had been recruited because I had a particular talent for finding what was lost or hidden. Therefore this object, whatever it was, could hardly be in some great lord's manor house, because that surely did not count as *lost*. No; it seemed far more likely that the object was something Romain and Sibert knew about but of whose precise location they were unaware. What had Romain said, exactly? I strained my memory to bring his words to mind. *I know the rough location where the search must be carried out and Sibert knows about the object of the search.* Yes. It appeared I was right. It also sounded, I thought optimistically, as if this object were hidden out in the wilds, where the possibility of being apprehended and accused of theft would be unlikely.

In this way I persuaded myself that I had made the right decision.

Thinking about what Romain had said had brought his face vividly to mind. I saw the wide smile, the well-cut, glossy hair, the expensive clothes under the worn and shabby travelling cloak which had certainly seen better days and which, I realized, he must be wearing to disguise the fact that he came from a stratum of society that could afford to spend a lot of money on good clothes.

He was a rich man. By my standards and those of my family, he was *incredibly* rich. He had talked at length to me on our first meeting. Now he had sought me out, danced with me, been on the point of kissing me (my fertile imagination had already taken a firm hold on that scene at the feast) and he had asked for my help. A man like him had appealed to a girl like me, so very far beneath him, because I had a unique talent (silently I spared a moment to bless Sibert, for surely it had been he who had told Romain of my gift). I was virtually certain that I could bend this promising situation to my own advantage and have Romain falling in love with me before our week in close proximity was out. How grateful he would be when I found his treasure for him! In my mind's eye I saw him fall on his knees at my feet, take my hands in his and cover them with sweet little kisses. 'Lassair,' he would say, 'my clever, precious girl, you have made one dream come true and now I beg that you will indulge my second wish by agreeing to become my wife.'

Yes, I knew I had been rash in agreeing to be a part of Romain's mission. But I also knew that, given how I felt about him, there had never been the slightest chance whatsoever that I

76

would refuse.

I made a soft pillow out of Elfritha's shawl, put it on top of my small pack and, my fatigue catching up with me despite my tense excitement, went to sleep.

As darkness fell, Romain and Sibert made their careful way to the place where they had arranged to meet the girl. Romain was rigid with tension and the long wait for the relative safety of night had all but undone him. He and Sibert had slept in the clearing on the fringe of Icklingham – not that Romain had managed more than a light doze, and that had been interrupted by frightening, anxious dreams – and in the morning Sibert had gone foraging, returning with a pail of milk, rye bread and a large linen-wrapped package that turned out to be a spice loaf. Sibert admitted he had filched it from the remains of last night's feast. Someone, Romain thought wryly, would be missing a carefully set-aside treat.

He had passed the daylight hours in obsessively checking through his plans. On occasions he came very close to panic. What did he think he was doing? Not only had he embarked on this brash, foolish errand but he had compounded the folly by involving two other people, one little more than a child and the other a youth whose introspective silences seemed, to the increasingly nervous Romain, nothing short of ominous.

But I cannot do this without them! he

reasoned with himself. Sibert knew more than any living man concerning this thing they sought and Romain needed his instinctive awareness of both its nature and that of the man who made it. In addition, Sibert was familiar with the area that they must search and, equally important, the long and potentially hazardous journey across the higher ground to the coast. Sibert, as Romain well knew, had made the trip several times, although not recently. It was unlikely that anyone in Aelf Fen was aware just how often, since he had grown towards manhood, Sibert had managed to slip away and brood over what he had lost. Or, to be strictly accurate, what had been lost to him, since he had had no more of a hand in his own dispossession than Romain had in his.

It is indeed as I have insisted to him, Romain thought. We are natural allies, both of us heirs robbed of our inheritance.

But he did not allow himself to pursue that thought. It would only serve to increase his apprehension.

Instead he thought about the girl. What was her name? Lassair. He must try to remember it. He was well aware she liked him. He had deliberately flirted with her, although in a far more innocent manner than he would have adopted had she been a few years older and his intention had been serious. But it would do no harm to foster in her the belief that there might be a happy future for the two of them together once she had performed the service which, according to Sibert, she was uniquely qualified to provide.

Oh dear God, he prayed with sudden fervour, please let Sibert be right.

The long day had at last come to its end. Trust me, Romain thought ruefully as he and Sibert had at last left the clearing, to select Midsummer Day to embark on my great enterprise. But then, of course, the selection had not been up to him. It had been determined by events far away to the south where a castle in Kent had endured a horrible siege and in the end fallen to the king. Even Romain had not expected that retribution would have followed with such amazing speed. But the king, so they said, was very, very angry.

Now they were approaching the meeting place. Romain had the sudden conviction that the skinny girl would not be there; she too, he reasoned, had had the whole day to reflect on what she had agreed to do and surely, *surely*, she would have seen how stupidly risky it was and would now be safely tucked up inside her fat sister's house, quite out of his reach.

She was not. She was sitting huddled under the hedge, a small pack beside her, a very pretty woollen shawl wrapped tightly around her arms and crossed over her flat chest.

Romain put what he hoped was a captivating and vaguely suggestive smile on his face. 'Lassair,' he said softly, pleased with himself for having brought her name to mind when he

79

needed it, 'how pleased I am to see you. I hope you have not grown chilly, sitting there?'

He sensed Sibert, just behind him, draw breath as if to say something; apparently he changed his mind. Lassair looked up and Romain saw the bright moonlight reflected in her wide eyes. Pretty eyes, he thought absently, of some light colour that he could not determine. Blue, probably, or perhaps green, to go with that copper-coloured hair. She might, he allowed, be attractive one day. For now she was just a child, and a boyish one at that.

But he must not let her know his opinion of her. Reaching out a hand, he helped her to her feet. 'We must get going,' he said. 'Sibert will lead us, for of us all he is most familiar with the route.'

'But—' she began, surprise evident in her face. She stared at Sibert. 'He lives in Aelf Fen,' she whispered, puzzled. 'How does he come by such knowledge?'

Sibert looked at her for a moment. Then he said, 'There's a great deal that neither you nor anyone else in the village knows about me.'

He turned and strode away. After a short pause, first Lassair and then Romain fell into step behind him.

Romain made them march for all of the dark hours. Not that there was any need of coercion, for if anything they were better walkers than he and, despite the fact that both were slim and lightly built, it soon became obvious that their stamina exceeded his. He had contemplated bringing his horse on this mission but there hadn't appeared to be much point; he would have been the only one mounted and they would have had to proceed at a human walking pace. However, as the night went on and his feet in their smart boots began to ache and grow hot with the prickle of incipient blisters, he wished fervently that he had ridden after all. Well, it was too late now.

The short night came to an end and in the east, over where the still-distant sea must lie, the sky lightened from the first shoots of brightness to a glorious rosy-pink dawn. They went on for perhaps another mile, looking for a suitable place to rest and sleep. Romain went to walk beside Sibert and asked in a quiet voice, 'We seem to have covered quite a distance. Do you know where we are?'

Sibert shot him a glance. His face was pale and set although whether from fatigue or fear, Romain did not like to ask. 'We've not done badly,' the youth said. 'We were following the Lark River south-eastwards for several miles out of Icklingham, then we turned due east and went round St Edmundsbury to the north.'

'Yes,' Romain said. They had agreed beforehand that it was wise to avoid towns and settlements wherever possible.

'We'd climbed a good bit by then, up out of the valley, and we struck out over the heathland. We gave Ixworth Abbey a wide berth – that's where we stopped for a wet and a bite to eat – and since then we've done maybe another five miles, going due east.' He pointed ahead to the dawn light as if to verify what he had just said.

'Sixteen miles,' said Romain slowly. 'How much further?'

'Thirty miles, maybe.' Sibert shrugged. 'I don't know.'

'How long does the journey usually take you?'

Sibert glanced at him, his expression hard to read. 'I can do from Aelf Fen to the coast in three marches,' he said neutrally. 'But I'm well used to walking.'

'Of course you are,' Romain said, putting a careful note of admiration in his tone. 'But for the three of us, how soon can we reach our destination?'

Sibert looked at Lassair, who was standing on the track behind them staring from one to the other. 'Two more marches,' he said. 'We should eat and rest now, sleep up for the heat of the day. If it's as quiet around here as it appears to be' – Romain, staring round, could see no sign of any habitation amid the heathland, and the narrow path was rough and showed little signs of heavy use – 'then I reckon we'd be safe to set out again in the early afternoon. Another rest soon after dark, then we'll proceed to the coast.'

It sounded an ambitious plan but Romain, driven hard by his desperate impatience to get on with the mission, thought it was not impossible. He turned to Lassair and said courteously, 'Could you manage that, do you think?'

'Of course,' she said, raising her chin and staring levelly at him.

Ah, a burst of pride, he thought. Well, that's all to the good as it means she'll be reluctant to moan when she gets tired.

'Very well.' He unslung the leather satchel he wore over his shoulder and gratefully dropped it to the ground. 'We'll stop and refresh ourselves.'

They found a dell among the heather that offered protection from curious eyes and also from any wind that might spring up. Sibert unpacked the food and handed round a flask of small beer, from which they all drank deeply. The beer was good, sweetened with honey and lightly spiced with rosemary and mint. Romain hoped Sibert had more of it in his pack. They each ate a slice of the spice bread and Sibert gave out apples, small and wrinkled with long storage but still sweet. Then one by one they made themselves comfortable and Romain watched as the other two went to sleep. Sibert lay quite still on his back, his head on his pack and his hands folded on his chest. Had it not been for the rise and fall of his belly, he might have been dead.

Romain, wondering where that morbid thought had come from, dismissed it. He looked over at the girl, curled up in a ball like a young animal and wrapped snugly in her shawl. Her copper hair reflected the light of the waxing sun and he noticed the fine texture of her pale skin. Suddenly her eyes shot open – they were grey-green, he noticed, with very clear whites and an indigo ring around the iris – and he felt guilty for having been caught staring at her.

She gave him a small and tentative smile which, in an older woman, might have been read as invitation.

He turned away.

# SIX

I woke stiff and uncomfortable, with sharp bits of heather sticking in my back. I think the heat had woken me, for I was lying in full sunshine and I was tangled up in Elfritha's shawl. Romain and Sibert were still asleep, so I crept out of the dell and, behind the meagre cover of some hazel bushes, passed water. I had been worrying about how I was going to manage my bodily functions; it was not proving to be easy, on the road with two men, so I was glad that, for the moment at any rate, I had solved the problem.

I returned to the dell, sat down and looked around me. We were on a sort of heath, bracken and heather mostly, and there were no more signs of life up here now than there had been at first light. I stared up the track, first one way, then the other. There was nobody about.

Sibert was asleep, on his back. Romain had turned away. With a small stab of pain, I remembered how I'd opened my eyes soon after we had settled down last night to see him looking at me. I had risked a smile – how lovely it would have been if he had lain down beside me and we had slept side by side – but instantly he had looked away. I tried to excuse him – he'd probably been embarrassed because I'd caught him watching me. He was that sort of man – courteous, mannerly – and it was probably against some code of manners that existed among his kind to make approaches to young girls when you happened to be camped out with them in the wilderness.

All the same, I wished he had been bolder. I would not have turned him away.

Sibert woke and sat up, stretching. He smiled at me – the first time he had done so for I couldn't remember how long – and said, 'Hello, Lassair. Did you manage to sleep?'

'Yes. Very well,' I replied.

Our voices woke Romain. He came up to consciousness more slowly – probably he was used to a gentle awaking, perhaps with some man-servant bringing him a reviving drink and a bowl of water to wash his face and hands – and for a moment or two he looked puzzled. Then his face cleared and he too smiled. There was an air of excited happiness among the three of us; any fears we might have had last night had gone. The sunshine and a good long sleep had thoroughly revived us and after a bite to eat and a drink, we were ready to resume our march.

Romain knew that he was the weak one out of the three of them but, as the eldest, the instigator and the leader in every other respect, he could not allow his fallibility to show. As afternoon turned to evening and the total of the miles steadily augmented, he watched the slowly lowering sun and reflected that so far on this journey, at least they had not had to bed down to sleep in the Fens.

Romain's mistrust of that mysterious marshland region was profound and he had only gone there out of desperate need; the Fens were where Sibert was to be found. As far as Romain was concerned, once this business was over he never intended to set foot there again.

He had once been told by an elderly family retainer who came from the Fens that once, long ago, an ancient horse-loving people had risen up against the invading armies from the hot south. They had fought ferociously under their red-haired queen and burned the towns of the newcomers to the ground. But the military might of the incomers proved too strong and the people were defeated, their proud queen taking her own life by poison before she could suffer the humiliation of capture. The remnants of that once-great people, leaderless, disorganized, had scattered and fled. Many of them, according to the old servant, had sought refuge in the one area where the newcomers barely troubled to venture: the Fens. And their ghosts – perhaps even their descendants – were still there...

Romain had believed he was too mature and sensible to go on being scared by a tale told by an old man to entertain a little boy. Reality proved different. But then, Romain reminded himself as he trudged on, buoyed up by the happy thought that tonight he was far from that dread region, that original childhood impression had been fed and kept alive by what he learned of the Fens as he grew to adolescence and manhood. Raised as he had been on the coast, where the wind blew fresh off the wide grey sea to the east, he had been all too ready to accept the horror stories of that dark, unknown inland place. Malign creatures inhabited the pools and the bogs, and they would entice a traveller along what seemed to be a safe path, only to create a strange white mist that swirled and billowed so that a man could not see where he was placing his feet. Then he would find himself tumbling into the stinking black mud, clouds of stinging insects round his head, leeches and eels sucking and biting at his legs. If the threatening water did not get you then sickness would, for ague and quinsy were rife and if you risked eating the bread, then the poisonous mould that grew on the crust would drive you to terrible visions that drove you out of your mind. Frightful, abominable creatures lived hidden in the Fens, from the terrible monsters that swam in the deepest, most secret waterways and lived on human blood to the nimble elves who were so successful at hiding themselves that a man only knew they were near when he felt their elf-shot pierce his skin. It was said that there were dragons, too, living in their barrows deep underground where they guarded their treasure hoards with their fearsome weapons of claws, spiked tails, vicious jaws and deadly fire.

Romain was less afraid of the dragons than of the other Fenland inhabitants. To an extent he was familiar with dragons, and familiarity had driven out some of the fear.

Not all of it; but he would not allow himself to think about that.

It was fully dark now. His feet were hurting badly and he could tell from the unpleasant wetness inside his right boot that the blister on his heel must have burst. He knew he must stop, for if he didn't there was little chance of his marching even one mile in the morning.

He glanced at his two companions, mere shapes in the darkness, for clouds had blown up across the moon. The girl still walked with a spring in her step, although he had an idea that she was deliberately making herself look fresh because somehow she sensed his eyes on her. She had, he had noticed with some apprehension, certain talents that were not given to most people, and a highly developed awareness of others seemed to be one of them. Sibert, a few paces ahead, was trudging with his head down.

He had not spoken a word for some time, not since they had stopped at a river crossing for a sip of ale. Back then – it seemed like hours ago – he had said the river was the Alde and that they had about another fifteen miles to go.

Oh, God, Romain thought, please let him have been right, for we must have walked five miles at least since then, which would leave just ten to cover tomorrow. For now – abruptly he made up his mind – I cannot walk another step.

'We're stopping,' he announced, his voice suddenly loud in the damp night air. 'There's a stand of pine on that rise to the left. We'll settle there and sleep for a while.'

Sibert and the girl followed him, neither speaking. They found a dry patch of ground where three trees stood close together and the slippery pine needles made an aromatic bed. They each stretched out in their own chosen place and Sibert gave them large slices of his spice bread and several mouthfuls of beer. Then he assumed his sleeping position on his back and soon his gentle snores suggested he was asleep.

Romain eased off his boots and then untied the strings that held up the hose on his right leg. He rolled down the fine wool and then winced in pain as he got to his heel, where the blood and the fluid from the huge blister had begun to dry in a crust, sticking the fabric to his raw skin. What should I do? he wondered. Peel it away? Put a dressing on the wound? He did not know how.

He sensed movement beside him. The girl said softly, 'Have you got a blister?'

'Yes.' There was no point in being proud and denying it.

But she made no remark about the youth and herself being better walkers than he. Instead she reached in the pouch at her waist and soon he smelt lavender.

'Pull your hose off the raw skin and press this on to it,' she commanded, handing him a pad of some soft fabric that was damp to the touch.

He did as he was told, expecting it to hurt like fire. It didn't. 'Oh!' he exclaimed.

'It's lavender oil, both soothing and cleansing,' she said. 'Before you put your boots on tomorrow, I'll give you some alcohol to rub into your feet. I carry a small bottle of it in my pack,' she added with a touch of pride. 'It'll harden the skin.'

'Thank you,' he said.

He hoped she would now go back to her sleeping place. He was grateful, very grateful, but now he felt embarrassed by her nearness.

She said, 'You must have taken the journey over to the Fens in easy stages.'

'Yes,' he agreed. 'How did you know?'

'Your feet are not used to long marches.' He could tell from her voice that she was smiling. 'Still, if you keep this up, they soon will be. Good night.'

She crept away and he lay down in the darkness. There was now only a gentle throbbing from his blister and he sent her his silent but profound gratitude.

When we woke up after the second night of our journey, I had the feeling that we were close to the sea. I could not have said how I knew, never having experienced the coast before, but there was a new quality in the light over in the east. I got up, stretched and, hearing in the utter silence the sound of running water, went to find its source.

We had crossed a river last night – fortunately there was a little wooden bridge – but this was much smaller, nothing more than a stream. Still, the water looked clean, running bright and fast over pebbles, and I could see fish in it. I bent down and drank greedily, splashing my face to wake myself up, then washing my hands and feet. The water was cool but not cold and very refreshing.

I was thinking about Romain's blister. The best thing, I decided, was not to disturb the dressing I had placed over it in the night but instead bandage it to his foot, to make sure the raw flesh was protected from the rubbing of his boot. Yes. That would be best.

I was deliberately forcing myself to think about the practicalities of how to make a man with a huge blister comfortable enough to walk another ten miles. I did not want to go on thinking about how I had held his naked foot between my hands and gently, so gently, touched his soft skin. The remembered sensations

91

had kept me awake long after he and Sibert were asleep. They had disturbed me in the night and they threatened to the same now in the day.

There was something different about our little company this morning and I detected it as soon as I rejoined them. The men were awake and already busy, Sibert with setting out food and drink, Romain with getting his boots back on. Before he attended to his right foot, I rushed forward to fix the dressing over his blister.

When I had finished I packed up my small bag and wound Elfritha's shawl around my waist. The day was already too hot for me to wear it. I watched the two men, trying to work out what had changed.

Romain was pale; perhaps from nerves, for we were surely now close to the climax of our mission. He stood a few paces out from the shade of the fir trees staring out towards the east, where we would shortly be going. He was frowning and chewing at the inside of his cheek. But nervousness was not the main emotion I sensed in him: what I felt emanating from him in powerful waves was a restless, barely contained excitement.

Sibert's mood was very different. I know him well – or I thought I did – and he had always been subject to steeper ups and downs than most of us. This morning he was clearly uneasy, and I could hear him muttering to himself. His frown made a crease like a knife cut between his eyes. Out of nowhere I felt a stab of sympathy for him, so sharp that I almost gasped.

What was the matter? Why was he not as excited as Romain? This mission concerned them both, or so I had been told. Why was Sibert not as thrilled as Romain at the thought of nearing its completion?

I stilled my thoughts and, relaxing, opened my mind to him as Edild had taught me. Straight away his distress flooded into me and I knew why he looked as he did.

He was afraid. He had assured Romain – older, tougher, more important, influential and powerful and infinitely wealthier – that he could lead him to the general location of this thing that we had come so far to find. Now the moment would soon be at hand when he would have to substantiate his boast and he did not know that he could.

I'll help you, Sibert, I said silently to him. All you have to do is tell me where to look. I can't scour the entire coast but if you narrow it down, I'll find your treasure.

My urgent reassurance could not have reached him. As we set off shortly afterwards, he looked like a man on his way to the gallows.

Around noon, to judge by the height of the sun, we passed through a broad band of forest. I was surprised, for what I had been told of the coast (by Edild, of course, my best and favour-ite teacher) suggested shingle or sandy shores and short, wiry vegetation tough enough to withstand off-sea breezes and salt in the air. Yet here we were, walking in woodland.

The trees thinned out and as we emerged into the sunshine, for the first time in my life I saw the sea. I stopped dead – just then I couldn't have moved to save my life – and stared. I heard myself go *'Oh!'*, but it was quite inadequate. There were no words to describe what I was feeling.

We were on a low sandy buff and I could see a large town in the distance below us. That in itself was quite awe-inspiring for someone who had lived her whole life in a small Fenland village. The greater wonder lay beyond.

The sea, restless under a light breeze that blew from the east, was like a huge sheet of beaten silver. It stretched from as far as I could see to my left to equally far to my right, and I had the sudden sense that we were nothing but a small outcrop in a vast watery world. Something in the sea called out to me, so that there and then, as I absorbed the effects of my first glimpse of it, I wanted to run towards it, give myself to it. It was just so *big*. Endlessly big, and the long line of the coast, stretching almost due north–south, seemed a feeble and inadequate defence against its might.

It will eat up the land, I thought. I didn't know where the image came from – I still don't – but I saw in my mind an image of low cliffs crumbling before the constant, effortless attack of the waves. Mighty buildings cracked and the lines that webbed out across them, tiny and insignificant at first, swiftly and inexorably grew into huge fissures, and then enormous chunks of masonry fell away and disappeared with vast splashes into the hungry sea. People cried out in panic, the church bells sounded their urgent alarm, and from out of the turmoil I thought I heard a sudden clear note ringing out, as if someone had struck a ring of metal with an iron hammer.

Then the image faded.

I was shaking, my knees suddenly weak. I would have liked to sit down but Romain, impatient now, was already striding on.

'Come on!' he urged, and Sibert and I hurried to join him. 'We'll look down on the town, then we'll proceed on to – to our destination.'

Had we further to go? I did not know, for Romain had only said vaguely that we were going to the coast and now we had reached it. I looked at Sibert, raising my eyebrows in enquiry.

'The port's down there,' he said quietly, jerking his head in the direction of the town. 'Romain's land' – a sardonic smile briefly crossed his face – 'is on the coast a few miles to the south.' He added, half to himself, 'Drakelow.'

Drakelow? Was that the name of Romain's manor? If it was, I didn't much like it. A drake is another name for a dragon, and it was surely inauspicious to call one's dwelling place after such a fearsome and aggressive creature. To compound the folly by adding *low* – our word for the roar of a wild beast – seemed to be just asking for trouble...

The bellowing of a dragon ... Why, I wondered, did that image seem familiar? But there was no time now to dwell on that.

I frowned as I walked, already deeply uneasy about the task before us. Before *me*, in fact, for I was the dowser and it was for me to pinpoint the location of whatever we had come to find. All at once I was very angry with Romain. He had been high-handed and arrogant, assuming my – our – ready compliance with his wishes and giving out so little information in return. I've been such a fool, I thought miserably; I've gone along with his wishes as meekly as a puppy eager for a pat on the head. I ought to have demanded to know what I was getting into before I even considered leaving the safety of my sister's house.

My sister. My fat, pregnant, complaining, cruel but nevertheless suffering sister. And I had abandoned her. Oh, well, I reflected, while I was castigating myself I might as well do the job thoroughly, so I gave myself a good scolding for being selfish and heartless as well.

Romain had stopped. I was so preoccupied with my unhappy thoughts that I almost walked right into him. I went to stand on his right; Sibert was on his left.

He stretched out his arm, indicating the scene before us. 'Dunwich,' he said grandly. 'It's one of the largest and most important ports on the east coast. Three thousand people live there' – *three thousand!* I could not believe it, nor begin to imagine how so many people could possibly be in one place – 'and there are half a dozen churches and quite a few chapels, and several religious foundations as well. The port exports East Anglian wool and grain and those ships you see down there' – he pointed to the harbour – 'are probably from the Baltic. They'll have brought furs and timber, mostly,' he added knowledgeably. 'We also receive ships from the Low Countries with fine cloth' – he brushed nonchalantly at the sleeve of his tunic – 'and from France, bringing good wine.'

He spoke with such confident authority and for a moment, scared and homesick, so far from my home and all that I knew and understood, I had an urgent need of his strength and self-possession. He'd said *we*. *We* receive ships. How possessive he sounded about this astonishing place. Well, if his manor were indeed close by, then it appeared he had every right to be. I was suddenly struck by the unpleasant thought that he can have had nothing but an abysmally low opinion of Aelf Fen. Oh, dear Lord, and I gave him some of the food my mother had prepared for Goda's wedding. Whatever could he have thought of it, he who was used to the very best that money could buy?

I felt my face flush with shame.

But then I thought – actually it was almost as if someone else had put the thought into my head, and the voice sounded very much like Edild's – that Romain might be wealthy and powerful but despite all that he had come looking for our help, mine and Sibert's. This vital task that he had to do could not, it seemed, be achieved without us.

After that, I began to feel less abject.

Romain was very aware of the two young people standing either side of him. The boy was trembling. Although the awareness of this disturbed Romain he was not surprised at it, for he had been aware of Sibert's growing fear for some time. He was fairly sure that he knew from where it stemmed: at the outset, the youth had said very promptly that he knew where the search must be carried out, no doubt about *that*. Now that the time had come, was he beginning to question himself? Perhaps he was thinking, *Oh, but it's all changed* – as indeed he well might – *and I'm no longer sure of my bearings.*

In a way, Romain hoped that this was the cause of Sibert's obvious distress. Romain could deal with it if it were; a few encouraging words, a few hearty phrases on the lines of 'Of course you can do it, Sibert! Just relax, take your time, study the area carefully and the rest will follow, you'll see!'

There was something else that could be causing Sibert's alarming tension. Studying him covertly, Romain wondered if at long last the boy had realized what Romain had tried so very hard to gloss over. Sibert was far from being stupid but he was obsessed, and such a violent and all-encompassing emotion did not always permit rational thinking. Romain had rather depended on this. So far, he had got away with it. *Please,* he prayed to a power he could barely envisage, *please don't let him realize now, of all times, what I've been so very careful never to mention!*

Sibert gave himself a shake, as if coming out of some bleak reverie. Sensing Romain's eyes on him, he turned and gave the older man a small smile. Romain, taking that as a good sign, returned it with a broad grin. 'Not long now!' he said encouragingly.

Sibert did not answer.

Romain twisted round to look at the girl. Something had shifted within her, too, although the change was subtle and Romain could not interpret it. He had sensed her awestruck reaction to her first sight of Dunwich – it was hardly surprising, she was a rural peasant who had probably never strayed more than a few miles from her ghastly little village before now – and he had compounded the moment by sharing a few of the impressive facts about the great port. Let her be in no doubt, he had thought, who is master in our enterprise. She's right out of her natural element here, as well as being absent from her sister's home without permission, and she's got to realize that I'm the only one who can protect her. I need her to be utterly dependent on me and on my good will, he reminded himself. That way she'll be completely in my power and there won't be any silliness when we find what we've come looking for.

To begin with she had seemed cowed and afraid, and he was sure that just for an instant as they stood there looking down on Dunwich, before she brought herself under control, she had leaned in closer to him. As if she desperately needed his kindly touch to reassure her that everything was all right.

But it had only been fleeting. Now she had edged a clear pace or two away from him and she had raised her chin in that gesture he had seen in her once before.

He wondered, just for an instant, if he had underestimated her.

# SEVEN

'Come on,' Romain said abruptly.

Even to his own ears, his voice sounded strangely harsh in the awed silence. He had suddenly realized that it was not wise to remain here looking down on Dunwich, for both his young companions seemed affected by the sight.

I have to keep control, he thought. He did not know exactly what he feared; perhaps it was better for his peace of mind not to put it into words.

He turned to his right and led the way at a smart pace southwards along the narrow track. They had kept away from all the main thoroughfares so far and this was not the moment to alter that prudent habit. Presently the path entered the welcome shade of a band of woodland. So much the better, he thought. The trees are in full midsummer leaf and they will give us excellent cover.

They did not have far to go. Drakelow lay two miles to the south of Dunwich and they would be in woodland most of the way. Romain had thought long and hard about this final phase of their journey, debating endlessly with himself whether they should go to the manor house first or to the shore. In the end he had settled on the manor house, although he was still not entirely convinced that this was the right decision.

A mile to go. The familiar landmarks were succeeding each other in swift succession now. Soon the house would come into view.

Half a mile. He risked a glance at Sibert. The boy was frowning, staring about him as if he were confused. Of course he was confused. He had not been here for several years and much can happen in that time.

They were close now, so very close. The woodland was thinning and here and there were the scars of recent timber extraction. So many trees had been felled ... Should I speak now? Romain asked himself, his heart beating fast. Would it be better to forewarn him?

The decision was taken out of his hands. Sibert gave a sort of groan – a dreadful sound of anguish and pain – and began running on down the path.

'*Stop!*' Romain yelled.

Sibert ran on.

Romain raced after him, pain from his blister-ed heel stabbing like a nail, but violent emotion had put wings on Sibert's feet. Romain was aware of the girl's light footfalls as she flew along the path behind him, but his attention was all on Sibert.

He caught up with him at last but it was too late. Sibert stood on a low rise at the very edge of the tree line, staring down at the great wounds that cut across the landscape like the scars of violence on a beloved face.

In the centre of a broad open space totally de-nuded of the softening trees rose a brash new building. To be accurate, it was a series of buildings, the group dominated by a squat, square tower topped with crenellations that stood on the summit of an earth mound. As befitted a structure designed as the last defence for the inhabitants, the tower had no windows and the single door was stoutly made of oak and bound with iron. It was surrounded by a palisade of stakes, their tops sharpened to savage points. A gated opening in the palisade led to steps leading down to another enclosed area in which there was a large thatched house and a semicircle of smaller buildings, including barns and a smithy. One or two people could be seen in the lower yard and smoke came from the roof of the large thatched building.

Sibert turned to Romain and the power of the emotion coursing through him had so twisted his features that he looked like someone else.

'*What have you done?*' he bellowed. 'Where is my house?'

There was a sharp exclamation from the girl but Romain ignored her. He put out a calming hand, catching Sibert's sleeve, but Sibert flung him off. 'Sibert, be calm and I will explain,' he said. Sibert had bunched his hands into fists, his whole body gathered as if to strike. 'Please!' Romain pleaded. 'Hear what I must tell you!'

Tears collected in the boy's wide eyes. Romain watched in horrible fascination as slowly they spilled over the lower lids and slid down the boy's dirty face. Beside him, he heard the girl give a low moan – of pity? – and she moved a step closer to Sibert.

Sibert drew back, and the hand that the girl had tentatively put out to him fell by her side.

Straightening his back with a touching gesture of pride, Sibert said, 'Go on, then. Say what you have to say.'

It was Romain's only chance. He knew he must get it right.

'Come back into the shade,' he said gently, 'for although the afternoon is passing, it's still hot out here in the sunshine. Come – yes, that's right!' He made his voice light and encouraging, for the youth had slowly and reluctantly begun to move. 'We'll sit down here by the side of the path, and you will be told what you ask to know.'

He sat down, indicating a patch of grass beside him. Sibert lowered himself on to the ground, and the girl did the same. She was watching him intently, he noticed uneasily, her eyes narrowed in concentration. Romain waited for a few moments, taking a few calming breaths, and then, well aware that he had their full attention, he began to speak.

'Before us lies the manor of Drakelow,' he said, 'which was awarded to my grandfather Fulk de la Flèche by William the Conqueror in recognition of my grandfather's contribution to the victory at Hastings in 1066. My grandfather was a wealthy and influential Norman nobleman,' he added, unable to keep the bragging tone out of his voice, 'and he supplied the Conqueror with a band of well-armed, well-drilled fighting men, many of whom did not live to enjoy the fruits of the victory. Fulk de la Flèche's prize was a fine one, for he was awarded extensive lands on the coast, close to a thriving port where the produce of the estate could be taken away by sea and sold for a handsome profit, and the lands themselves were fertile. Naturally, the king's largesse was not entirely without self-interest, for in a newly conquered land it was to his advantage to have his own supporters installed in castles and fortified manors so that they could come to his aid in the event of rebellion.'

'Like Hereward,' the girl piped up. 'He led a rebellion from Ely.' Romain started with surprise. Caught up with his tale, he had all but forgotten her presence, and he was astounded that an ignorant village girl would speak with such authority of matters surely so far removed from her sphere.

'Yes, like Hereward,' he agreed, turning to beam at her. He had become so accustomed to the shy blush that flooded her face as she diffidently returned his smile that it was remarkable now because of its absence. Instead the clear grey-green eyes stared levelly back at him and he thought he saw the corner of her wide mouth turn down in a swift wry quirk.

Again he was struck by the faintly alarming thought that he did not really know her very well...

But there was no time for that now. 'So, my grandfather was given the manor of Drakelow, everything and everyone in it,' he said, taking up his tale. He sensed Sibert's sudden tension, as if he were about to speak, but, not wanting to be interrupted again, he hurried on. 'Fulk had brought with him to his new home his wife, my grandmother Mathilde, who was like him of noble Norman blood, and their two sons, Baudouin and Athanase, who at the time of the Conquest were fifteen and fourteen. Baudouin, I am told, had pressed to be allowed to ride with his father into battle but the most that my grandfather permitted was that he might be a part of the reserve troops, and in the end he was never in any great danger. In due course the family settled in their new home and the younger brother, Athanase, wed the daughter of another Norman. Her name was Amarys and she was my mother.' He paused, but it was purely for effect. 'My birth was difficult and my mother did not recover from it. She died in 1071, a few months after I was born.'

He had half expected some sort of sympathetic acknowledgement from the girl; none came.

'It was not the end of tragedy for my family,' he went on. 'The summer of 1076 brought sickness to the region. The symptoms of the illness were a high fever, a rash and a violent, destructive cough that frequently brought on a spitting-up of blood. It was thought that the malady must have come in with a sailor on one of the ships that docked at Dunwich, for few suffered from it beyond the immediate vicinity of the port. Once the patient coughed blood, he was as good as dead.' Again he paused. Then he said softly, 'I lost my father and both my grandparents in the space of a week.'

'You did not fall sick?' the girl asked, but he detected curiosity in her tone rather than pity. They say she is a healer, he reminded himself. Perhaps her interest is professional. Nevertheless, the absence of so much as a single compassionate word still seemed strange.

'No, I did not,' he replied easily, putting aside his misgivings. 'My nursemaid was an old countrywoman and when the first of my family fell ill she shut me up in my chamber, burned rosemary and sandalwood and made me wear an amulet.'

'And what about your uncle?' she persisted.

'He was away from home. Word was sent to his hosts and he was warned to keep away while the sickness ran its course.' He waited but it appeared she had no more questions. 'My uncle Baudouin adopted me and made me his heir,' he went on. 'He is not a naturally paternal man and he has never given me much affection, but he supported me, provided a luxurious home and saw to it that I was educated as he saw fit. It is more,' he added, 'than most people have.'

He heard the girl mutter something under her breath. Sibert was silent and he sat as still as if made of stone. No doubt it would not last; the tricky part of the story must now be spoken.

'Even while the Conqueror lived,' Romain said, 'we were anxious about what would happen when he died.'

'*We?*' the girl said.

For a simple and ignorant villager, Romain thought, there was quite a lot of irony in the one short syllable.

'I am sorry. By *we* I mean my own family and the wider community of Norman lords.'

'*We*, by which I mean the people of my village, were quite worried as well,' she murmured.

He chose to ignore her.

'We expected that Duke Robert would probably have Normandy and William Rufus would inherit the throne of England,' he continued, 'and, on the Conqueror's death last September, this is what happened. However, many of our number would have preferred Robert to rule in England. We knew what he was like as a ruler, and the majority of the Norman landowners had already sworn fealty to him during his father's lifetime. Once someone had the temerity to propose ridding ourselves of William Rufus and putting Robert on the throne of England, a great many of the Norman lords chose to follow him. So this past Easter, when Odo of Bayeux whispered the details of his plot, he discovered that he had a great deal of support.'

'But not yours?' the girl suggested.

'No,' he agreed. He had not been aware of revealing his own feelings on the matter; he resolved to be more careful. 'No, indeed. My uncle Baudouin, however, declared for Duke Robert and Bishop Odo. I tried to counsel him against acting rashly, for I feared that if King William were to predominate in the coming struggle it would go badly for my uncle.'

'And for you as his heir,' the girl put in.

'Yes, naturally,' he said sharply. Then, forcing a smoother tone, 'My uncle was going off to fight, however, and I did not wish to see him wounded, or worse.'

'Naturally,' she echoed faintly.

'The fighting was fierce and in places quite devastating,' he went on firmly. He was not going to allow a skinny little girl to take over the impetus of this account. 'My uncle was wounded but fortunately it was not life-threatening, and he returned to Drakelow where he was tended by—' No. He must not think about that. 'Where they looked after him. But meanwhile the fighting in the south was going from

108

bad to worse and earlier this month we received news that Odo had surrendered to the king. Then the disaster which I foresaw indeed came to pass.' He paused for effect and then said, 'Drakelow was taken from us in punishment for my uncle's part in the rebellion.'

There was a moment of utter stillness. Then the girl said, 'So you have lost your inheritance and your home.'

He could not detect much sympathy in her voice.

He turned to look at her. 'I have,' he agreed. 'But I plan to win it back by—'

'By buying yourself back into the king's favour via this thing you've brought us here to find for you,' she finished for him.

He was totally taken aback. 'Well, yes, I suppose that is the case, although—'

'What's in it for me?' she demanded. He noticed that she kept darting furious glances at Sibert, as if to say, *Come on! This is your battle too!*

Sibert maintained his state of stony silence.

And Romain, who could think of nothing to say, fell mute as well.

I was shaking, although quite determined not to let him see. I edged away, so that I sat by myself a few paces off. Then I went back over all that I had just seen and heard.

The manor must look very different now from when Sibert had last seen it, that was for sure. Poor Sibert – he had been absolutely shocked by his first sight of that horrible new building down below us. I couldn't blame him. *Where is my house?* he said. *His* house ... I was still trying to work that out. I knew a little of Sibert's history, how his father Edmer fought at the Battle of Hastings and later with Hereward in the rebellion, and I understood now what that had meant: Edmer must have belonged to the rich and the powerful elite who held sway in England before the Conqueror came. He must, if I was right, have owned this manor of Drakelow, and it was him from whom it was taken when the first King William awarded it to Fulk de la Flèche.

I sat there, thinking so hard that my head ached.

Sibert was two or three years older than me, so he was about sixteen; I did not know exactly. His mother Froya was quite young, for all that her careworn air made her look older, and would have borne Sibert in round about 1071 or 72. I had always been led to believe that Edmer had died as a result of the wound he received fighting with Hereward, but in fact he must have lived on for a while if I was right about Sibert's age. So, that was one misapprehension gone. What about the other part of that stirring tale? The bit that had Froya, heavy with the child that would be Sibert, making her secret, desperate journey with her dying husband through the Fens to the sanctuary of Aelf Fen?

I realized suddenly that I had no idea where I had come by these scant details of Sibert's life.

Perhaps I had made them up. Perhaps I had been fed a lie. That hurt, for as a consummate liar myself, I pride myself on my ability to detect when I am being lied to.

There was no mistaking the honesty of that terrible cry that broke out of Sibert when he saw Drakelow: *Where is my house?* I knew this did not necessarily mean that he had lived at Drakelow; it was equally likely that he had been brought up believing it was his true home, which would be enough to make anyone possessive about it. So, someone – presumably his mother or his uncle Hrype, his father being dead – must have fed the poison into Sibert. *Drakelow is your home. It was ours, it has been in our family since time out of mind* – since when? I wondered, but I would come back to that – *and it ought to be yours.*

They must have encouraged Sibert to come and look at his ancestors' home. When he returned from each visit, did they increase the pressure on him? Did they present a future when he might win it back for them? Oh, but if they did, how cruel, for what could a slimly built youth do against the might of the ruling Norman lords, especially the one who now owned Drakelow?

Only, of course, he didn't own it. This Baudouin de la Flèche had been kicked out of his grand manor and his strutting new castle, just as Sibert's forefathers had before him.

Which appeared to open up all sorts of possibilities ... and all at once I had a flash of understanding and I believed that I knew Romain's mind. At the same time I perceived the major flaw in the argument that he must have employed to win Sibert's help.

I made myself sit very still and I relaxed the muscles of my entire body, from my feet to my scalp, just as Edild had taught me. It worked, as it always does, and the nervous tension dissipated. I knew I could not return to Romain and Sibert until I had regained control. I breathed slowly and gently – in ... out ... in ... out ... and finally I was ready.

I stood up, brushed down my skirt and wrapped Elfritha's shawl around me, for the afternoon was over and evening was approaching, bringing a lowering of the temperature. Then I strolled back until I stood before Romain.

'I had hoped, when I first set eyes on that rather crude habitation before us, that you would offer us accommodation there tonight,' I said. His head shot up and I noticed that he was eyeing me warily. Good. 'But, of course, if it isn't yours, I suppose you won't be.' I gave a little sigh. 'I shall have to say goodbye to my images of a good, hot meal, some of that fine French wine you spoke of and a luxurious night's sleep in a warm, snug bed on a goose-feather mattress.'

He had the grace to lower his eyes.

'I suppose we had better move on,' I continued. 'You won't really want to be found loitering in the vicinity, will you, Romain? Under the circumstances, it would hardly be wise.'

He dropped his face into his hands. 'No, it wouldn't.' His words were muffled.

Suddenly I felt very sorry for him. I wanted to reach out and touch the bowed, defeated head, and with that urgent desire all my starry-eyed feelings for him came rushing back.

Why was I being so unkind to him?

'I'm sorry,' I whispered.

He must have thought I was saying I was sorry about his misfortune in losing his inheritance. He looked up, gave me the shadow of his bright, beaming smile and said reasonably, 'It's not your fault, er, Lassair.'

It was, I believed, only the second time he had used my name since we had set out. But all the same it touched my heart.

He stood up and between us we got the mute Sibert to his feet. 'We're moving on,' I said to him, giving his arm a squeeze. Then, because his continued silence and unresponsiveness was starting to worry me, I added, 'Are you all right?'

What a stupid question. Of course he wasn't all right. He had just seen what the new owners had done to his former home and clearly he didn't like it. I didn't blame him. When the rich and powerful men of the previous regime had built, they had taken into consideration the location and the nature of the surroundings, so that the long halls that they constructed grew, in time, almost to be a part of the landscape. They lived as their forefathers had done, within wood and wattle walls and beneath reed roofs, their pastoral way of life generally peaceful so that there was no need for extravagant defences. They were not like the Normans, conquerors and invaders who forcefully and violently imposed themselves, their way of life and their harsh rule on an unwilling, unwelcoming populous.

Poor Sibert. I could only imagine what the manor of Drakelow had looked like before Baudouin de la Flèche had rebuilt it to answer his own need. Sibert must have—

No. That could not be right. I had taken a wrong step in my reasoning, for surely the old Drakelow would have been replaced years ago, when Baudouin's father was first given it not long after 1066. It was impossible for Sibert to have seen the original structure built by his forefathers, for he had not been born until seven or eight years afterwards.

Yet he had uttered that heart-stopping cry: *What have you done?*

What did it all mean? For the moment I could make no sense of it.

I fell into step beside him as we set off. I did not know where we were going and merely hoped that Romain had somewhere in mind where we could shelter overnight. Sibert, who claimed to know the area so well, was for the moment quite useless; I reckoned I would even have to take over his job of dishing out the food and drink. I felt so very sorry for him. I would have liked to take his hand but I held back, instead hoping to comfort him by my presence at his side.

We walked in the woodland for a while, then emerged into the open. Sibert raised his head and stared around him. 'I don't understand,' he muttered, frowning, 'it all looks so very different. I can't – can't—' He gave up, his frown deepening.

'Perhaps it's a while since you've been here,' I said kindly. 'Places do change, you know.'

'I was last here a little under two years ago,' he said.

'Well, perhaps – perhaps—' But I was at a loss to explain how a location with which someone had once been familiar could have altered so drastically in two years. Instead I said bracingly, 'Come on. I'm hungry, and you must be too. Romain seems to be leading us somewhere, so let's hope it's dry, out of the wind and provides us with somewhere comfortable to sleep.'

He glanced at me but it was as if his eyes slid over me as he continued his worried gazing around. I was about to start urging him again when all at once he jerked into action and staggered off after Romain.

I hurried after them.

# EIGHT

We were all tired after the long hours of walking and, after our unnatural pattern of being awake for the night and asleep in the daytime, the prospect of settling down to sleep at the appropriate time was surprisingly good. We ate reasonably well before we turned in. Romain had gone scavenging and returned with a dry heel of bread, a large onion squashed on one side, a piece of mouldy cheese and some spindly carrots. I didn't ask him where he'd found the food; all the items looked suspiciously like the leftovers from a market, usually abandoned for the dogs and the starving to clear up. Still, we were grateful, and cheese savoured by the bite of onion – even a squishy onion – was welcome after a diet that consisted mainly of spice bread.

I knew that Romain had money. I also knew why he could not stride up to some beautifully laid-out stall and purchase the best provender on offer: because around here his was a familiar face and we had come on a secret mission. For the time being, until we had succeeded in our aim, it looked as if we were going to have to go hungry.

I went to sleep quickly and slept profoundly; I don't think I even dreamed. Then all at once I was wide awake. I lay quite still in the darkness – the sky was cloudy and there really was barely any light at all – and used my ears and my nose. I could hear the sea; or I guessed it was the sea. It was how I imagined waves beating on the shore in the dead of night would sound. I could hear Romain, who lay over to my right. He was fast asleep, breathing deeply and evenly and with a little click in the middle of each in breath, as if something were caught in one nostril. The leaves of the trees above us were moving restlessly in the breeze off the sea. The wind must have changed, I thought absently. I couldn't hear the sea when I went to sleep but now I could, so the wind must have gone round from west to east so that now it was carrying the sound of the waves.

Then I heard stealthy footsteps. I stiffened in alarm and felt for the small knife I carry in a sheath on my belt. Not that it would have helped me much against an assailant, as it's only as long as my hand and I would need a very lucky stab to reach a man's vitals, but nevertheless holding its horn hilt gave me a tiny bit of confidence.

The footfalls were coming nearer.

Should I wake the men? Oh, but if I did and whoever was out there heard me, then he'd know where we were, whereas now there was a slim chance that he was out on his own business and not concerned with us.

I lay in an agony of indecision, the sweat of fear breaking out all over my body.

Moving very slowly, I turned my head to locate Sibert, asleep on my left. He wasn't there. And as I realized who those terror-inducing footsteps belonged to, he crept into our little hideout and lay down under his cloak.

I was furious with him for scaring me so badly, which was not entirely reasonable as he had probably got up to pass water and that was nothing to do with me. But it happens like that, I find; when something deeply frightens or disturbs us, we need someone to put the blame on.

I was still fuming when Sibert spoke, his voice barely above a whisper. 'Lassair? Are you awake?'

Several possible replies flashed through my head. In the end I just hissed back, 'Yes.'

He rolled closer. 'I need to talk to you,' he said, right in my ear and tickling me with his warm breath. I noticed that he smelt powerfully of onions, but then undoubtedly I did too. 'Will you come out there with me' – I sensed movement as he jerked his head – 'so we don't wake Romain?'

It was rather nice to be needed. I nodded, but of course he couldn't see, so I whispered, 'All right.'

He crawled away and, wrapping myself in my shawl, I followed. When we were out of our sleeping place we both stood up and on silent feet tiptoed fifty paces or so into the breeze. I was very aware of the sound of the sea. Sibert stopped and, taking my hand, led me to a shallow indentation in the ground where, as we sat down, we were sheltered from the wind.

'Are we near the sea?' I asked in a low voice.

'Yes. I've been to look and it's only a short walk away. There's a cliff, then the shore and the sea.'

'A cliff.' The night was pitch black! 'Sibert, wasn't it foolhardy to go wandering along cliffs on a dark night?' Then I remembered that he knew this area. 'But I suppose you're well aware how the land lies.' He didn't answer. 'Aren't you?'

He turned to me. His head was a darker patch in the darkness but I caught the glint of his eyes. 'That's just it. I thought so, but— Oh, Lassair, it's changed! What has happened here? What have they done?'

I watched as he dropped his face in his hands. I felt his body shake and wondered if he were silently weeping.

'I don't understand,' I said. 'What's changed?'

'Everything!' he said in a suppressed wail. 'The house is quite different, and the fields and the woods, and it's as if some sorcerer has put an evil enchantment on it!'

I was already feeling decidedly uneasy. There was no need to bring sorcerers and enchantments into it. 'Well, of course the house has changed,' I said in my no-nonsense tone. 'The one we saw yesterday was built by the Normans, and they have a way of stamping their mark on a place, probably to make sure the rest of us know who's in charge. So you—'

'Lassair, listen!' he interrupted. 'Yes, I know all that! But the manor and castle we saw – the place Romain said was Drakelow – isn't. When the de la Flèches were given the estate, of course they weren't going to live in the hall my forefathers built, but they left it standing and built their new castle close beside it. They used my ancestral home as a grain store,' he added bitterly.

Yes, I reflected. That sounded like the incomers. They won, they invaded, they built their castles and, not content with that, rubbed the faces of the vanquished in the dirt by demeaning their former treasured homes.

I brought myself back to the moment. 'You said you were last here two years ago?'

'Yes. A little more – I made the journey just before the Easter feast.'

'And at that time Drakelow was as you remembered it?'

'*Yes.*'

'Yet now it's changed.' He did not even bother to reply to that, and I didn't blame him. 'Were you out there wandering about just now to try to make sense of it?' I asked, filled with sympathy.

'I wasn't walking for the good of my health.'

I could hear that he was smiling and I hoped it was an indication that his mood was lifting a little. 'It's a very dark night, Sibert,' I said gently. 'Wouldn't it be better if we waited till morning?'

'Of course it would,' he said, impatient suddenly. 'But you forget, I think, what I shall be called on to do tomorrow.'

'I – *oh!*'

He was right. I had forgotten. Poor, poor Sibert. We had reached our destination and in the morning Romain would undoubtedly demand that he begin on his appointed task. Sibert must find the general location of the treasure we had come to find and then I must use my dowsing powers and pinpoint its hiding place.

And Sibert had lost his bearings because an enchanter had broken up the familiar landscape into little pieces and set them down again in a new pattern.

'Perhaps,' I ventured when the silence became unbearable, 'it'll look better by daylight.'

He actually laughed. 'Good old Lassair, ever the optimist,' he remarked.

'I'm sure it will!' I said urgently. 'It must!'

'Maybe.' He didn't sound at all confident.

I couldn't speak for him but I felt wide awake and I was sure I would not sleep if we returned to our shelter. 'Tell me about Drakelow,' I said. 'It was your father's house, I know, but obviously, from what you say, he didn't build it, did he?'

'Oh, no. It's been in my family for – oh, generations.'

'Will you tell me?'

'Yes.' He settled himself more comfortably and, I noticed, closer to me so that our arms and shoulders touched. It was probably just for warmth. 'My ancestors came from the Baltic, where the lands of the Swedish homeland were threatened by a series of years that brought flooding to the coastal plain. There wasn't room any more for everyone and they needed a new place to live, so they joined in the movement westwards, to Britain, where many of their people were going.'

'How many generations back?' I asked. 'Your grandfather? His father?'

'Oh, long before that. It was five hundred years ago.'

'How do you know?' I demanded.

'You have your grandmother Cordeilla to memorize and guard your family history. Well, we have our bards too.'

'Yes, but who told you?'

He hesitated. Then he said, 'Hrype.'

'Your uncle the cunning man,' I said without thinking; Hrype is a bit scary and people in Aelf Fen usually refrain from voicing their suspicions concerning exactly what he is.

'Yes,' Sibert agreed. 'He's my father's brother.'

'Your *father's* brother!' I was very surprised. Although I couldn't recall that anyone had ever actually said so, I – and everyone else in Aelf Fen – had assumed that Hrype was Froya's brother, and had come to support his sister when she lost her husband.

'You think you know the story, I'm sure,' Sibert said dryly, 'but since we're here in the lands of my forefathers, concerning ourselves deeply with their deeds, perhaps I ought to tell you the true version.'

'I'm listening.'

He hesitated, as if gathering his thoughts. Then he began to speak. 'They came from the coast that borders the Baltic Sea on its eastern side, near a place where the great funeral mounds of the early kings rise up. They were important people, for they knew how to make the things that the kings craved. Hrype is not the first magician in my line, and his forebears had the skill of transferring their power into metal, so that the finished artefact was an object of power.' Awestruck, I murmured an assent; I had heard tell of such things. 'The men who led the people into the new lands had need of such aids, for the migration was perilous and they knew they would not only have to fight others who also coveted the lands but, in addition, there would be resistance from those who already inhabited the places they were intent on taking over.'

My people, I thought, for the incomers sailing ashore out of the dawn landed in the east of England. They landed in my East Anglia. Perhaps Sibert was thinking the same thing, for quickly he went on, 'They settled on the coast, for they loved the sea and did not wish to live away from it. The king and his line went south and built their great halls at Rendlesham. My

ancestors settled at Drakelow and they prospered and grew wealthy.'

I expect they did, I thought, if they and their
strange powers remained so crucial to the king.
'Were they not commanded to live nearer to
Rendlesham?' I asked. 'Surely, if the king depended on them, wouldn't he want them close
at hand?'

'You don't know where Rendlesham is, do
you?' He laughed softly.

'Well, no, but you said the king went south
and so I thought—'

'I meant south of where they landed, which
we are told was to the north of Dunwich.
Rendlesham is only some fifteen miles from
here. It lies at the mouth of a river, to the south-
west.'

'Oh.'

'They were close enough to reach the king's
side within a day when summoned,' he went on,
'and they preferred to keep a little distance
between themselves and the king. They worked
their land and looked after their people, and by
the time of my grandfather Beorn, they felt as if
Drakelow had always been their home.' After
five hundred years, I reflected, I should think
they would.

'My grandfather had two sons, my uncle
Hrype and my father Edmer,' Sibert continued.
'Hrype was very strange and my grandfather
was wary of his power, so that when the threat
from the Normans came, it was Edmer whom
he commanded to fight with him. Hrype,' he

124

added, 'would not make a good soldier.'

He would if he could blast a few of the enemy out of their saddles with a bit of magic, I reflected, but I kept the thought to myself. 'So your father and your grandfather rode away to the great battle?' I asked.

'Yes. Nobody thought that they would lose, for King Harold had already won an impressive victory against the Viking Hardrada and everyone was saying that he was invincible. My grandfather and my father joined the king's army as they marched south to Hastings.' He sighed. 'But, of course, King Harold lost.'

'And Drakelow was given to Fulk de la Flèche.' For the first time, I was beginning to understand just a little of what a devastating, life-changing blow that had been.

'My grandfather died on the battlefield,' Sibert said, 'so he was saved the ignominy of seeing his enemy in his own hall. My father escaped both death and capture, and he sent urgent word to my grandmother Fritha, telling her what was going to happen. She and Hrype made their escape, taking with them everything they could carry, and fled westwards inland to the Black Fens.'

I nodded. 'As many have done before them,' I observed. It takes a very determined enemy to chase his quarry into the heart of the Fenland. Many who have tried found only their own deaths. You really have to have been born there to be confident of finding the safe ways, and even then we have been known to make mistakes.

'My grandmother and Hrype were not caught,' he went on. 'In time my father found them, and they made their way to Ely, where they had been told that resistance was gathering. My father fought with Hereward, as you know, although Hrype counselled him against it, saying it would end in death. Not Hereward's death; my father's.'

'Hrype was right,' I whispered.

'Yes. He usually is. My father was shot in the thigh and the wound became infected. Hrype did his best for him, even to the extent of amputating the leg. He—'

'He must be very skilled,' I interrupted, 'to attempt such surgery.'

'He is. He knows how to render his patient insensate, and by so doing he can take his time over the cutting.'

I knew that such powerful magic existed, for I had picked up occasional hints that Edild had let drop. Not that she had elaborated, for quite clearly she deemed that as yet I was far too young to be instructed in this surely most dangerous of skills. To render a man insensate, so that he did not feel the agony of amputation! How would anybody dare to do that and be sure of being able to wake the patient up again when it was all over? I thought that were I not so in awe of him – oh, all right, downright scared – I would have given much to talk with Hrype. Maybe when I was older and had begun to earn myself a reputation as a healer...

'He did not work alone,' Sibert was saying, 'for by now my father was married to my mother, and at one time she was Hrype's pupil. Together they patched my father up and prepared him for travel.'

'It was very risky to move him,' I protested. Edild had taught me about life-threatening wounds and how a patient must above all else have rest; complete immobility, if at all possible. If the amputation of a limb was not a life-threatening wound, I did not know what was.

'They had no choice,' Sibert said grimly. 'The rebellion had failed and there was a price on the heads of each of the main protagonists, my father included. Hrype had to choose between staying where they were and seeing his brother arrested and probably hanged or else taking him on a difficult journey over uncertain terrain and perhaps watching him bleed to death.'

'What did the others say? Your mother, your grandmother?' I did not suppose that poor Edmer would have been up to making a contribution to the discussion.

'My grandmother was dead. She was never the same woman after the flight from Drakelow to the Fens. According to Hrype, she suffered some sort of a seizure that left her partly paralysed. She gave up on life after Edmer received his wound.' He paused. 'She lay down, turned her face to the wall and she died, and there was nothing Hrype could do to save her.' Poor Hrype. What sorrow his family had endured, I thought, my sympathy making tears form in my eyes. 'My mother was terrified of moving my father,' Sibert went on, 'but she saw the sense of what Hrype was saying and in the end she agreed that flight was better than arrest. Hrype volunteered to remain at Ely, doing all he could to give the impression that he was still tending my father there, and my mother slipped away in the dead of night, leading a docile old mare that bore my father.'

'She brought him to Aelf Fen,' I said wonderingly. 'And then he died.'

'He did.' The two curt syllables fell like hard drops of cold rain.

'Your mother was already pregnant with you,' I went on, recalling what I had been told, 'and you were born after your father's death.'

'Yes.'

'You must have—' I stopped. Something in his tone made it clear that he did not wish to dwell on that, and I understood. I cannot imagine what it must be like not only not to know and love your own father but never even to have had the chance to meet him.

'Now,' I said, for a change of subject seemed to be necessary, 'now you have to face what the Normans have done to your home.'

'I do,' he agreed. I sensed a different mood in him suddenly and I felt him straighten up, as if he were lifting his head and squaring his shoulders. 'This is my people's home,' he said slowly, 'and a knowledge of it is in my blood.' He turned to look at me. 'I will succeed,' he whispered. 'For all that I cannot see my way, tomorrow it will be better.'

'That's the spirit!' I said encouragingly. I got up and, reaching for his hand, pulled him to his feet. The sudden note of optimism seemed to be a good time to turn in. 'We should sleep,' I added. 'Then you'll be fresh for the morning.'

'Lassair,' he began, 'I—'

'What?'

'Nothing.'

Side by side, we crept back to our sleeping place and, each going to our separate corners, settled for what remained of the night.

Romain awoke with the same sense of foreboding that had been with him when he went to sleep. The boy, Sibert, was behaving so oddly and, although Romain suspected that he knew why, all the same it was very worrying. Sibert had to achieve his task; this whole mission would fail otherwise and Romain's future would be—

No. Don't think about that.

I must tell him what I probably should have warned him of before, Romain decided. It would help, once the boy was over the shock. It *had* to help, otherwise...

Again, he reined in his panicky thoughts.

There was little to eat for breakfast. I will purchase good, fresh food today, Romain vowed, whatever it takes. His stomach was grumbling with hunger and he felt light-headed if he got up too quickly.

They packed up their few belongings and the

little that remained of the food and drink. Romain looked at the girl and then the boy. 'Ready?' he asked.

They both nodded.

'Very well. We shall go to the sea.'

He led the way back on to the path that wound through the springy grass between the band of woodland and the distant sea. He heard their footsteps behind him but neither spoke. He went on, and the line of the cliff top steadily drew nearer.

Any moment now, he thought.

Suddenly the girl called out to him, 'Romain, Sibert has stopped!' There was urgency, perhaps fear, in her voice.

Romain turned round. Sibert's face was ashen and, as he stared with wide eyes at the scene before him, he was slowly shaking his head. Romain took a few steps towards him. 'What is it, Sibert?' he asked quietly. 'What do you see?'

Sibert raised his arm and, with a hand that shook as if with the ague, pointed. 'That's my tree,' he said in a horrified whisper. 'When I came here first I used to climb it so that I could watch the comings and goings at Drakelow and not be seen by those within. But – but—'

'What?' cried the girl, anxious eyes fixed on Sibert.

Romain watched in deep apprehension as Sibert stared out at the scene before him, the expression on his face like that of a man who has wakened to find himself in a world he does not recognize.

130

After what seemed like an agony of waiting, Sibert whispered simply, 'It's moved.' Then, power filling his voice, he cried in anguish, *'It's moved!'* He was almost sobbing. 'I don't understand, but my tree is in a different place – it used to be much further from the sea, and the hall was perhaps fifty paces away on the shore side...'

Very slowly, as if reluctant to look, he turned all the way around in a circle. Then, pathetically, he looked at Romain. 'What have they done? Have they moved the cliff?'

*'They* have done nothing,' Romain said gently.

For, indeed, what had happened here was far beyond the power of any human agency and could not have been brought about even by the full might of the powerful, aggressive, ruthless and violent Normans.

A large strip of land on the coast at Dunwich and to the north and south of the town was no longer here. The cliffs that had so puzzled Sibert had moved some distance to the west.

Almost half of the manor of Drakelow had fallen into the sea and it had taken the ancestral hall of Sibert's ancestors with it.

# NINE

Standing beside Sibert, Romain could almost feel the boy's horror prickling against his skin. He waited. Instinct told him that anything he might try to say now, either in sympathy or in explanation, would either go unheard or else release the fury that was so evidently building up.

After an initial moan of distress, quickly suppressed, the girl, too, was silent.

Finally Sibert turned to him. The blue-green eyes burned with fire and he said, 'Why did you not tell me? A word of warning about this – this *catastrophe*' – he swept an arm in the direction of the sea, now deceptively calm as if for some reason wishing to disguise its furious, destructive potential – 'would have prepared me!'

Trying to speak soothingly and reasonably, Romain said, 'I did not think you would agree to come if I had spoken.' He hesitated. Was it better to say what he had in mind, for it had to be said some time, or wait a while until Sibert was less emotional? He decided to speak. 'Also, I feared that if I told you what has happened at Drakelow, you might have said you would no longer be able to locate the – the thing

132

we seek.'

'You feared right!' Sibert shouted. Now both arms waved in the air, making great wind-milling gestures expressive of his pain, his frustration and his despair. 'How am I to begin to look, when half of the place I knew and loved has vanished beneath the sea?'

Romain made himself take several steadying breaths. Then he said, 'The landfall is alarming, I admit, at first sight, but—'

'*Alarming!*' Sibert's echo was harsh with sarcasm.

'—but, if you give yourself time to consider what has been happening here, you will under-stand that it's just another step in a process that has been going on for a very long time. The sea comes in hard out of the east, forced on by the winds, and—'

'I don't care,' Sibert said coldly.

Romain cursed himself. Now was no time for wordy explanations. In a flash of memory he recalled his own reaction when he had first seen the apocalyptic damage. I must move the boy on from this, he thought. Putting some iron in his tone, he said firmly. 'We have come here for a specific purpose. Yes, I admit that your role in our mission will be far more demanding now that the landscape has changed so drastically, but it is my belief that you can still perform it. I would not have brought you here otherwise.'

On Sibert's other side, the girl moved closer to him and Romain heard her mutter something; it sounded like, *I'll help you all I can.* Sibert turned and gave her a brief, absent smile.

'We shall go up to the cliff edge – don't worry, the drop is neither very far nor very steep – and we shall make ourselves comfortable in the sunshine,' he went on, now subtly changing his tone so that it sounded as if he were a commander and the young people his troops. 'You, Sibert, will look all around you and establish where you are in relation to how the lie of the land used to be. Then you will be able to work out the location of the spot you seek.'

There was a long pause. Then Sibert said, 'Very well,' and the three of them made their cautious way to the cliff edge.

Romain left Sibert and the girl sitting in the sunshine at the top of the low cliff. He had an idea that the boy would do better without him there. Also they were now in grave need of food and drink. Romain had resolved to trudge a mile or so inland to a small settlement that he knew of and see what he could purchase. He wrapped his stained old cloak around him, covering the rich fabric of his tunic. There was no need to dirty his face for he guessed it was already filthy, and he had several days' growth of beard. It was highly unlikely that anyone would recognize Romain de la Flèche beneath the grime.

In any case, he had no option. The alternative was to collapse from exhaustion and dehydration.

I sat beside Sibert for what seemed ages after Romain set off. I wanted to comfort him, to help him, but he had shut me out and I could do neither. I hated sitting doing nothing; everything in me always seems to rebel at enforced idleness. I stared north, towards the town, then south, at the long coastline stretching into the far distance. I counted seabirds whose names I did not know. I wondered how long Romain was going to be finding food and drink; my stomach was hollow with hunger. Finally I counted the waves breaking with soft, hypnotic regularity on the shore below.

When eventually Sibert spoke, it made me jump.

'The hall used to be there.' He pointed.

I waited. When he did not elaborate, I prompted him. 'And the treasure was kept in the hall?'

'No, oh, no, it can't have been.' He shook his head emphatically. 'Our halls were always built for communal living and nobody in their right mind would hide a valuable object where there were constant comings and goings. The hiding place must surely have been in some secret location, Lassair. I did not even know there was need of such a hiding place until Romain told me about the – about the treasure. I'd never even heard of any treasure. I imagine that nobody was meant to know about it and no doubt the penalty for speaking of it was severe.' He frowned, as if by keeping something so important so very secret his people had some-how let him down.

'Did you really know nothing at all of this until Romain sought you out?' I asked, although I felt that I already knew. If Sibert had dis-covered that there was a hidden treasure, un-doubtedly he would have gone to hunt for it alone. Although there were those mysterious trips he admitted to have made to spy on his ancestral home...

He smiled bleakly. 'No, not really.' He glanced at me briefly and, as if he read my mind, added, 'It wasn't why I kept coming here. I had heard whispers,' he went on, 'but the little I overheard made no sense. I'm not supposed to know anything at all. Hrype would kill me if he found out.'

'I won't tell him,' I said fervently. I spat on my finger and drew it dramatically across my throat. 'On my life.'

I don't think he heard. He was far away, lost in memory. 'I've always spied on Hrype,' he said dreamily. 'You would too, if you had to live with him. He's just – weird, and he's so secretive all the time that sometimes I— Well, once I woke in the night and he was in some sort of a trance. He was sitting cross-legged by the hearth, where a small fire burned. There was something smouldering on top of one of the logs and it gave off a really pungent smell. It gave me a headache, and I started to feel dizzy. Anyway, Hrype had his eyes almost closed, just slits showing between the lids, and he was muttering. Sort of chanting. I kept back in the shadows and tried to make out what he was saying and I realized with a shock that he was talking about Drakelow. Of course, I had to go on listening then because although I didn't know a lot about it, I knew where and what it was and what it meant to my family.'

'And he was speaking about the treasure?' I butted in. I couldn't help myself.

'He must have been, although I didn't realize it at the time. He was *chanting* to it, I think, as if the object was there before him and he was communicating with it. Sensing its power, perhaps.' He shook his head impatiently. 'I don't know, I don't have Hrype's knowledge or his gifts. But he spoke of something he referred to as the sea sanctuary. He *talked* to the thing, telling it that it was safe there in this sanctuary place because its location was a secret and quite soon it would be hidden for ever, and – *oh!*'

His gasp of realization came an instant after mine.

Sibert turned to me, wide eyed with awe. 'He knew!' he whispered. 'He predicted this landfall!'

'He did,' I agreed. I was struck by a further thought. 'Sibert, they must have known that this was going to happen, all those hundreds of years ago at the time the thing was put there in this sea-sanctuary place.' I felt the hairs on the back of my neck stand up as a shiver of atavistic dread went through me. To foresee the future with such clarity was quite alarming. But then a more prosaic explanation occurred to me. It was surely more likely that this eating away of the land by the sea had already been under way five hundred years ago. The men who had hidden their precious treasure had simply taken advantage of a natural phenomenon.

Edild once said to me that the best magicians maintain their scepticism and always keep one foot on the ground. My web of destiny might well show me to be earth-poor and not firmly grounded, but it didn't mean I was totally lacking in common sense and logic.

I glanced at Sibert. He was shaking his head in wonder, his expression distant and dreamy.

Oh, dear. I was not at all sure he was open to common sense or logic just then.

'So,' I said brightly, 'where and what was this sea sanctuary?' He must have some idea, I thought. Not only that, he must have believed he could find it. Why else had he come along on this mission?

'I think I know where it used to be,' he said slowly. 'When Romain approached me, my first thought was that the – the *thing* he was after must be whatever it was I overheard Hrype chanting about. I had no idea what it was but I had already worked out where and what the sea sanctuary must be. When Romain told me about the— When Romain explained, it – er, seemed as if everything suddenly fitted together,' he finished lamely.

He was being deliberately vague. I was sure, however, what it was he was trying not to say:

somehow Romain had discovered what Sibert had not. He might not know where this magical treasure was but he knew precisely what it was.

I thought about that. Romain knew *what* it was and Sibert knew roughly *where* it was, and they both needed me to pinpoint it for them. The thought gave me a warm glow of satisfaction.

'Very well,' I said, deliberately keeping my emotions out of my voice. 'Where was it, this sea sanctuary, and what sort of a building was it?'

'It was not a building. It was a circle of wooden posts, in the centre of which there was the stump of an oak tree, its trunk buried in the ground and its roots open to the air. It used to be some distance inland. Now' – slowly he shook his head, as if he still could not absorb the vast change in the landscape – 'now it's out there somewhere.' He waved an arm in a sweeping gesture towards the smooth sea, where no structure of any size or shape broke the surface for as far as the eye could see.

But I hardly registered his last words. I was almost in shock; I could not have been more amazed. What he had just described was a replica of one of the places Edild had told me about. It was up on the coast to the north of the Fens and one of the most sacred locations of our ancient ancestors. It was one of the deep mysteries – that much I knew. The upturned tree stump was a symbol of the link between the living and the dead; between us and the world of our ancestors, which was a mirror image of our own that co-existed beneath the earth, so that they walked the same ground as we did but upside down. It sounded quite bizarre to me and I was confused because I thought it was something to do with Yggdrasil, the world tree, but that, Edild said, was because I did not yet understand. How right she was. She had promised to take me to the sanctuary in the north one day when I was further advanced in my studies and, at my present lowly stage of learning, the prospect was more frightening than exciting.

Now it appeared that there was another such structure here at Drakelow. Well, I knew from my granny Cordeilla's tales that the forefathers had lived on the coast at Dunwich, so it was possible. Did Edild know about this one? Had she seen it? If not, it was too late now because it had gone.

I realized suddenly what I should have appreciated straight away: Sibert's people had not built their sea sanctuary. They had utilized a place of power that already existed, and had done so for thousands of years. Something about it had called out to them in their urgent need and they had responded.

I felt shaky with the impact of what I had just learned. I wished fervently that Edild were with me; she would have calmed me, helped me to understand and, I was quite sure, told me what I ought to do next. For I was – we were – faced with a problem. The place that Sibert must locate and where I must use my special skill

140

was under the water and, for the present, I had no idea what we were going to do about it.

Then Sibert said matter-of-factly, 'We'll have to wait till low tide.'

I have already said that this was my first sight of the sea. I was an eel fisherman's daughter and I knew how the water washed in and out of the creeks and the best time to hunt for eels. I knew about the sea – of course I did – but I did not know *much* about it. I certainly wasn't relating this huge, gently moving expanse stretched before me with the tricky, treacherous, ever-changing waterways of the Fens.

I said, and I must have sounded so stupid, 'What do you mean?'

And he told me.


Romain's apprehension had grown to an alarming level by the time he got back to the cliff top. He tried to judge by the two figures sitting there so still, in surely exactly the positions they had occupied when he left, what the prevailing mood might be. Had Sibert recovered from the shock of seeing the landfall? Had he got his bearings, and could he lead the girl to the place where the thing was hidden?

Unable to contain himself, he broke into a run. Hearing him approach, Sibert turned round. 'Oh, good,' he said, 'you've brought us our meal. Hurry up, Lassair and I are ravenous.'

Slowly Romain knelt down and, unfolding the linen wrapping, revealed bread, cuts of cold meat, a knuckle of ham, pickles, cheese, some tiny, wrinkled apples and a large sweet cake. He stared intently at Sibert and thought – hoped – he detected a smile. 'Well?' he demanded.

Sibert made him wait. He picked up some bread and hacked off a slice of ham, dipping it in the little pot of pickle. He took a huge bite, chewed vigorously and then through the food, said, 'Lassair, have some, it's delicious.'

'Sibert, I—' Romain began. He felt the blood surge into his face. He was on the verge of losing control.

'It's all right, Romain,' the girl said. She had been eyeing him apprehensively and he wondered wryly if she feared for his health if he was made to wait in his agony of suspense much longer. 'Sibert's done it. He knows where the search must be carried out.'

Romain flung himself on the boy, hugging him and slapping him on the back. 'I knew you could do it!' he cried. 'Didn't I say so?'

'Yes, Romain, you did,' Sibert acknowledged.

He stood up again, surprised that they did not instantly do the same. 'Come on, then!' he said excitedly. 'What are we waiting for?'

Sibert indicated the calm, silvery sea with the last portion of his bread and ham. 'The tide.'

Romain looked out to where he was pointing. The new shoreline was already deep in shingle and the waves washing to and fro made a soft, hypnotic sound. There were at present some ten or twenty paces of exposed foreshore, littered with slabs of stone, pieces of tile, fragments of planking, beams and bolts of wood. It was not that long since the sea had swallowed its latest meal and the remnants were still being spat out. Beyond the foreshore a vague, circular shape was slowly appearing and suddenly Romain understood.

'You mean – you're saying it's there?' he asked in a whisper. 'Under the sea?'

'Under the sea now, yes,' Sibert agreed, calmly helping himself to more bread and a chunk of cheese. 'When the tide has gone out, it ought to be exposed. At least,' he added cheerfully, 'it might.' He chewed reflectively for a while. 'Otherwise, it'll all depend on how long Lassair can hold her breath.'

They waited. The sun reached its zenith and began the long, slow descent into the west. Slowly, steadily, the sea fell back and the outline of the timber circle became clearer. At last Romain could contain himself no longer; he felt as if his blood was fizzing and frothing in his veins and he was light-headed and slightly nauseous.

He stood up, his head spinning. 'We're going down there,' he said decisively, fighting the vertigo. 'Come on.'

Giving his companions no time to protest, he led them away. The cliff was less than a man's height here, the ground soft and crumbly. There was a place nearby where a stream must once have cut its way down through the newly exposed soil, and they paused to inspect its now bone-dry course. It would be easier to go that way than trying to drop straight down the cliff. Low it might be, but all the same an awkward fall could have broken an ankle. Romain went first, turning to hold out a hand to the girl, but with a faint shake of her head she declined his help and scrambled down on her own, jumping the last few feet and landing neatly like a cat. Sibert followed, sliding on his backside and setting off a small avalanche of earth and pebbles.

The cliff, Romain reflected anxiously, was indeed deeply unstable...

They struck out across the spoil from the cliff and presently it gave way to shingle. Romain, his eyes fixed on the strange circle of ancient timbers straight ahead of him, worn by time to stark fragments, hardly noticed when he reached the first of the little pools left behind by the retreating tide. Soon his boots were soaked and he felt the sharp sting as salt water found the raw skin under his burst blister.

Now he was intent on the peculiar upturned tree stump that, with a vague sense of menace, squatted in the middle of the timber circle. Its roots were spread wide, held up to the summer sky like arms reaching out in supplication. A sudden huge shiver ran through him, all the way from his head to his toes. It had nothing to do with the chill of the water now surging around his ankles; it was fear, pure and simple. We should not be here, he thought. It is a forbidden place and there is danger lurking.

It seemed to him as he splashed through the

shallow waves that all at once the bright sun faded. Looking up in alarm, expecting to see a black storm cloud coming up against the wind, he was amazed to see that the sky was still clear, undisturbed blue.

But he was in shadow; he *knew* it.

Another shiver ran through him. Get away, a voice seemed to whisper inside his head. Go, while you still can.

He stopped dead.

Sibert came up behind him, panting. 'What is it?' he demanded. 'We should hurry – we've left it too late and I think the tide's turning.'

Romain looked up. Was Sibert right? He did not know. But the sea seemed to be pushing hard against his legs. Then his mission and its vital importance broke through the enchantment and he said roughly, 'Come, then.'

He waded inside the timber circle.

Sibert was right beside him. The girl, hampered by having to hold up her long skirts, was still several paces behind.

Romain made himself wait in silence. Sibert stood quite still, looking around him. He was sensing the place, Romain thought. He would not necessarily know straight away where to tell the girl to start looking. He would probably have to poke around and find the most likely area within the circle. And what of her? Romain shot a surreptitious glance at the girl, whose face was white and set. How close did she have to be to an object before she could pick up its presence?

So many questions, he thought in frustration. And all he could do was wait for the other two to act. Impotent, he clenched his hands into fists.

Sibert was walking around the circle, stopping by each ruined timber post to push his hands down under the rapidly deepening water. Romain watched him, aching to order him to hurry up. Then Sibert went to the upturned stump. Now he knelt down in the water, leaning forward and supporting himself on one hand while with the other he explored the gnarled and sodden surface of the tree that had died in another age of the world.

His frown of concentration was suddenly replaced by a different expression.

'What is it?' Romain cried, hurrying to crouch beside him, sending up a wash that drenched Sibert to the waist. With a curse, Sibert straightened up, scowling at Romain.

'You've soaked me!' he complained.

*'What did you find?'* Romain shouted. 'Have you got it?'

But Sibert shook his head. 'No. I had something, though, or I thought I had. There was – I don't know how to describe it. I was feeling down the tree trunk and I found a line that felt as if it was too straight to be natural. I was trying to see if it could be the outline of a recess of some sort when you came over and now' – he was once more feeling about beneath the water – 'now I've lost it.' He sent Romain an accusatory glare.

Romain wasted no time on apology or recrimination. Spinning round, he called to the girl. She was standing outside the timber circle and she had her back to him. He thought for a moment that she was moving away, but that couldn't have been right. 'Come here and see if you can detect anything,' he called urgently. 'Over here, on this side of the stump. Sibert thinks there may be a hidden opening and—'

She turned round and he saw her face.

It was deadly pale, and the grey-green eyes that had turned to silver in the light off the water were wide with fear. 'We cannot stay here,' she said, her voice an anguished whisper as if it were vital that nobody overheard. 'There is death here and we are in its shadow.'

He heard her words, which so faithfully echoed what he had sensed only moments before, in a kind of numb horror.

Death. Shadow.

*But the thing I have come to find is almost within my grasp!*

'We must go on looking!' he shouted. He lunged towards her, intent on grabbing her and forcing her inside the circle. She saw what he was going to do and, turning, splashed back towards the shore, skirts trailing in the water. Romain went to go after her but then a sudden very cold wind blasted out of the east and with it the speed of the incoming tide picked up alarmingly.

Sibert was at his side, and he had a firm grip on Romain's sleeve. 'I don't want to drown even if you do!' he yelled. 'It's madness to stay out here – we'll be out of our depth very soon and there's already a vicious current pulling at our legs. *Hurry!*'

Still Romain pulled against him, drawn to that unearthly stump and whatever it held inside itself as if it had cast a monstrous, invisible net over him and was slowly drawing him in.

Another powerful wave hit him in the back of the legs and he would have fallen but for Sibert holding him up. Salt water splashed up into his face and went up his nose and into his open, gasping mouth. Coughing, choking on the harsh brine, at last he allowed Sibert to drag him away.

The first attempt had failed.

# TEN

I think it was that evening, as we sat round a driftwood fire and tried to dry our soaked boots and clothing, that what I had worked out ages ago first really dawned on Sibert.

Which, very simply was this. Romain, Sibert and I were all vital to this mission, Romain because it was he who had found out about the hidden *thing*, Sibert because he knew where it was concealed and I because my particular skill would allow me to locate lost objects. I had been naive and had omitted to agree a fair recompense for my trouble; it had been enough, when Romain approached me, that I would be escaping from my sister for a while and going off on an adventure with two young men, both of whom I liked quite a lot and one of whom I was *really* attracted to.

What terms had Sibert agreed?

Unless this treasure was easily divisible – which I seriously doubted since all along it had been referred to in the singular as *an object* – then only one of them could have it. Romain had been forced to admit I was right when I'd said he planned to use the treasure to buy himself back into royal favour, so it was possible he intended to sell it and give Sibert a share of the proceeds, reserving the rest for his own purpose. I wanted to believe it but I could not make myself. It really wasn't very likely because the king probably had plenty of money already but it wasn't every day an abject subject came grovelling to be pardoned for his father's sin with an object of power in his hands...

No. If I was right – and every instinct was shouting out to me that I was – then Romain had no intention of sharing the treasure with anybody. He would allow me and Sibert to find it for him and then at best he would offer us something for our trouble. At worst, he would betray us and desert us and we would never see either him or the treasure ever again.

I had worked out this truth long since and I

was biding my time, not sure yet what I ought to do. Now, as we sat digesting what I have to admit was a pretty decent meal accompanied by the great luxury of smooth red wine, watching dreamily as the steam rose off our drying garments, I sensed that Sibert was at last realizing it too.

He shifted around for a while and I felt that he was wondering whether or not to raise the matter and, if he did, what he should say. Eventually, staring at Romain with an angry frown on his face, he opened his mouth to speak.

And in that instant I knew that he must not. Something was telling me urgently that this was not the moment. I did not wait to try to work it out but instead coughed loudly to cover Sibert's first words and at the same time kicked him hard on the shin.

'*Ouch!*' he exclaimed, rubbing at his leg. 'What did you do that for?' Now he was glaring at me.

'Cramp,' I said shortly. 'Sorry.'

While he was still frowning at me I mouthed, 'Not now!' and, thankfully, he seemed to understand.

I lay back, the tension seeping out of me. I had obeyed the inner warning without hesitation, partly because I trust my own instincts, which usually do not let me down, but also because of what I had sensed as I approached the sea sanctuary. There was such a sense of threat out there that I had wondered that

Romain and Sibert had kept on their feet; as for me, I was so beaten back by the silent power emanating out of it that I couldn't have gone on even if they'd dragged me. *And I was so afraid.* I knew that the sea was angry, for I could hear crashing waves like marauding ships breaking out there on the waterline. The wind was angry too, blowing straight out of the east. From somewhere – perhaps within the timber circle itself – there had come a low, forceful, unearth-ly sound that I could not begin to identify. But then I had recalled the name of this place: Drakelow.

I was hearing the muffled boom of the dragon...

I was not only afraid for myself, although in truth that fear was more than enough to cope with. I had seen a dark cloud over Romain. As it billowed and waxed right above his head I recalled my granny's words: *He walks in the shadow of death.*

Was this what she had seen? All those months ago in Aelf Fen when she stared at Romain, had her more practised eyes detected what was hidden to me until today? I did not know, but I strongly suspected it.

I liked Romain. Oh, more than that; despite the fact that I was fairly certain he intended to cheat Sibert out of a share of the treasure, I was drawn to him powerfully. In my foolish heart I still entertained the fanciful, optimistic hope that if and when I succeeded in bringing off what he wanted of me, he would stop treating me like an anonymous child and see me for the alluring and fascinating woman I was.

Some hope.

I was faced with a dilemma. My only – and very slim – chance of making Romain see me with new eyes involved my steeling myself to go back out to that terrifying timber circle and find the treasure. But I was afraid of the circle's power and I also knew it was very dangerous for Romain. I could not bring myself to admit that I believed it would bring about his death; my mind kept hedging away from that. And I might be wrong...

So, was I to do what I knew I should, and try to persuade Romain to give up the whole venture – finding the thing, giving it to the king, winning back the royal favour and with it his forefathers' home – and slip away to the safety of whatever refuge he had found for himself? Or did I curl up like a frightened little animal and, when Romain deemed it was time to try again, meekly do what I was told?

I might be wrong, I reminded myself. And the rosy, pink-tinted daydream spotted its chance and slipped back seductively into my mind. I was in a beautiful velvet gown in a sea-green shade that brought out the colour of my eyes and on my head I wore a precious gold circlet. I strolled in a beautiful garden scented with pinks and roses and, beside me, lovingly holding my hand, walked my husband. He was broad-shouldered and very handsome, dressed like me in new finery, and behind us was our home. The home was Drakelow and the husband was Romain.

I can see now that my fantasy was childish and quite unrealistic. I couldn't make myself see it *then*.

Presently we settled down to sleep.

I was wakened by a soft whisper in my ear and a firm hand over my mouth.

'It's me,' Sibert hissed. 'Don't make a sound.'

Again I crawled after him out of the place in which we were sleeping. Again we crept away until we could speak without waking Romain.

'What is it this time?' I asked resignedly.

I truly had no inkling!

He said, 'Dawn is close. The tide is almost at its lowest point and the water is well clear of the sea sanctuary. It's gone quite a lot further out than it did yesterday afternoon. Let's go.'

'Wait.' I spoke the single word so sharply that he did.

'What?' he demanded.

'It's dangerous,' I said. It was pretty feeble but I had just been shocked out of sleep and I wasn't at my best.

'It's not,' he countered. 'Weren't you listening? I just said the tide's a lot further out this time. The sand around the circle's virtually dry.'

He had to be exaggerating. What about all those pools we'd splashed through when we made the previous attempt? Some of them were pretty deep. I was far more wary of the main enemy, however. 'But the sea comes back in so quickly,' I protested, 'and we might get caught unawares.'

'We won't.' He grabbed my hand and we hurried over to the dry stream bed, trying to wriggle down without dislodging too many stones whose rattling fall might disturb Romain.

Romain...

Suddenly I was eager, willing to overcome my instinctive fear of the sea sanctuary and what it contained. Now it was I who was urging Sibert, running down the long shore and into the slowly paling eastern sky in pursuit of the retreating tide. For I had just thought this: if Sibert and I succeeded, we could slip away in the night with the treasure. Romain would know nothing about until he woke and by then we would be long gone.

His involvement with the sanctuary and what it contained would be over and perhaps – I was almost sure – that would mean the shadow of death would no longer hover above him and he would not have to die.

My actions tonight might well save his life.

We had reached the timber circle. I was shaking, once again cowering before its force. The low booming had begun again, louder than before. Now whatever power was making the eerie sound had eyes as well as a voice, for the tingling and prickling on my skin told me I was being watched. Somewhere out there in the

154

pinkish, unearthly light, something was aware of us. Sibert looked pale and scared. I wondered if he too heard the sound and felt the eyes...

'We have to do this,' I said. My teeth chattered with fear.

'I know.' He sounded no less terrified.

I don't know who made the first move but suddenly we were holding hands. I'm sure it was as much of a comfort to him as it was to me. He stepped up to the upturned stump and crouched down. Letting go of my hand, he put his fingers on the exposed trunk, just above where it disappeared under the sand. This time, it was almost clear of water and as I stared I thought I could make out what he had felt: a sort of line that seemed to have been cut into the wood.

'I think,' he said, 'that it might be time to see what you can pick up.'

Of course it was; that time had come quite a lot earlier, only I had been too awed by the sanctuary – too terrified of it, if I am honest – to act. Now I knew I had no choice.

I straightened up, stepped a deliberate pace away from Sibert and closed my eyes.

It was far, far worse with my eyes shut. The force lines that I had sensed whirling and spinning around us became visible behind my eyelids and they were harshly coloured, jagged and shocking. They touched on my bare arm and I felt as if I had been cut. I wanted to cry out, to scream, but I controlled myself. *I wish you no harm*, I tried to say silently to whatever it was that fought me, but it was a lie and the power out there must have known it; I did mean harm, for I intended to locate the hidden thing that the men of old had placed there so that Sibert could take it away.

I gathered my puny strength and fought back. Now they used different weapons, playing on my mind. My eyes were still tightly closed but yet I seemed to see the shore stretching away before me. The sea was out there; I could smell it and hear it and it was angry. Dawn was near and the sky in the east was lemon yellow, steadily filling with flame-coloured streaks. There was a ship on the horizon, sailing in out of the light. As yet she was just a black outline, but I could see by her profile that she was a longship and her proud prow was in the shape of a dragon. She was beautiful and graceful, but she brought horror.

I was so afraid, for I knew what her crew had come for.

Then I saw other men, behind me on the shore. One of them was a king, his high fore-head bound with a narrow silver circlet. Beside him was a robed figure of dark aspect and I knew him to be a sorcerer, for magic hummed and thrummed around him and he glowed faintly as if lit from within. Lines of brilliant blue-white light ran across his body, down his arms and legs and out into the wild air of the shore, stretching away to link with other lines until they joined to make a vast web connecting everything and everyone on the earth.

156

The sorcerer carried something in his out-stretched hands. Something in which he had captured his own power, for it shone brightly in the first rays of the rising sun.

Behind them a procession of figures slowly paced. On they came, on, on, until they reached the sea sanctuary. Still they came on, and the king and his sorcerer stopped beside the upturn-ed stump. The king nodded and the sorcerer bent down, placing the object he held so rever-ently in his hands into the tree...

...where as if by magic it seemed to meld with the very wood and disappear.

The vision faded.

My downturned palms felt as if great jolts of power were shooting through them. It hurt – oh, it hurt! – but I gritted my teeth against the agony. I opened my eyes, and tears of pain ran down my face. I discovered that I was up against the tree stump, my hands close together hovering right above the strange line that Sibert had discovered.

I crouched down. The force stabbing into my hands changed, first fading and then, as I held my palms down below the etched line, sud-denly coming back so strongly that at last I cried out.

'There!' I said, my voice not sounding like my own. *'There!* No, not where the line is, below it and to the right!'

It was as if the line had been carved into the wood as a pointer. Sibert, on his knees in the damp sand, was digging frantically like a dog after a rat, sending up showers of coarse grit. I stood at his shoulder, my hands still out-stretched, enduring the pain because I had the strong sense that, if I stopped doing whatever it was I was doing – acting as a receiver, perhaps – the power would switch off and the *thing* would just not be there any more...

It was a long way beyond anything I had learned with Edild.

I did not dare ask him if he had found any-thing. I could not have spoken at all; the effort of holding in the scream I was so desperate to let go was such that I had clamped my jaws shut. He dug on, deeper, deeper, desperate now. I watched him, aching for him to say some-thing, to cry out in triumph, to slump in dis-appointment. Above all I wanted him to stop, so that the pain I was enduring would go away.

He was still. Suddenly, after all that desperate digging, he was perfectly still.

Then, so slowly that at first I had to look closely to detect he was actually moving, he backed away from the hollow he had dug under the tree stump. He had something in his hands. It was an object, roughly circular, wrapped in an earth-stained, salt-stained, torn and ragged piece of coarse cloth.

He stood up, turning to face me.

He unwrapped the cloth.

The first rays of the new day's sun blasted out of the dawn and found their reflection in the object in Sibert's hands.

The object was solid gold.

# ELEVEN

It was a crown. A very simple one, really no more than a heavy circle of gold, unadorned with any stone. As the sun rose above the eastern sea and the light strengthened, Sibert and I, leaning over it, our fingers exploring it and quite unable to look away, noticed that there was a faintly etched pattern of leaves.

'Laurel leaves,' Sibert breathed.

I looked more closely. He was right, for the leaves had the distinctive shape of the bay laurel. Edild had warned me of the power of its berries, which could make a pregnant woman abort, and she told me that a bay tree by the door warded off the plague. Chewing on the leaves was dangerous, she had warned, as it brought on violent hallucinations.

I wondered why an ancient crown should have bay leaves carved on it. My fingertips still running over the vividly intertwining pattern of leaves, I noticed something else: the lines were made up of tiny, beautifully-worked runes. Whoever had crafted this crown, whoever had harnessed his power and put it into this incredible object, had sealed it inside with a rune spell.

I began to shake. For an instant it was as if a window in my mind opened and I saw the unbelievable potency of the thing I held in my hands. I saw light, so bright that it hurt my eyes. I sensed the incredible shock as mighty forces clashed together. I heard a loud humming sound echo and bounce inside my head, as if the aftermath of a cataclysmic thunderbolt.

Then with a sort of jolt – quite a violent one – I came back to myself. The bright early light was dimmed by a bank of cloud and the crown seemed to change – diminish, somehow – until it was merely a circle of metal.

I shook myself back into the here and now.

We had found a crown. Sibert and I had Romain's treasure in our hands. But it wasn't Romain's treasure now.

'We must get way from here,' I said urgently. 'Wrap it up again, Sibert. Quick!'

He glanced out to sea. 'The tide's turned,' he observed, 'but we have a while yet.'

But I hadn't meant merely that we must get away from the sea sanctuary. I thought carefully – this was a crucial moment – and then said, 'Sibert, we have to leave the area. We ought to be well away by the time Romain wakes up.'

His blue-green eyes met mine and I thought that he understood. In case he was not entirely sure of my meaning, I added, 'There's only one crown and it was undoubtedly put here by your forefathers.' I did not tell him about my vision. 'It's been under the tree stump for far too long to have been placed there by Fulk de la Flèche.'

'I know.' He nodded slowly. Then he said, 'Romain implied he'd make sure I got my share. But he's not going to do anything of the sort, is he?'

'I don't think so.' I didn't know, to be honest; I was probably maligning Romain, who could well have been planning to treat both his accomplices honourably and fairly. But my overriding purpose was to stop Romain in a headlong pursuit that, as far as I could see, would only have one outcome: his death.

'We'll go and fetch our packs and set off immediately,' Sibert said. I could feel the nervous energy building up in him. 'It's mine. This' – he hugged the crown to his chest – 'belongs to me. I will not let him have it. I found it' – *we* found it, I corrected him silently – 'and I intend to keep it.'

We turned our backs on the timber circle, whose power, I detected, had diminished noticeably now that we had violated it and robbed it of its treasure. We hurried across the damp sand, and I was very conscious of the sea at our backs. It felt threatening, and I had to keep turning round to make sure it hadn't sneaked up on us. I pictured the water gathering itself into a mighty wave which would break over our heads, swirl us around like leaves in a mill race and then withdraw, taking our drowned bodies with it. We had made the sea very, very angry; I was quite sure of it.

We were running, racing each other in our urgency, by the time we reached the dry stream bed that led up the cliff face. We stopped to get our breath back and Sibert tucked the crown, securely wrapped once more, under his belt. Noticing my eyes on him, he said softly, 'I have a leather bag rolled up in my pack. I'll put the crown in it and buckle it to my belt, under my tunic. It'll be safe there right next to my skin.'

I was worried by that. I knew very little about power objects but what I did know suggested it probably wasn't wise to wear them right against the body for any length of time...

We crept up to the place where we had left Romain. He was still fast asleep and he did not stir as, very carefully and cautiously, we collected our belongings and edged away. We walked on light feet for perhaps fifty or sixty paces, keeping to the shadow of the trees in case he woke and spotted us. Then the track rounded a shallow bend and we were out of sight of our camp. Without saying a word, we broke into a run and our speed barely eased until we were almost level with Dunwich, below us on our right.

'When we came here we emerged from that path over there,' I gasped, panting and leaning forward, my hands on my knees, trying to get my breath back. I nodded to where a sandy track wound its way off through the thin woodland.

'Yes,' Sibert agreed. He was looking around, a frown on his face. 'We should go back another way. He'll follow us, and he'll expect us to return via the same route we took on the way out.'

It made good sense. 'Do you know an alternative road?' I asked hopefully. He had been in the habit of coming here quite often, I reminded myself, and so it was quite possible.

He looked around again. Then he said, 'Yes, I think so. We'll go on past Dunwich and turn inland further to the north. There's a good road that runs from Lowestoft to Diss and we can pick that up, if I can remember the way. We'll journey westwards and cut across Thetford Forest, approaching Aelf Fen from the northeast.'

'I have to get back to Icklingham,' I reminded him.

'Yes,' he said vaguely. He sounded as if that was no concern of his. He glanced up at the sun. 'It's still very early. If we keep up a good speed we can be on the good road by sunset.'

I picked up his sense of haste. I could see as well as he could that if Romain picked up our trail we would be in a much safer position on a well-used road, with the presence, or at least the reasonable expectation, of fellow travellers and passers-by, than all by ourselves in the wilds.

We set off. We were not quite running but our pace was not far short of it.

Romain knew he was on the right track when he came to a place on the narrow path where some moisture remained in what had been a shallow puddle. Either they hadn't seen it – he knew from the speed at which he had been covering

the ground that they must have been hurrying –
or else they believed themselves safe from
pursuit. He did not much care. What was important – so very important – was that he could
see two clear footprints in the mud, one of a
man-sized boot, the other of a girl's coarse,
stout shoe. He could easily picture what the two
of them had been wearing on their feet, having
watched the footwear of all three of them
slowly drying out by yesterday's fire.

Where were they going? Romain wished he
had a better knowledge of the geography of the
region and the layout of its tracks and roads.
The narrow, ill-defined path along which he
was now pursuing Sibert and the girl – *and his
treasure*, although he tried not to dwell on that
as it made him apoplectic with rage – ran
roughly north-west. Romain could make little
sense of that, since Aelf Fen, where Sibert
lived, and Icklingham, where the girl was lodg-
ing, were surely due west. If they are trying to
put me off the scent, he thought grimly, then
they have failed. And as for that simpleton's
trick of going back via a different route, what
did they think he was?

He set off after them.

After the muddy footprints he had found no
more signs of them and he was beginning to
think he was wrong and they had returned some
other way. The sun was high in the sky and,
driven by thirst, for he had been running for
much of the way and sweating copiously, he

knew he must find water.

He came upon a tiny settlement in a clearing among the trees; one or two hovels, hens and a pig scratching in the dirt; a small child with trails of snot from nostrils to mouth sitting bare-arsed in the dirt. There was a ripe stench of ordure, either animal or human or both. The hamlet had a well, thankfully positioned a good distance away from all the shit, and as Romain approached, a fat woman was drawing water in a bucket. Holding out his cup, he asked if she would give him a drink and, after staring at him suspiciously for several moments, she nodded.

The water tasted like cool white wine in his parched mouth. He thanked her briefly, hoping she would retreat back to her hovel, but to his dismay she was disposed to chat. She perched her ample rump on the wall that ran around the well and, refilling his cup, urged him to drink some more.

'Now there's a thing,' she said cheerfully. 'I can be out here tending my little bit of land every day for a week and never see a soul, and here you are, filling your mug from my old bucket there, and you're the third person today to do so!'

He managed to contain the flare of excitement. 'Really?' he replied.

'Oh, yes,' she assured him, nodding to emphasize her words. Leaning closer – he caught a waft of warm air and smelt unwashed flesh – she dropped her voice and said, 'There were two of them, a youth and a girl, and the lass was quite a bit younger than the lad. I think they were runaways. Looked ever so anxious, they did. The lad kept staring back down the path as if he feared the devil was on his heels.' She folded her arms and nodded, as if to say, What do you think of that?

Fool of a woman, Romain thought. Did it not occur to her that he could be that devil? Apparently not, for she was still chattering. 'Pretty little thing she was, what was with him,' she said. 'She had lovely hair, coppery, like, but she was scrawny, not a lot of flesh on her.' She glanced down fondly at her own large bosom. 'But then she were young still,' she acknowledged charitably, 'no more than a girl.'

'Really?' he said again. Careful to keep a disinterested tone, he said, 'Which way were they heading?'

She pointed. 'Up there. Going to pick up the Diss road, I reckon.'

'Hmm.' He made himself drink several more slow mouthfuls. Then he wiped his cup and tucked it back inside his pack. He stretched, looked at the fat woman and said, 'Well, I must be on my way.'

'You've far to go, my lord?' she asked.

He gave her a lazy smile. 'Only another few miles, then I shall be home in my own hall.'

'God's speed,' she said.

He sensed her eyes on his back as, forcing himself to saunter when he wanted to run, he returned to the track.

\* \* \*

I must catch them before they reach the road. He repeated it to himself over and over, trying to dull his fatigue, his growing sense of hopelessness and the sharp, hot, constant pain of his blistered foot. He did not dare risk a look at it. He had the fearful suspicion that it was beginning to smell; did that mean infection? He did not know.

He made himself hurry on.

He heard them before he saw them. The path ran through a belt of trees and, welcoming the shade, he had been very tempted to stop and rest. He had resisted the temptation. Now, as he stared ahead to the sunshine beyond the trees, he heard voices. A young man's voice and a girl's.

He turned off the path and slipped through the trees, hiding behind each trunk, spying ahead to make sure he saw them before they saw him. They were moving quite slowly now and as Romain drew near he heard Sibert say, 'It can only be a few miles now till we get on to the road, and then we'll—'

Romain pounced.

I picked up no warning signs and the first I knew of his presence was when he flew through the air and landed on Sibert's back. He was making a terrible noise – a snarling, ferocious, wild-animal noise – and he was raining down such powerful blows on Sibert's head and shoulders that I was amazed Sibert could still stand. He was taller than Romain, but Romain was broader and had a man's muscles where Sibert had those of a boy.

Sibert, however, seemed to be possessed. Spinning round very fast, he released himself from Romain's grip on his tunic and for a moment turned defence into attack. He got in a hard punch to Romain's jaw that jerked his head back; I heard his teeth snap together and I think he must have bitten his tongue, for blood started to spurt from his mouth. He took a pace backwards and tripped, and Sibert was on him like a hound on a deer, knees on Romain's chest and fists flying in the general direction of his face.

Romain was gathering himself. I could see it and I yelled, 'Sibert, watch out, he's up to something!' Sibert shot me a look and then, bunching his right hand, swung it in a wide arc towards Romain's head. Romain saw it coming – anyone would have done, Sibert didn't seem to know much about fist-fighting – and caught it easily in his left fist. With his right, he hit Sibert very hard on the side of his head and Sibert slumped over to his right.

If he fell he would be done for. I sprang forward and got my arms under his shoulders, then using all my strength humped him first to a sitting position and then to his feet. He was very unsteady, rocking to and fro, his face white except for the vivid scarlet mark on his temple. Beyond him, I watched in horror as Romain leapt up and drew a knife.

'*I want my crown!*' he screamed.

'It's not yours!' Sibert yelled back. His hands were on the leather bag concealed under his tunic. 'You were going to rob me of it, but it's mine, it was made by my ancestor!'

His ancestor. Of course. From all Sibert's talk of sorcerers in the family, I had pretty much worked that out. I forced myself back to the perilous present; Romain was watching Sibert's hands and I knew that he had guessed what Sibert was guarding.

As I stared at the crown in its leather bag beneath Sibert's tunic, I had the strange thought that it was neither Romain nor Sibert who was controlling events. It was the crown, steadily sending out its power and driving both the man and the youth to madness. For a frightening moment as my eyes flashed from one to the other, I recognized neither of them. Romain's handsome face was ugly with urgent greed and Sibert – oh, Sibert looked like a man of forty, thin, haggard, lined and grey.

I screamed in horror.

Romain lunged for Sibert, the knife in his right hand. I did not think for an instant that Sibert would stand his ground. For one thing, I had already seen he wasn't much of a fighter and for another, only a fool faces up to a man with a knife when he himself is unarmed.

Sibert was unarmed but he was possessed. I watched, horrified, as the crown commanded his actions. He stood like stone and I sensed the power of the crown throb and thrum in the air. Romain leapt at him and even as the knife flashed in its descent, Sibert acted. He was considerably taller than Romain and this, together with the fact that Romain had jumped up and was now coming down again, gave Sibert the one advantage that he had.

I do not think to this day that Sibert would have realized this for himself. He was, as I have said, possessed, and the crown was thinking for him.

But there was no knowing precisely what the crown had in mind so, just to be on the safe side, I added some advice of my own. I cried out, *'Now, Sibert! Get your leg up!'*

As Romain descended on Sibert, the knife in one hand and the other stretched out to grab Sibert's shoulder, Sibert calmly raised his knee. It caught Romain between the legs and I winced at the force of the impact. Romain gave a great cry of agony and fell on to his left side. The knife flew out of his hand and Sibert went over to pick it up. Staring down at Romain, he gave a curt nod. Then he looked at me and said, 'Let's go.'

I wanted so much to stay. Romain had failed and Sibert had the crown; at that moment all my sympathies were with Romain. Not only had he lost the treasure he had tried so hard to win but he'd also lost what he had hoped to acquire with it. He had, in short, lost his future.

But if I had not aided Sibert against him, I reasoned with myself, fighting back my tears, then he would have lost his life. He'd been in danger – Granny said so, and now I had seen it

170

for myself. I couldn't have let him die, for he meant far too much to me.

I stood over him, watching as he rolled to and fro in a futile attempt to ease the pain, settling on his back with his knees clutched to his chest. There was nothing I could do.

I turned away and set off after Sibert.

We did the journey in three marches. That night we slept deep in woodland just short of the road we'd been heading for and the next night we were on the fringe of the Thetford Forest. Early in the evening of the third day, we were approaching the place where our roads diverged.

'I'm not coming all the way to Aelf Fen,' I said wearily. The idea of the long miles I still had to cover before I reached Icklingham was daunting but it was even further to Aelf Fen. I'd been tempted to go on to the village with Sibert and knock on my aunt Edild's door to beg a bed for the night – after all, I'd used her as my excuse for absenting myself from Goda's house – but I thought I had better not involve her in any other way. If Goda ever checked up on me, that would be a different matter but otherwise, the less anybody knew about where I'd been and why, the better. As far as Edild and everyone else in Aelf Fen were aware, I was over in Icklingham looking after my sister.

Sibert and I stood eyeing each other. We had shared so much and we had done a momentous thing. Were we thieves, in the eyes of the law? I did not know. Romain would say that we were, and only a couple of weeks before he would have had some justification, in that what Sibert carried in his leather bag had been hidden on Romain's land. But now the king had taken the manor and everything in it, so in truth, I supposed, we had stolen from him.

It was alarming, to say the least.

I reassured myself with the thought that morally, if in no other way, the crown belonged to Sibert as the descendant of the man who had made it. I had longed to ask him about this all the long miles of our journey home but he had changed. The Sibert who possessed the crown – or, more likely, it was the crown that possessed him – was not a man of whom you could ask unwelcome questions, and every sense told me that this was not a matter he wished to discuss with me.

I turned away, leaving him standing at the crossroads, and headed off down the track to Icklingham. I was dog tired, my feet ached, I was hungry, thirsty, filthy dirty and my face was hot and prickly with sunburn. I had done what I had been asked, and what had I got for my troubles? Nothing.

I trudged on, deep in self-pity.

But then as I drew near to my destination and at last a proper bed to sleep in, I realized that I was wrong. I had got something, and its value far outweighed money or treasure.

Romain – who, I admitted to myself, I liked so much that it felt like love – had been in deadly peril. Death had shadowed him and I had seen its black cloud over his handsome head as we stood by the sea sanctuary. Somehow the crown had endangered him; that was where the threat lay. By my actions I had seen to it that Romain and the crown were kept apart.

I had saved his life.

Happy, smug in this secret knowledge of my own power and skill that could outwit death, finally I got to Goda's house. It was fully dark now and I could hear my sister's snores. I didn't look to see if Cerdic was home – it didn't really matter – and, being as quiet as I could, I let myself into the lean-to and fell on to my bed.

It had taken Romain some time before he felt able to straighten out his curled body. Whenever he risked movement, the pain ripped up from his groin with such ferocity that it was as if Sibert's knee was driving into him all over again. Slowly, agonizingly, he rolled on to his side, then up on to hands and knees. Then he tried to stand up.

Besides the injury, however, he was suffering from dehydration and he had not eaten anything of any substance for hours. He had raced along the track in pursuit of Sibert and the crown; he had been in a fight that had left him badly hurt. His blistered foot was a constant agony, throbbing in repeated waves of pain in time with his fast heartbeat. It was little wonder, then, that the moment he was upright, his head began to swim and he fainted.

When he came back to himself he was lying

on his left side, knees drawn up, his face pressed into the soft ground. He tried to remember how he had got there. He felt dizzy, sick and disoriented and his memory would not oblige him.

When eventually he recalled the events of the recent past, he groaned aloud. They had deceived him, that crafty youth and the skinny girl who looked so young and scared but whose true nature was so very different. They had crept out of the sleeping place in the night, gone back to the sanctuary and stolen his crown. He had tried to fight the lad to regain it but he had failed and they had escaped him. Now they were somewhere on the road ahead and, injured and sick as he was, there was little chance that he could overtake them.

Little chance? he thought. There was no chance at all, for by now they would be deep in those pestilential, haunted Fens and he knew he would be hard put to follow and find them.

Very cautiously he sat up. The swimming sensation flooded back but he gritted his teeth and endured it. When it faded a little, he tried once again to stand up. This time he succeeded.

'What should I do?' he said aloud. 'I must have my crown' – it was the one thought that was in his mind, banging insistently against his skull until he thought he would go mad – 'and so I have no choice but to follow them.'

His footsteps dragged as he made his slow way over to where the path emerged from beneath the dark shadow of the trees. It was then that he knew he was no longer alone.

He could not identify the sound that had set his nerves tingling and jangling with fear. Was it a footstep? A soft intake of breath? He stood quite still, heart hammering, sweat breaking out on his body, and listened.

The silence ached around him.

His control broke and he yelled, 'Where are you? Come out and show yourself!'

Not a sound.

I am being stupid, he tried to tell himself. There's no one there or, if there is, it's some poacher up to no good and probably far more frightened of me than I am of him.

But in his heart he knew that this was no poacher.

He believed he knew who it was and the thought terrified him.

'I haven't got it!' he cried, a sob in his voice. 'The boy and the girl took it and now they are far away!'

He stared around him, eyes wide and wild. He thought he saw movement and spun his head so swiftly to look more closely that the threatening faintness came rushing back.

He fought down the nausea and went on staring.

It seemed to him that there was something black creeping out from under the trees. He blinked and it vanished.

'Where are you?' he sobbed again. 'Show yourself!' Whatever horror lurked there out of the deep past, it would be better to face it, to see what it was.

Wouldn't it?

He thought he smelt the sea. Oh, dear God, what was it? Some dread magic conjured up by the sorcerers of old? Some projection of their vast, unearthly power, disguised as the terrible dragon whose roar gave Drakelow its name?

'Help me,' he whimpered. 'Oh, God, help me!'

They – *it* – had come for the stolen treasure. He knew it. He was the thief, for all that he did not have the crown. Dark, frightful and all-knowing powers such as these, whatever they were, knew who was to blame.

They blamed him.

And they had come for him. They had followed him stealthily all the way from the sea and now they would take him.

With a moan of pure terror, Romain sank to his knees. Holding up his clasped hands as if in prayer, he wept. 'Spare me!' he begged. 'Oh, spare me!'

There was a whistling noise, as if something heavy was flying through the air. The pain burst with unbelievable, agonizing force inside Romain's head and then the dark took him.

# TWELVE

In the morning I entertained my grumpy and by now all but immobile sister to a lively account of my week back in Aelf Fen. She didn't seem particularly interested but all the same I elaborated and embroidered my tale, describing this person's concussion, that person's severe bruising and how I had helped Edild reduce a fracture. In the end Goda shouted at me to shut my mouth, get on with cleaning the house and then fetch her something to eat.

Meekly I did as I was told. The house certainly needed cleaning and it looked as if whoever had been keeping an eye on my sister during my absence – probably the village mid-wife – had contented herself with the briefest of visits and done no more than make sure Goda was still alive and not giving birth. As I worked I continued to volunteer further details about life back in Aelf Fen until Goda lost her temper and threw a wooden platter at me. Advanced pregnancy had, however, weakened her aim and the platter's trajectory was feeble. I ducked it with the ease of long practice.

I decided it would do no harm to describe my fictitious stay in Aelf Fen to Cerdic, too. I wanted to make sure that if ever anyone accused me of having journeyed all the way to the coast south of Dunwich where I assisted in the theft of a gold crown, at least two people would protest that I couldn't possibly have done because I was staying with and helping my aunt Edild. I reminded myself that if the day ever came when more verification was called for, I must enlist Edild's help too so that she supported my story as well.

I was, however, quietly confident that no such day would ever come.

It came two days later.

I had been occupied in the mammoth and complicated task of changing the rough and worn sheets on Goda's bed. The task was well overdue and exhausting right from the start, when I had to help her to get up and sit on the bench by the hearth. Immediately she began to harangue me for not working fast enough. The bed was horrible and I won't describe exactly in what way. I stripped it, put the straw mattress outside the door and gave it a vigorous beating. Then I sponged down the sacking that covered it, opened one end and stuffed in some fresh sprigs of pennyroyal to discourage the fleas. I took the sheets down to the stream and plunged them into the water, then picked up Goda's block of lye-and-tallow soap and began rubbing it into the worst of the stains.

I had the sheets washed, rinsed and spread out on gorse bushes to dry when I heard the sound of horses' hooves. Looking up, my heart beating fast in alarm, I saw three of the lord's men riding into the village. They were bareheaded – clearly not expecting the least sign of trouble in a small village full of humble people minding their own business – and their surcoats were maroon and bore a device in black. Even if they weren't expecting trouble, all the same each of them had a sword at his side.

They went to my sister's house and I knew they had come for me. They went inside, stayed for a short while, then one of them came hurrying out again, leapt on to his horse and rode away. Was he going to check on my story?

I cursed myself. Why hadn't I gone on to Aelf Fen with Sibert that night and spoken to Edild? She would back me up, I knew it, but she could not if she didn't know I needed her to! Oh, what an idiot I had been.

I waited, holding my breath.

I heard my sister screech, *'Lassair!* Come here!'

I went.

I had left her sitting on the bench in nothing but her shift, stretched impossibly tight across her swollen belly and none too clean. I had intended to see to her once the sheets were drying, and for now she was sweaty, smelly and greasy-faced, her hair hanging in sticky rats' tails and so dulled by dirt that its bright carroty-red colour was totally hidden. I felt a stab of sympathy for her, as this was no condition in which any woman would wish to greet two

179

well-dressed, important men.

The sympathy was short-lived. 'What have you done?' she yelled at me as I stepped through the door. 'You're in for a beating, my girl, bringing shame to an honest household, and I'll—'

One of the men – the elder of the two – held up an imperious hand and my sister fell silent, her mouth left hanging open.

'You are Lassair?' he asked.

I tried to read his expression but his face was bland and gave nothing away.

'I am.'

'Your sister here tells us you have recently been at Aelf Fen.'

'Yes, that's right. I was staying with my aunt, her name's Edild and she's a healer, and we were—'

Again he held up his hand. 'So I am given to understand. I have sent one of my company to verify the truth of what you say.'

I said nothing. Across the miles that separated us, I was concentrating on feverishly willing Edild to back me up.

'You are required to come with us to Aelf Fen,' he stated baldly.

To my own village? Why? I wondered frantically. If as I suspected all this flurry of activity was because they'd found the crown, then why did I have to go to Aelf Fen when the act of theft had been at Drakelow? But then I thought, ah, yes, but the crown is with Sibert, and he's at Aelf Fen.

I almost blurted out the question that they must have known I was desperate to ask. But somehow I managed to hold it back. I was innocent, I reminded myself firmly. I had been nowhere near Drakelow but closeted with my aunt Edild, helping her in her healing work. Innocent people did not demand anxiously why they were wanted. Confident that it could be for no sinister purpose, they simply smiled and said, very well.

Which was exactly what I did.

They were obviously in a hurry because they were not content to go at my walking pace. Instead the younger man swung up into the saddle of his great chestnut horse and, bending down and catching me under the arms, lifted me up and sat me down in front of him. Then both men put spurs to their mounts and we were off, cantering smartly in the direction of Aelf Fen.

All the way there I was thinking about Sibert.

How could I help him? If they suspected what he – we – had done, how could I defend him? Perhaps he, like me, had prepared a good story and, if what I dreaded had happened and they had accused him of stealing the crown, he would be able to hold his head high and offer proof that he had been nowhere near Dunwich.

Then it would be Romain's word – for surely it could only be he who had brought the accusations – against Sibert's and mine. Two against one, but the trouble was that the one was a rich Norman lord's son. A rich lord, however, I reminded myself, who had just fallen so far out of favour with the king that his manor, his lands and his property had been seized.

Perhaps it did not look quite so bad after all.

I concentrated very hard on making my expression sweet and innocent. A decent girl, hard-working, caught in the act of helping her pregnant sister and only lately returned from a stint of dedicated nursing and healing with her aunt; that was the way they must see me.

Trying like fury to send a mental message to Edild – *When they ask, support me! Oh, please, Edild, say I've been with you the whole time!* – all too soon we were riding into Aelf Fen.

I had never seen so many people gathered together in my village. We do not have a central meeting point such as I had seen the villagers enjoy at Icklingham, for Aelf Fen is, as the name implies, a Fenland village and grew up, I suppose, from a series of dwellings constructed over time above the upper line of the tidal wash. There have always been dwellings there, we know that, and sometimes when people dig over a new piece of ground they find evidence of ancient houses, circular where ours are rectangular, huddled close together as if in fear of the great world beyond. The track sweeps through the village in a sort of wiggle, with the little houses situated on one side and the wetter ground leading down to the water in the other. Such was the avid curiosity of the villagers this morning that some of them, standing at the rear of the crowd, were ankle-deep in black, muddy water.

The man I was riding with deposited me – quite gently and carefully – on the ground, and then dismounted and went to join his two companions. They spoke briefly and one of them looked in my direction. There were another lord's men there too, wearing a different device on their breasts. I counted half a dozen of them. Standing with them was a tall and burly man of perhaps thirty-five or forty, dark hair club-cut in a fringe, clean-shaven and dressed in clothes that must have been expensive but which now looked well-worn and travel-stained.

Nobody seemed particularly interested in me, although I had a feeling this state was not going to last. For now, I slipped in between two of my neighbours and tried to make myself invisible. I looked around for my family and saw my parents, my granny, my sister Elfritha and my brother Squeak. My mother held the baby. My brother Haward stood behind one of the lord's men. He caught my eye and sent me a worried frown. I was wondering whether to slip through the crowd and go to speak to him when I saw Edild. She was standing with the rider who had been sent to question her and verify my tale of having spent the past week with her. She too caught my eye and I thought I saw her give a very small nod. Had I not been looking so anxiously for some such sign, I don't think I would have seen it.

I breathed a huge sigh of relief and began praying fervently, saying over and over again,

*Thank you. Thank you. Thank you.*

This must be the reason why the lord's men seemed so unconcerned with me. The rider who hastened away from Goda's house had sought out Edild and she, bless her, had backed me up without hesitation. I knew I had some explaining to do and I guessed she was none too pleased with me. But she had supported my story. At that terrifying moment, that was all I could think of.

The relief that coursed through me was short-lived for just then they brought forward Sibert. Tall though he may be, he is slim and lightly built and I could not think it really needed two heavy-handed guards to hold him. It seemed that the two different companies of manor officials had each provided their roughest, toughest guard and one stood on Sibert's right and the other on his left. Sibert looked petrified.

The man who had questioned me in Goda's house now stepped up on to a large wooden box that some helpful villager must have provided. He said in a loud voice, 'An accusation of theft has been made against the young man Sibert of Aelf Fen, here before you. He has just been brought from the house of his mother and his uncle' – I stared round frantically and there were Froya and Hrype at the back of the crowd, Froya tugging and twisting anxiously at her white linen apron, her face as pale as her light blonde hair, and Hrype scowling thunderously – 'and he will now be searched.'

They must already have searched the cottage,

I thought wildly, not that it would have taken long to rummage through the family's few belongings in their one-roomed house. Clever Sibert, not to have hidden the crown in so obvious a place! I wondered where he had put it. Perhaps he had thought up a suitable place on our long march home – he'd passed enough time in silence to have come up with several likely spots, and—

They had dragged him out in the open where everyone could see and they were starting to pull off his clothes. He cried out in protest and started to struggle, and one of the guards hit him quite hard on the jaw. I heard a gasp and then a moan from Froya. His tunic was lifted over his head and two of the guards felt it carefully to see if anything was hidden in its folds. Someone made him lift his feet, one after the other, and they drew off his boots. Then one of the guards who had been holding him untied the drawstring around his narrow waist and his baggy breeches fell to the ground and bunched around his ankles.

Sibert stood there naked but for a leather bag that hung over his flat belly, fastened on a thin strap around his hips. In his shame he hung his head. I wished I had looked away sooner, for as I screwed my eyes shut I could still see him. His face, throat and lower arms were sunburned, dark against the pale flesh normally covered by his garments, and his body looked frail, the ribs and the collarbones very prominent. His legs were long, the sinews straight and wiry. His penis, shrivelled with his fear, hung limp beneath its thatch of fair hair.

I kept my eyes shut while silently I sent him the strongest support I could muster. If he looked up and saw me, I thought, he would see that at least one villager was not staring at him in his humiliation and—

Oh, but what was I thinking of!

I was almost weeping with sympathy for my friend because he stood stripped and shamed in front of the whole village. But that was nothing. For, obsessed and driven young man that I now knew him to be, he had not hidden the crown at all.

Perhaps he tried. Perhaps he got out to whatever place he had selected for its concealment and then when the moment came, discovered he was unable to tear himself away from it.

The little experience I had had of the crown told me that its power was such that it was more than capable of such a feat.

However it had happened, the fact remained that Sibert stood before those who had come looking for what he and I had stolen and he was carrying it – *wearing* it, almost – in its leather bag around his body.

I had to look.

One of the guards had unfastened the bag and was on the point of untying the thongs to see what was within. Then the burly man stepped forward and took it rather roughly from the guard's hands. Only a man as big and powerful as he would risk that, I thought, for the guard was very broad and bore the signs of more than one fight on his coarse features. For an instant he stared at the burly man through narrowed slits of eyes, then he stepped back.

The burly man thrust his hand into the bag. He must have known full well what was in there, for the shape was unmistakable. He paused, and I saw a cruel smile twist his thin lips. Then he extracted his hand and held the crown high above his head.

There was no need for words and he said nothing. The guards closed in around Sibert as if they feared that, faced with incontrovertible truth of his guilt, he might think he had nothing to lose and try to make a run for it. I could have told them they were wrong; Sibert, I realized, was in a state that verged on total collapse and only the guards holding his arms stopped him from slumping to the ground.

Then I realized something strange. The burly man was not the only one who was suddenly mute; nobody else was speaking either. And Sibert's guards were ashen-faced.

The little group made up of Sibert, his guards, the lord's men and the burly man formed the centre of the crowd and they were closest to the crown. But as the burly man continued to hold it high in the air, it was as if a wave of its power broke over the rest of us. Some seemed impervious, continuing to stare blankly at the drama unfolding before them. Some – Hrype, Edild, my sister Elfritha – went so white that they looked deadly sick and I knew I must look the same. My knees shook and it was all that I could do to keep standing. There was a rushing sound in my ears and my skin felt as if it had been blasted by hot air. I wanted very much to throw up.

The invisible wave passed.

The burly man must have recovered for suddenly he was shouting in a loud, confident voice, 'Here is the object that was stolen from me and that I now reclaim!'

*Stolen from me.*

I knew then who he was.

I fixed my eyes on him, using all my puny, fledgling power in an attempt to make him look at me. He did, and for the first time I stared into the glittering black eyes of the man I knew to be Baudouin de la Flèche.

*It is not yours*, I said silently as our gazes met. *It was hidden centuries ago by men who were not of your blood. Even the feeble excuse that it lay hidden on what for a time was your land no longer applies for Drakelow is no longer yours.*

I don't know if he knew what I was thinking. Probably not, but it made me feel better to be doing something.

He stared at me blank-eyed for a moment. Then he gave a very horrible smile.

He held up his hand and at once the agitated hiss of muttered comments that had broken out among the villagers ceased. 'Sibert of Aelf Fen here is guilty of theft,' he stated forcefully. I saw one of the lord's men step forward as if to protest, to say, perhaps, that Sibert would have to be put on trial to determine his guilt, but Baudouin de la Flèche ignored him. 'The proof of his theft was found on his body and all here present saw it!' He looked round as if daring us to challenge him. Nobody did.

'There is more,' he said, still staring round and now speaking in a low, dramatic tone that carried right to the back of the crowd. He spun round to face Sibert. Then, his face working with the violent emotion that tore through him, he shouted, 'This young man is a murderer! He killed my nephew and he will hang!'

The horrified mutterings of the villagers rose to a crescendo and with it, blending like two lines of melody, I heard a ferocious humming like a skep of angry bees. It came from the crown, but whether it was jubilant or protesting I did not know.

The sounds climaxed inside my head to a roar. I felt dizzy with sudden violent vertigo and my knees gave way. I was vaguely aware of the ground rushing up to meet me and then everything went black.

# THIRTEEN

When I came to I was lying on the floor in my own home and my mother and my aunt were bending over me. My granny sat beside the hearth, watching me very closely. I could see her deep eyes glittering. Ignoring both her and my poor mother, who had clearly been crying and was red-eyed and puffy-nosed, I grabbed Edild's hand and said, 'I'm so sorry! I'll explain, I promise!'

She knew, of course, what I referred to. 'Don't worry about that now,' she replied. My mother looked mystified and Edild turned to her. 'Essa, could you find a blanket, please? Lassair's shivering. I think it's the shock.'

'Of course!' My mother leapt up. She has a lot of respect for her sister-in-law and would never dream of challenging her in her healing role. Besides, they are very fond of each other.

'Quickly, now,' my aunt hissed, bending low over me. 'You've been with me for the past week or so, is that what you've said? I've already told them you were but we'd better agree on the details.'

'Yes,' I hissed back. 'I told Goda I had to come back to the village to help you with the injured from an accident with a hay cart.'

'The accident that happened rather longer ago than a week.' Edild nodded. 'Any specific injuries?'

'I helped you with a fractured leg,' I whispered. 'A nasty injury, with bits of bone sticking out. I had to hold the man's shoulders while you pulled on his leg, but you gave him something to numb the pain.'

She nodded again. 'Otherwise, mainly cuts and bruises?'

'Yes.'

'Clever girl,' she muttered. 'Except for the fractured leg, exactly what we did do. We'll just have to hope,' she added, speaking swiftly because my mother was coming over to us, 'that nobody thinks to check the time of this accident and its aftermath with the victims.'

With that awkward little conversation out of the way, I relaxed for a moment. Then, of course, I remembered about Sibert. Even worse, if anything could be worse, I remembered about Romain, whose uncle, his face distorted with grief, had said he was dead. I felt two large tears roll out of my eyes and slide sideways on to the pillow. My mother bent down and hugged me wordlessly. It was, as it always has been, a great comfort. Edild offered to make a soothing drink for me and hurried away, leaving my mother by my side holding my hand.

I needed, however, comfort of a different sort. I needed to know what was happening to Sibert and – for no matter how badly someone we're fond of is suffering, we still put our own safety first, or at least I did then – I had to know why they had come looking for me.

How had they possibly known I was involved?

I had to think. I had to try to piece together what might have happened, and for that I needed quiet. In case my mother felt she ought to talk to me to take my mind off the morning's awful events, I closed my eyes and made my breathing deep and steady. Presently I sensed her get up and tiptoe away. Please don't think she was being callous; it's just that she always has so much to do that she couldn't afford to spend time at the side of her distraught daughter if that daughter had just fallen asleep.

I had imagined at first that it was Romain who had organized the lord's men to come searching for Sibert, me and the crown, but it could not have been because he was dead. He could, I supposed, have told his uncle about what we had done before he died, so that it was Baudouin and not Romain who tracked us down. I thought about that for a while and it seemed to make sense. Romain had somehow got word to his uncle, then, that I had helped Sibert steal the crown, yet I had told a different story, one verified by my aunt and, to a lesser extent, by Goda and Cerdic. It was my word against Baudouin's and although he was a Norman lord and I a village girl, for one thing I had someone to verify my story and for another he had rebelled against the king and lost everything. My position was beginning to look more secure.

Then I thought, aghast, but Romain is dead!

Romain was *dead*. I could still barely believe it. Baudouin claimed that Sibert had murdered him, but that wasn't possible. Was it? He certainly hadn't murdered him in the time it took us to walk home from Drakelow because we had been together every minute. He could, I supposed, have got up while I was asleep, found Romain and killed him, but I didn't think it at all likely. Sibert and I had both been very scared on that journey home and we had barely slept. Even when I did manage to drift off, the slightest sound had brought me back to full consciousness. I didn't think Sibert could have left my side without my noticing, since to comfort ourselves we had slept with our backs pressed tightly together. Besides, was it possible that a slim youth like Sibert could have attacked and killed a much broader, stronger man like Romain without a considerable amount of noise? And then returned and calmly gone back to sleep as if nothing had happened? That presupposed that Romain had recovered sufficiently from Sibert's knee in his testicles to get up and follow us, and I was not at all sure he could have done.

No. I was willing to swear that Sibert had not murdered Romain on the course of that journey. It was possible that Romain had followed him back to Aelf Fen and Sibert had slain him then, but surely Froya and Hrype would be able to prove that he didn't because he lived with them and they would know his movements.

Unless, of course, he had actually managed to evade them and he *had* gone out and killed Romain...

Romain was dead.

I had been so busy rushing in my mind to Sibert's defence that I had barely taken in that stark, horrible, heartbreaking fact.

Romain was dead. With him went my happy daydream of him discovering how I had helped Sibert take the crown and so saved Romain from its deadly threat, and coming to Aelf Fen to rescue me from my village life and marry me, turning me at a stroke from peasant into lady. Drakelow would, of course, have been restored to him (how this would be achieved without the crown I had not quite worked out) and we would live in blissful happiness for the rest of our days.

But he was dead.

Despite what I had done, that shadow had still found him and death had claimed him, just as my granny had predicted. I risked a quick peep to see if she was still sitting there watching me. She was. Knowing Granny, even if she hadn't seen the quick flutter of my eyelids she would still be well aware that I wasn't really asleep. I didn't think I could bear to talk to her just then. She had warned me, months ago, and I ought to have taken more notice. Instead I had thought I knew better. I had believed in my overconfident faith in myself that I could outwit death when it had put its mark on someone. What a fool I had been, for now I had lost him.

Soundlessly, secretly, I wept.

When I finished weeping, I had a thought. If Sibert did not kill Romain – and I was quite sure he did not – then who did?

I was not allowed to get up. Had it not been for my grief over Romain and my gnawing, constant anxiety over Sibert, I would have relished the chance to lie there in comfort while my family ministered to me. While I needed to be looked after – and clearly they all thought I did – Edild had taken up temporary residence and, because there was so little room, my brother Haward was going to sleep in her house, taking Squeak with him. He's a kind man, my brother, and he did not complain at all about being cast out of his home for my sake.

Later that day, when darkness was falling and all was quiet, Hrype came to our house. I was sitting up by then, propped up on a pillow and regularly sipping the concoctions that Edild prepared. They had tried to make me eat but my stomach was tying itself in knots and I knew I would be sick if I did.

Hrype accepted a place beside Granny on the bench by the hearth and as he sat down he stared at me. I made myself stare back. He is, I suppose you would say, quite a handsome man, always giving the impression that he takes care of himself. His hair is long, dark blond, parted in the middle and hanging glossy and smooth down to his shoulders. His eyes are light – grey, I would say – and the bones of his face are graceful, almost kingly – he has high cheekbones and a proud nose. He rarely smiles. He was for sure not smiling now.

I tried to read what was in his eyes but his skills are so far above mine that he knew I was searching and blocked himself off. Edild might have penetrated him a little way but she did not even appear to be trying, instead looking after him solicitously as if he had been taken ill. In a way, he had; he looked grief-stricken and he was white with shock.

He did not waste any time. As soon as we were settled, my parents opposite Hrype, Edild and Elfritha on low stools and the baby asleep in his cradle, he said, 'They have taken Sibert away and he is in prison. They say he will face trial but Baudouin de la Flèche speaks of dragging him out and hanging him.'

There was a horrified silence. Then my father said, 'What happened? I mean,' he corrected himself hurriedly, 'what does Baudouin claim happened?'

Hrype was watching me. It made me feel very uncomfortable. He said, 'He claims that Sibert stole the crown from its hiding place at his manor of Drakelow.' I almost protested that it wasn't his manor any longer but then I remembered that I wasn't supposed to know that. I wasn't supposed to have been anywhere near the place, never mind knowing who it did or did not belong to. 'Then he set off to make his way secretly home to Aelf Fen.' He paused. 'Baudouin suspects that Sibert was not alone.' Again those strange silvery eyes with their unreadable expression glanced against me. 'He claims that his nephew Romain knew of the theft and pursued Sibert with the intention of reclaiming the stolen crown. He says that, worried for his nephew's safety, he set out to look for him. He encountered men searching for *him*, bringing the awful news that Romain was dead and offering to take him to the place where he had been slain. He says that he has a witness to the moment when Romain caught up with Sibert and this person saw with his own eyes how Sibert doubled back on his tracks and so came upon Romain from behind.' Then Baudouin's witness has identified the wrong man, I thought fiercely, for Sibert did no such thing. 'It is claimed that Sibert leapt out on Romain, taking him by surprise, and hit him very hard on the back of the head with a heavy branch. The witness heard the crunch of the shattering bones and Romain fell dead to the ground. Sibert ran away.' He stopped abruptly, wiping his hands over his face several times.

After a while my father spoke, very hesitantly expressing what I was thinking. 'Er – if this is true,' he said, 'if we are meant to believe that there is a fragment of truth in it, then, as soon as Baudouin learned from the witness what had just happened, why did he not immediately set off after Sibert – er, after the assailant, and catch him? He had just been told that his

197

nephew had been brutally slain, yet he would have us believe he did nothing to apprehend the killer? He is a big, strong man,' he added thoughtfully, 'and surely he could have outrun a slight youth like Sibert.' He thought some more. 'He'd surely have had a horse,' he added.

Hrype looked at him intently and then said neutrally, 'He says he was preoccupied with looking after Romain.'

'But he'd been told that Romain was dead when he fell! If Baudouin knew that, surely he realized there was nothing he could do and much the better course of action was to catch the killer!' My father sounded quite cross, as if such irrational behaviour were more than any decent man should be asked to believe.

My mother gave a quiet sound of distress. Putting a hand on my father's arm, she murmured, 'He was grieving and surely not himself, Wymond. The poor man had just been led to where his nephew lay dead and was that very moment bending over the body.'

My father grunted something.

Hrype was still looking at him. I saw him give a very small smile of approval. 'I thought precisely the same thing as you,' he said. 'It is what, indeed, I tried to say to the men who are holding Sibert.'

'How is he?' my mother asked softly. Now it was she to whom I was grateful, for I longed to ask the same question.

'He – has suffered a profound humiliation and a severe shock,' Hrype said. 'He does not

198

believe, however, that he is guilty of theft and he knows he is not guilty of murder. I hope,' he said with a sigh, 'that these firm beliefs may sustain him in his time of trial.'

'He's going to be tried?' I asked. I had not really wanted to draw Hrype's attention to me – any more than it was already there, for all the time he was engaged in talking to my parents I sensed that a part of him was probing me – but I could not hold back the question.

Hrype gave me a wry smile. 'I did not speak literally,' he said. 'As to whether he will be tried, I cannot say. I hope so, for it is better than summary execution, but then the trial will be performed by Normans and we are not of their kind.'

We all knew what he meant by that.

'If there is a trial,' he said, 'then Sibert will have to prove that he could not have done the deeds of which he is accused. Somehow it will have to be demonstrated that the object he stole did not belong to Baudouin de la Flèche.' He did not elaborate but I thought I knew what he meant; Sibert had said the crown had been made by his own ancestor and placed beneath the tree stump by men of his family. This surely made the crown his, and you can't be convicted of stealing from yourself. 'It will also have to be proved,' Hrype went on, 'that Sibert did not leap on Romain and batter him to death. For that to happen, it will have to be shown that he was elsewhere.' I knew that his full attention was on me now, for all that he was staring down into the hearth, and it was a frightening feeling. 'Someone,' he concluded, 'will have to speak for him.'

Silence fell, the echo of Hrype's words slowly dying. My mind was whirling and I felt the vertigo returning. I shut my eyes, but that was worse. *Someone will have to speak for him.* Hrype can only have meant me, and it appeared he knew much more about Sibert's and my escapade than I had thought.

My father, who must have been thinking as hard as I was, said, 'Does Baudouin say where and when his nephew was killed?'

Hrype looked at him. 'He does. He says the attack happened a few miles short of the road that goes from Lowestoft to Diss, and that it was five days ago.'

I counted. I had been back with Goda for two days and for the three days before that Sibert and I had been making our way home following the fight with Romain. This meant, I realized, that whoever had killed Romain must have caught up with him shortly after Sibert had laid him low with a knee in the crotch.

We had left Romain alive and fairly well, other than the bruised testicles. And from then on I had been with Sibert all the way home.

Despite everything, I felt a cry of triumph inside my head. Sibert was innocent, and I knew it.

Whether I could prove it – whether I even had the courage to try – was a very different matter.

# FOURTEEN

In the morning I was up and quietly preparing to go out before my mother, my granny or Edild could try to stop me. We had talked late into the night, at first with Hrype and then, once he had gone home to the unenviable task of trying to comfort Sibert's poor mother, among ourselves.

I had slept for a while but not long. My dreams had been deeply troubling and when I opened my eyes in the pre-dawn darkness and knew I would not sleep again, my waking thoughts were no more reassuring.

I knew what I had to do and I did not want to do it. I was very scared, for one thing, and as well as that I was nervous because I was about to make myself do something I would not normally have considered in a hundred years.

I had not said much more during the long discussions last night but I had listened very carefully, especially to a certain question posed by my father and answered by Hrype. This morning, as a consequence, I knew not only what I had to do but where I must go to attempt it. The *how* I would leave to what I hoped would prove a benevolent providence; having no clear idea yet, I prayed that inspiration would strike at the appropriate moment.

I did not want to do this at all. The problem was that I didn't see I had any choice.

My mother was surprised to notice, on waking, that I was pulling my boots on. 'Where are you going?' she asked, brushing back her long plait. She wears her lovely strawberry blond hair like this for sleeping.

Her voice disturbed Edild, who had been asleep by the hearth. She propped herself up on one elbow and watched me, waiting for my reply.

'Back to Goda's,' I said shortly.

My mother looked very surprised, as well she might as she would, I'm sure, have expected me to use the drama of Sibert as an excuse to stay in Aelf Fen as long as possible and certainly for today. 'I think you should stay here and have a restful day,' she said, sounding worried. 'You were quite ill yesterday and we were anxious at how pale you were.' She turned to her sister-in-law. 'Don't you agree, Edild?'

I met my aunt's eyes and sent her a pleading look. She seemed to understand – really, I was asking a great deal of her just then – and said, after a moment's consideration, 'She looks better this morning. I believe that a walk in the fresh air followed by the resumption of her duties will be better for her than staying here and brooding.'

The voice of authority had spoken and my mother seemed to accept it. 'Very well,' she said, not sounding entirely happy. 'But if you feel at all unwell, Lassair, you are to come home. Do you hear me?'

'Yes, Mother.'

She muttered something under her breath, something about Goda having to get off her fat backside and manage without me, and I realized then just how disturbed my mother was, for in the normal way she never runs down one of her children in front of the others. Not even Goda.

Before either of them could say anything else – or, even worse, before my father could awake and get the chance to weigh in to the discussion – I said a swift goodbye to Edild and my mother and slipped out of the house.

Baudouin de la Flèche disliked having to stay under another man's roof but, as he frequently and sourly reminded himself, he ought to have thought of that before he joined Bishop Odo's rebels and by that action found himself on the losing side with his manor taken away from him. Its loss had followed the defeat at Rochester with breathtaking speed and he was still reeling from the blow. He had quit Drakelow with the clothes he wore, his knife, his sword, a saddlebag of provisions and one of hastily packed spare linen and his horse. Everything else in the house, the tower, the outbuildings and the whole estate was now under the care of the king's representative.

Baudouin tried not to think about that.

There was plenty to distract his thoughts, although the labyrinthine cast of mind of Baudouin de la Flèche meant that some of his deepest, darkest thoughts and deeds were sometimes all but hidden even from himself. He was a man who acted with ruthless decisiveness and, if he did not actually regret things that he had done, he was on occasion faced with consequences that proved challenging to surmount.

Now was such a time, although he believed that already the way was becoming clearer. The boy was in captivity and the treasure was restored to its rightful owner. Or very soon it would be...

Baudouin heard footsteps coming along the passage into the hall and, with some difficulty, composed his features into a smile of welcome.

The stranger's roof under which he had slept the previous night was that of Gilbert de Caudebec. Gilbert's father Ralf had fought with William the Conqueror and, having proved himself an efficient administrator rather than a ruthless and inspired soldier, his reward had been not one of the castles deemed crucial to the Conqueror's defence of his new realm but the relative backwater of a small manor on the edge of the Fens known as Lakehall. There Ralf de Caudebec had settled quite happily, in due course marrying an English heiress, Alftruda, who gave him a son, Gilbert, and two daughters. On Ralf's death Alftruda had gone to live with the elder of her daughters, leaving Lakehall to Gilbert and his young wife Emma.

The plump and easy-going Gilbert showed no

more flair as a fighting man than his father but, unlike Ralf, he was not a particularly talented administrator either; probably the shrewdest thing he had ever done was to appoint a hard-working and highly efficient reeve. The estate that Gilbert controlled on the king's behalf was a mixture of arable land on the higher, drier ground and waterlogged marsh out in the Fens. Happily for Gilbert, the people of the latter seemed content to carry on the way they had always done, back through the long decades and centuries before the Conquest, and that suited him very well.

He was rarely called upon to fulfil his judicial role, which suited him too, but now trouble had come and lodged itself right in his own house. He found it hard to meet the dark eyes of his guest, for the man seemed all but unhinged by his nephew's death. The dead young man was also his guest's heir, Gilbert thought astutely, and we Normans set a great store on having a suitable male heir to inherit from us, so that the loss of such a man would indeed be a heavy blow. Yes, he thought with a sigh. Trouble was here all right, and he was uncomfortably aware that he must step forward to deal with it.

Now, on this bright summer morning when he would far rather have stayed in his own chamber with his pretty wife and the enchanting baby boy with whom she had recently presented him, he had been forced to rise, dress and go into his hall to entertain Baudouin de la Flèche.

Baudouin stood up smartly as Gilbert strode into the hall and they exchanged polite greetings. When Baudouin deemed there had been enough pleasantries, he said quite curtly, 'So, Gilbert, have you come to a decision concerning the crown?' He almost said *my crown* but that could have been seen as provocative.

Gilbert did not immediately answer, instead walking over to the open door of the wide hall and gazing out for a few moments over the peaceful scene outside. Gentle country sounds floated up: the quacking of ducks on the pond just beyond the courtyard; the barking of a dog; light voices and laughter as two young maidservants enjoyed a gossip; the rhythmic sound of someone sweeping muck and old straw out of a stable. Ah, he thought, with a soft sigh. If only these small, pleasurable, everyday matters were to be the sum of my concerns this day. Then he turned to face his guest.

Even before Gilbert had said a word, Baudouin's heart sank, for he knew from the fat man's uncharacteristically solemn expression what he was going to say. Gilbert was weak – Baudouin had detected that after a very short acquaintance – and, like all weak men, he could on occasion stick with stubborn tenacity to some small point which, among the minutiae of everyday occurrence, for some reason presented itself as a matter of principle.

It was Baudouin's misfortune that the point on which Gilbert had stuck was the ownership of the crown.

Go on, you moon-faced fool, Baudouin thought bitterly as he waited for Gilbert's judgement. You don't care in the least who ends up with these particular spoils and it would make no difference to you if you said now, *Here, Baudouin, take your treasure, with my blessing.*

Gilbert frowned, as if what he was about to say pained him, and then repeated what he had said the previous day. 'It would certainly seem, my dear Baudouin,' he began pompously, 'that the right of title to this precious object is yours, for nobody is disputing that it was found on the shore at Drakelow. I understand that there is some confusion over *precisely* where it was found, which raises the question of the ancient and inalienable right of the king to anything found between high and low water, but I do not think we need bother overmuch about that if you assure me it was found on Drakelow land.'

'As I do,' Baudouin said firmly. He did not even flinch as he spoke the lie.

'However,' Gilbert added, his voice dropping to a new level of portentousness, 'unfortunately Drakelow is not at present in your hands, although we all hope that this will prove but a temporary state of affairs, as indeed it surely will if the king opts for leniency.'

He won't opt for anything of the sort, Baudouin thought, unless I persuade him, and I can't do that without my crown. He stared at Gilbert, fighting to keep his despair and his fury out of his eyes.

When he was reasonably sure that he could speak without his voice giving him away, he said, 'And what of the boy?'

'There again,' Gilbert said regretfully, 'although I do indeed sympathize most sincerely with your loss, I fear I cannot accede to your demand that he be immediately hanged.' Some tiny portion of the emotions that seethed and boiled through Baudouin must have been visible, for Gilbert took a step back and said in a placatory tone, 'Oh, I am sure that it will come to that in the end, for you have a witness who has given a clear statement that he saw Sibert attack your poor late nephew, and of course your word on this is more than enough.'

*Then do it!* Baudouin raged silently. *Take the damned impudent youth out and string him up!*

'However,' Gilbert went on – and Baudouin had reluctantly to admire his surprising refusal to be browbeaten – 'I do feel that it is necessary that I instigate some further enquiries, both here and at Drakelow. I must—' He broke off, frowning, and Baudouin guessed that he had little idea how to go about his self-appointed task. 'I shall speak to the youth this morning,' he said instead. 'He was distraught last night when the guards put him in the lock-up but after a night's sleep he may be more approachable. I shall—'

He was interrupted by voices coming from the courtyard; the male tones of a couple of grooms and the lighter but far more insistent voice of a girl. Gilbert strode over to the doorway and, from the top of the stone steps, looked down at the scene below; Baudouin hurried after him.

The grooms were remonstrating with a thin copper-haired girl who wore a shabby woollen tunic and, tied around her waist, a rather beautiful shawl. She was demanding admittance to the lord's house and the two grooms were telling her to go away although, Baudouin observed, not in such polite terms.

'I *will* see him!' she insisted, wresting her arm out of the grip of the younger of the grooms and kicking out at his shins for good measure. He skipped neatly out of reach. 'It's my right,' she added, 'my father's one of his tenants and he's a *good* tenant, he fulfils all his obligations and what's more he's an eel-catcher and he sees to it that the lord gets the best of the catch!'

'Ah,' Gilbert murmured, and Baudouin saw him smile.

'You know this girl?' he demanded.

'No, but I know her father.' Gilbert was rubbing his round belly. 'She's right, he does bring me fine eels. His name's Wymond and he lives with his family out at Aelf Fen.' His eyes rounded. 'Where your young man comes from!' He turned to Baudouin, amazed.

So, Baudouin thought. This is the girl. He stared more closely and, as she edged closer, he realized that he had seen her before. She it was who had stared at him so belligerently over the heads of the crowd when he accused the boy of murder.

'You should not allow her to push her way in,' he said. 'There is a proper procedure if a tenant has a matter to discuss with the lord of the manor, and bursting in on your privacy is not it.'

'Oh, I don't mind,' Gilbert said mildly. 'She's here now and what's more she's putting up quite a fight.' He chuckled. 'I like a bit of spirit in a girl.' He beckoned to the grooms, calling out an order. 'I may as well see what she wants now she's here.'

Baudouin could have told him what she wanted. Filled with sudden apprehension – what, after all, could a slip of a girl do against a man like him? – he stepped back into the shadows and waited to hear what she would say.

I was glad that the grooms had been so offensive (especially the younger one, who had the cheek to call me a scrawny little cat and then told me to go away, only not in those terms) because they made me angry and being angry was a far better way to go up the steps and face Gilbert de Caudebec than being terrified, which was what I'd been before I encountered the grooms.

He led me across his enormous hall – it was awe-inspiring and my whole house could have fitted inside about three if not four times – and invited me to sit down on a wooden seat, long enough for about half a dozen people, with a straight back and carved dragons or something on its front legs. He waited till I had done so and then sat down in a huge chair opposite me. I stared wide-eyed – I couldn't help it – and a succession of vivid images flooded my mind. A flagged floor – no damp beaten earth and smelly, soggy rushes here; a huge wooden chest, elaborately carved with an intertwining design of flowers and imaginary beasts; a huge pewter tray on which stood a jug and several goblets; and, as a softening, human touch, a baby's silver rattle attached to a coral teat. Stop it, I commanded myself. You're not here to make an inventory of Lord Gilbert's hall.

As I entered the hall I'd had the strong sense that there was someone else there but, peering round as well as I could without making it too obvious, I could see nobody. There were some beautiful hangings embroidered in rich red, brown and gold wool at the end of the hall that I guessed concealed the door to the kitchens, so maybe whoever it was had gone out that way.

'Now, who are you and why do you wish to see me?' Lord Gilbert asked, kindly enough.

I studied him, trying to obtain a sense of him. I saw a fat man of perhaps twenty-five whose face smiled readily and, to judge from the lines around his hazel eyes, frequently. He slumped rather than sat in his chair and his rich velvet tunic had small greasy stains down the front. He likes his food, I thought, and his girth suggests self-indulgence.

I was probably far too hasty in deciding that I could manage Gilbert de Caudebec, but the sudden confidence gave me the ability to speak.

'I understand that my friend Sibert is imprisoned here,' I began. I knew he was; Hrype had told us so last night. 'He is charged with the theft of a gold crown from a place called Drakelow and the murder of a man called Romain de la Flèche.' I had to press my lips together for a moment as I said his name. His loss was still very raw. 'I have come,' I hurried on, 'to protest his innocence.' I hoped that was the right phrase. 'He did not kill Romain.'

'Indeed?' said Lord Gilbert. 'And how can you be so sure?'

'Because he was with me,' I said firmly.

'I see.' Lord Gilbert went on looking at me, smiling vaguely, and I sensed he was playing for time while he thought how to respond.

'He was!' I insisted when he still did not speak. 'We went to Drakelow together – well, Romain was the leader, I suppose, since it was all his idea, but we—' I realized I was entering difficult territory. I had been about to say that Sibert and I had parted company from Romain after we'd found the crown, but since that was a lot to admit straight away and I'd very likely live to regret my frankness, I held back. 'We came back together, just Sibert and me,' I finished feebly. 'But I know he didn't kill Romain,' I went on, trying to make my voice sound firm and confident, 'because Romain was killed six days ago and Sibert was with me then. I will speak for him,' I finished, in what I hoped was a dignified tone.

'You will speak for him,' Lord Gilbert mused.

'Yes indeed, he said that you would. He too tells this tale of the two of you journeying to Drakelow, finding the crown and returning with it, he to Aelf Fen, you to your sister's house at Icklingham.'

'He tells it because that's exactly what happened!' My cool, authoritative voice seemed to have flown away and I was screeching like a seagull. But Lord Gilbert was frightening me; I sensed that he did not believe me and I have learned to trust my senses. 'I was with Sibert all the time and he didn't kill *anybody*!'

Lord Gilbert's suspicious expression softened and I thought for one wonderful moment that I had convinced him. Then he said, quite kindly, 'But you are lying, aren't you?'

'*No!*' I leapt up, stamping my foot for emphasis.

Lord Gilbert actually chuckled. 'As I observed, didn't I? A spirited girl!' he said over his shoulder.

I *knew* there had been someone else in the room! I cursed myself for not having tried harder to see if I was right. My skin prickling with apprehension, I stared into the shadows at the back of the hall where I had supposed that the hanging concealed a door. Slowly, as if he was reluctant to show himself, a man walked forward into the light.

I stared at him and his intense dark eyes under their strongly marked brows stared right back. The lines of his face were pronounced and he had deeply etched grey circles under his eyes.

His mouth was no more than a thin, hard line. He was, I reminded myself as I tried not to recoil, a man in mourning, for he had just lost his nephew and his heir.

It was Baudouin de la Flèche.

My fear came racing back, multiplied a hundredfold. It had been scary enough nerving myself to face Gilbert de Caudebec, and I knew his reputation as a benevolent lord who did not harry and bully his peasants and his tenants like many Normans did. Baudouin de la Flèche was a very different matter; I had no logical reason to be so frightened of him but I was. I tried to tell myself that his fearsome expression was undoubtedly the result of his grief – some people, especially men, adopt anger as a way of dealing with the pain – but it did little to reassure me. As I stood there forcing my knees to hold firm and stop shaking, commanding myself not to do as I longed to and turn and flee, I knew he brought with him danger. Terrible danger.

He smiled, a ghastly expression that I detected had not a jot of sincerity in it. Then he said – and his light, cheerful tone, like his smile, was so incongruous and so clearly forced that I was amazed Lord Gilbert did not spin round to stare at him – 'You did indeed, Gilbert, and *spirited* barely describes our young visitor adequately.' He moved closer, and I forced myself to stand firm. 'I would say also that it is very brave, for a little village girl to stride into her lord's hall and contradict him so forcefully!' He laughed, a short *ha!* which sounded unpractised, as if he did not do it very often. 'But sadly,' he went on, his face falling in mock sympathy, 'we already know the truth.' He turned to Lord Gilbert. 'Is that not so?'

'Yes, yes!' Lord Gilbert beamed. 'The young man, Sibert, tried to make us believe this highly imaginative tale, of you accompanying him and Romain de la Flèche to Drakelow, and even as he did so we all doubted that he was telling the truth.' He broke off, looking at me closely. 'How old are you, child?'

'Fourteen.' My midsummer birthday seemed months ago.

'Fourteen,' Lord Gilbert echoed. 'But you look so much younger, like a little girl who has yet to bloom into womanhood and still needs the security and protection of her family.'

I seethed with silent fury. If only he knew, fat, condescending pig that he was!

'Little village girls do not go on illicit, un-authorized journeys half across the country,' Lord Gilbert stated flatly, and there was a worrying note of finality in his voice. 'In addition,' he added, smiling at me, 'as soon as Sibert made this claim – that you were with him all the time and would vouch for the fact that he committed no murder – I sent men to find you, as you know, but also to question your kin.'

Oh, no! I had caught myself in my own trap! I had lied so convincingly that everyone had believed me.

'Your sister and her husband repeated the

account you gave of your week of absence from their house,' Lord Gilbert went on, 'in such detail that there can be no doubt they were telling a true story. In addition, my men spoke to your aunt, with whom you were staying, and she verified the fact that you never left her house.' He eyed me with sudden interest. 'You are skilled as a healer, I am told?'

He stared at me expectantly and I had to answer. 'I'm learning,' I admitted grudgingly.

'Good, good,' said Lord Gilbert. 'I must remember that. I have a pretty young wife and an adorable baby son, did you know that?'

'Er—'

He did not wait for me to answer. 'They are in fine health at present,' he said, smiling happily, 'but my wife will be reassured to know we have a young healer close at hand in case of need.'

He was patronizing me and I hated it. If he or this wife of his had wanted a healer they'd have sent for Edild, not me. He was being kind because he was sorry for me. I'd come on a silly, childish mission to try to save my friend by spinning a ridiculous yarn that nobody in their right minds would credit, and he had dismissed me out of hand. Now he was trying to comfort me. In a minute he'd be offering me a sugar cake, as if I were an infant who had fallen over and banged her head.

If my fury and my shame had not been so violent, I might have realized that it was actually quite decent of him. Many lords would, I am sure, have sent me packing with a scolding and possibly a thrashing to remind me not to tell lies.

Perhaps he did not wish to jeopardize the eel supply.

Baudouin had been silent during this hopeless exchange with Lord Gilbert. He had circled me – I had sensed his presence behind me and had found it deeply unnerving, my skin crawling in response to his proximity – and now he went to stand beside Lord Gilbert's chair. I looked at him. He – or more likely one of Lord Gilbert's servants – had brushed down his dusty tunic and polished his boots, and now he could be seen for the wealthy, powerful man that he was. Observing my eyes on him, he smiled faintly, as if to say, look well, child. Admit you stand no chance against me.

He wants justice, I thought. He is in desperate need of somebody to blame for Romain's death and he will settle for Sibert. He will not rest till Sibert hangs for the murder of Romain.

I quaked under his black stare but I made myself hold his glance. *You might once have been rich and important,* I said to him silently, *but that time has gone, for you have lost your manor. I don't know why you claim that Sibert killed your nephew but there has to be a reason and I shall find out what it is and save my friend.*

I don't know if he perceived my thought. If he did, he made no visible sign. But then I felt a horrible sensation – it was if a wave of heat from a huge, uncontrolled fire had just hit me. I flinched and his smile twisted until it was a look of pure evil.

I suspected, for all I hoped it was not so, that I had just made an enemy.

# FIFTEEN

I had told them at home that I was going back to Goda's house and as I left Lord Gilbert's manor, my face still burning from my humiliation, I thought I might as well do just that. I had nerved myself to do the one thing I could think of to save Sibert and I had failed, miserably and utterly. Lord Gilbert had all but patted me on the head and told me to go away and play. Baudouin de la Flèche had revealed himself to be a truly frightening man. But then, I reminded myself, trying to be fair, he had just lost his nephew and heir and perhaps was not in his right mind. Thinking of him in his lonely grief I almost felt sorry for him.

Almost.

I really didn't want to go back to Goda's house but I could not think of anywhere else to go. If I turned up at home I'd have to explain, and my failure still bit too deep for me to have any desire to talk about it. So, slowly, reluctantly, I plodded wearily off down the road to

Icklingham, thinking as I did that never had the miles seemed so long.

The day had become hot and I stopped by a stream to splash my face with cool water. I was straightening up again, preparing to attack the last leg of my journey, when I heard a rustling sound in the bracken behind me.

For no apparent reason, I was afraid. I stood quite still, only my eyes moving as swiftly I looked round, both for the source of the sound and for a hiding place or escape route. There was nowhere to hide – I was standing on a low bank above a watercourse that wound between low bushes and skinny alders – and the only place to run was on down the track to Icklingham.

I listened, my ears straining, but the sound did not come again. It was probably an animal, I told myself. A bird pulling at a worm. A stoat whipping round into the safety of its hole.

I did not succeed in reassuring myself at all. I knew that the sound had somehow been too big for a small, innocent creature. I was all but sure it had been made by a human.

I thought suddenly, someone killed Romain. It wasn't Sibert, no matter what this mysterious witness says, no matter how much Baudouin wants to believe that it was. I knew the truth and I realized with a cold shiver of horror that, other than Sibert, I was the only living soul who did. It was in this unknown somebody's interests to ensure that my version of events did not gain credibility and one sure way of doing that was to silence me. Permanently.

I leapt across the stream and ran as fast as I could towards Icklingham.

Goda received me with slightly more animation than she usually managed. It was not, after all, every day that her sister managed to involve herself in a murder. After the initial questions, however, Goda's attitude changed and soon she was screeching at me for bringing the family into disrepute. It was a relief to go outside into the warm sunshine to collect vegetables for our meal.

She found plenty of tasks of varying degrees of distastefulness for me to do for the remainder of the day. She was quite clearly making a point, that I had done something reckless and silly – she never specified what, exactly, since she didn't know – and must be punished. I accepted it, doing whatever I was ordered efficiently and without complaint. I too felt I needed to be punished, and far more severely than anything my sister could come up with, for I had failed my friend and he would probably hang.

As the long day at last descended into evening, it was all I could do to keep back my tears.

I finally got Goda settled for the night. She had been complaining of aches and pains all after-noon, but then she always complained about something and I did not take a lot of notice. I knew she must be near her time but, other than making sure I knew where to go for the midwife when the moment came, there was little else I could do.

I went to sit outside on the narrow little bench in front of the house. Presently Cerdic came home; he had developed to a fine degree the knack of knowing when his wife was asleep and only creeping into their bed when she was snoring rhythmically and all but impossible to wake. Since he was up and out of the house in the morning before she woke, I wondered if these days they ever exchanged as much as a word. Certainly, it seemed highly unlikely they would exchange anything else.

He saw me on the bench and nodded a greeting.

'She's asleep,' I whispered.

We both listened in silence for a moment to her snores. 'So I hear,' he whispered back with a grin.

On an impulse I patted the bench beside me and after a brief hesitation he sat down. We did not speak for some time – it really was a lovely night, clear skies and a glowing, golden moon – and then he said tentatively, 'Do you think she'll be better when the baby's here?'

I did not know how to answer. What exactly did he mean by *better*? She'd be less immobile and useless, probably, and there was a slim chance she'd remember that she was a wife and it was her duty to keep the house clean and tidy and get a meal ready for her hard-working husband when he came home at night. Her temper might improve marginally once she was no longer fat, sweaty and uncomfortable. But she would still be Goda.

I thought very carefully and then said, for he was stuck with her and it would do no harm to give him some hope, 'Lots of women feel quite differently about – er, about things once they have a baby to cherish. She'll have a big, strong child,' I went on, my confidence growing, 'that's for sure, and that'll be a joy. She'll nurse it and it'll thrive, and she'll be happy and I'm sure she'll try to be a good mother.' I was going too far and I knew it when I heard myself say *she'll be happy*, for I'd never known my sister when she wasn't discontented and moaning abut something.

But then miracles did sometimes happen.

I had said enough; more than enough.

Cerdic seemed content, however. After a time he said, 'Ah well, better get to bed, I suppose.' He stood up, looking down at me with a wry smile. 'Thanks for coming back,' he added. 'She'd never say so but she needs you.'

As I watched him let himself quietly into the house and close the door, I reflected that it was probably all the appreciation I was ever going to get.

I sat on for some time and I was only prompted to thinking that I too should go to bed when I realized I was growing cold. I wrapped my lovely shawl more tightly around me and stood up, heading for the jakes.

On my way back to my little lean-to an arm was thrown around my throat and before I could cry out a hand was pressed tightly over my mouth. My alarmed heart started banging against my ribs and, as in a flash I was transported back to the cliff above Drakelow where the same thing had happened, my instant thought was: *Sibert! It's Sibert!*

Something about my assailant must have added to that impression – a smell, or the feel of the skin on the hand clamped to my lips – for, despite my fear when I had heard something in the undergrowth, now, as the initial shock faded, I was not scared at all.

The hand lessened its pressure and the arm around my throat fell away. I turned round and saw not Sibert but Hrype.

I stared at him. His dark blond hair gleamed in the moonlight and his eyes reflected its glow. He was dressed in a long black cloak, its deep hood thrown back. He said very quietly, 'I must talk to you. Come.'

He led the way along the track that leads eastwards out of the village and when we were well past the last habitation, he turned off the path and in under the trees. We were not far from the place where I had waited for Romain and Sibert.

We settled on the bank beneath a beech tree. For a few moments we sat in silence. I was very aware of the night sounds all around me; even more aware of the unknown, unknowable man who was by my side. I shivered suddenly, wrapping my shawl more closely around me. Perceptive man that he is, Hrype noticed. 'I am sorry to keep you from your bed,' he said.

'It's all right.' I thought briefly about the coincidence by which I had not retired at the usual time but stayed sitting outside the house on the very night that Hrype needed to speak to me. Perhaps it was no coincidence at all; Hrype is, as I have said, a strange man with many powers.

'You tried to save Sibert,' he said. He knew, then, of my abortive visit to Lord Gilbert.

'Yes. I failed.'

'Nevertheless, I am grateful. My sister-in-law,' he added, 'loves the boy dearly. I too am very fond of him.'

Fond was an odd word to use, I thought vaguely. But then Hrype had not really chosen to be a substitute father; he had had to look after Froya and the baby Sibert when his brother Edmer died and for all I or anyone knew, he might have preferred a solitary life and only forfeited it because of duty...

'You have to know,' Hrype was saying, 'what is at stake.'

'Sibert's life!' I hissed.

'Yes, yes, of course.' He seemed to brush that aside; perhaps it was too painful to think about. 'There is something else, Lassair. Something which, although it pains me to admit it, is far more important than one young man's fate.'

What could he mean? The answer came in a

flash. 'The crown,' I breathed.

'The crown,' he agreed. Then, after a pause, 'You have sensed a little of what it can do, I think.'

'Yes. It affects me and I am afraid of it.'

'You are right to be afraid. It is an object of power and it is not something that a man like Baudouin de la Flèche, or indeed any man, should use for the base purpose he has in mind.'

'You mean buying his manor back with it.' I wanted to be quite clear.

'Yes.'

I frowned. 'Romain gave the impression that searching for the crown was his idea,' I said slowly. 'Yet now you say it's Baudouin who wishes to use it to persuade the king.'

Hrype stared at me. 'It seems he was aware of what his nephew was up to,' he said. 'He was, he says, anxious about the young man.' He sighed faintly. 'With good reason.'

I realized that Hrype knew far more than I had imagined. 'I think Sibert believed that his involvement with Romain and the mission to Drakelow were secret,' I said.

'Not from me,' Hrype said.

'He only knew about the crown because he heard you chanting to it!' I burst out. I needed someone to blame and if Sibert hadn't overheard Hrype and learned about Drakelow and what was hidden in the sea sanctuary, all this would not have happened.

Hrype sighed. 'I know. Because of that, Sibert was ready and eager to be involved when

Romain approached him.'

'So' – I tried to piece it together – 'Romain sought out Sibert, told him there was a treasure buried somewhere at Drakelow and the two of them should go and find it, and Sibert said he knew roughly where it was hidden, and so they—'

'They sought the help of a girl who is a dowser,' Hrype finished for me, 'and the three of them set off on their foolhardy mission.'

'If you knew it was foolhardy why didn't you stop us?' I demanded angrily.

'I did not know what you were planning to do!' His reply snapped through the air like a whip and with a shudder I felt the very edge of his power. It was enough to make my flesh contract into goose pimples. 'I have only understood why this has happened afterwards,' Hrype added more gently, 'when it is far too late.'

I thought about that. 'How did Romain know of the crown's existence?' I asked. 'Sibert only knew that an object of power existed – because he overheard you communicating with it – and not where or what it was.'

Hrype said, 'That is so. It was indeed Romain who enlightened him. As to how he knew, I do not know for sure but I believe I can guess the truth.' He paused. 'My forefathers built Drakelow when first they ventured out of their homelands and came across the whale routes to England,' he said, his voice sounding distant. 'They were the companions of kings and their hall had to be within reach of the royal dwelling place.' Yes, I thought; Sibert told me. But I dared not break into Hrype's narrative. 'My ancestors were sorcerers and they were known as cunning men,' he went on, 'and their worth for the king was inestimable, for he depended on their skill to keep safe the new realm that he had taken for his own. Drakelow was given to us as our reward, to be our family home for ever.' He sighed again. 'Neither the kings of old nor their cunning men, however, predicted the Conquest that would rob not only us but all the aristocratic families of their estates. Ours went to Fulk de la Flèche and we were forced into the role of powerless witnesses as our birthright was spoiled and abused.'

He fell silent, as if that old loss still had the ability to render him mute with pain.

I said tentatively, 'Could your father not have used the power of the crown? He had you as a son, you who understand that sort of—'

'No.' He breathed the word but with such force that abruptly I stopped what I was saying. 'It is true that I have certain skills, more apparent to you than to others,' – I stored that up to gloat over later – 'but the power that is within the crown is not there for the gratification of one family's wishes. Which, of course, is why Baudouin de la Flèche must not be allowed to use it in that way.'

I wanted to hear more about the crown but Hrype was obviously not prepared to tell me. Instead, he said, 'After the Conquest, the remnants of my family were forced to flee. There were, indeed, few enough of us. My father had died vainly trying to fight off the Conqueror, and his body lies somewhere among the heaps of the slain, buried close by the battlefield. My brother Edmer and I took our mother into hiding in the Black Fens and from there Edmer set out to join the Wake in his rebellion, and they held Ely against the new king. Edmer received the wound that killed him and my mother succumbed to her long grief over all that had been lost to her and fell an easy victim to fever. I sent my dead brother's wife to the safety of Aelf Fen, where in time she bore her posthumous child.'

'Sibert,' I said softly.

'Sibert. Yes.' Briefly he bowed his head. Then he went on, 'We were in exile but we kept our pride. We who had quit our hall and our home-lands carried our heads high; not so those despised ones of our blood who remained and sold their souls to the new Norman lord. One such, I confess, was my cousin, the son of my mother's sister. He was weak, greedy and, reluctant to give up the good things of life, he abased himself before Fulk de la Flèche, offered him his loyalty and his service and so betrayed his forefathers and his living kin.' I could hear the fury and the scorn in Hrype's voice. 'His name is Roger – it is not his given name but that he has left behind him in his bid to become as the Normans – and he it was who dropped tantalizing hints about the crown and its power. He knew far less than he claimed, for the crown was ever deeply secret among my people and none of us would willingly have shared the smallest, least significant detail with one such as my cousin.' The anger had built again and I sensed it like a flame on the bare skin of my face. 'In time, rumour of our treasure must have reached the ears of Romain,' he said, clearly mastering his fury, 'so that when Baudouin joined the rebels and, with Drakelow lost to the de la Flèches, the means to buy back the king's favour were so urgently required, immediately Romain thought of what lay hidden somewhere within the manor. He learned – from Roger, I would guess – the identity of the former masters of Drakelow; somehow he succeeded in discovering our whereabouts. He did not approach me, for he must have known what my reaction would be. He sought out Sibert, dreamy, hopeless Sibert, so full of anger and resentment that when a stranger offered him the chance of recovering a treasured family object, he barely paused for thought before leaping at it.'

'I'm quite sure he thought he was helping,' I said gently.

Hrype grunted an acknowledgement. 'I'm quite sure you are right,' he said wryly. 'But he did not know what he was meddling with. The crown is no bartering tool and will not permit itself to be used as such. Now as a result Sibert lies imprisoned and will hang' – his voice broke with emotion but quickly he regained control – 'and that will break his mother's heart.'

And perhaps yours too, I thought, compassion bringing tears to my eyes as I watched Hrype hunch in pain.

'Sibert is no murderer,' I said shakily. 'Whatever Baudouin's witness may say, he is wrong when he says he saw Sibert kill Romain. Sibert was with me, and I will swear it before the highest authority in the land.' I spoke grandly but I spoke true. Or so I believed.

Slowly Hrype straightened up and turned to look at me. His eyes held mine and I found I could not look away. It was as if he were searching my mind, testing me, assessing my courage.

I don't know what he concluded but I fear that I disappointed him, for he turned away and I thought he slumped a little.

'I will!' I repeated recklessly. 'If there's a way I can prove I'm telling the truth' – yet again I cursed my fluent lying, which had convinced those who counted that I'd been with Edild all along – 'then explain it to me and I'll do it!'

He stared at me for what seemed a very long time. Then eventually he said, 'We are told of this witness who claims to have seen Sibert's attack on Romain. You were on the road at the time. Did you see anybody? I am thinking,' he explained, 'that if you have the courage, you might retrace your footsteps, find this man and ask him to reconsider. If you were to say that you know Sibert is innocent because you were with him all the time, possibly this witness will realize he is mistaken.'

Once I was over the initial shock, I tried to calm my mind and think carefully. Had I seen anyone? Had there been someone on the track? Sibert and I had encountered fellow travellers in plenty once we were on the road leading inland from the coast, but on that journey across wild, empty country, there had been nobody and, indeed, few signs of human habitation at all.

Then I remembered.

'There was a woman by a well!' I shouted. Hrype instantly hushed me. 'Sorry,' I whispered. 'Sibert and I were so hot and thirsty. We'd kept up such a pace all the way from Drakelow – we were both scared that Romain would catch up with us and Sibert wanted to get out on to the road, where he thought we'd be safer because there would be other people about. But I could not go on any further without water and when we saw her with that bucket, dipping in her drinking cup and pouring the lovely cool water down her throat, I wouldn't go on until we'd begged her to give us some too.'

Hrype stared at me. 'This was close to where Baudouin claims Sibert killed Romain?'

'Yes. Very close.'

'Could she have witnessed the murder?'

'I suppose so, yes. Since we passed right by her, Romain probably did too, and she might have followed him for some reason.' I hesitated, but only for a moment. It was better if Hrype knew the whole story. 'We did see Romain that day,' I said. 'But it was he who

231

attacked Sibert, not the other way round. He was after the crown, of course. He jumped on Sibert's back, taking him completely by surprise, and they fought and Sibert managed to get his knee into Romain's – er, up between his legs. But Romain had a knife and he would have *killed* Sibert if he hadn't fought dirty!' I was trying not to cry. The memory was still far too fresh, caustic in my mind. 'And besides, Romain was so much bigger and stronger, and although I *really* liked him and I had no idea it'd lead to him being killed and I'm *so sorry* that he's dead, it wasn't fair on Sibert' – I was crying in earnest now, tears soaking my face and my nose bunged up – 'and anyway it was what the crown wanted. Sibert had it and it wanted to stay with him.'

I sensed Hrype nod and he murmured, 'Yes. It would.' Then very gently he asked, 'What did you do, Lassair?'

'I warned him,' I said between sobs. 'I saw that Romain was about to attack with the knife and I said, *Now, Sibert, get your leg up!* and he did and it hurt Romain so much and that's when he stopped fighting and fell, but he was alive when we left him, I swear on all the gods that he was!'

Hrype had his arms round me and it was very comforting because he smelled like Sibert. I relaxed against him and cried out all the pain, anxiety and grief of the past few days. For quite a long time he simply held me and waited – really, I hadn't realized he could be so kind –

and finally, when I sniffed, wiped my sleeve across my face and sat up away from him, he just said, 'Better now?'

I nodded. It was very restrained of him, I thought, when he must be dying to ask if I'd agree to his suggestion. It was the one tiny chance we had of saving Sibert; of course I would agree.

When I told him so, for the first time I saw him really smile.

# SIXTEEN

Baudouin discovered very quickly that living in the pampered style of Gilbert de Caudebec and his household was not to his taste at all. The focus of everyone's eyes, from Gilbert down to the lowliest scullion, was the baby, and Baudouin had little or no time for babies. It was, he decided, trying to force a smile as he endured yet again Gilbert's exhortation to watch and admire what seemed to him an unexceptional infant, far too feminine a household for a man such as himself to find comfortable. The young wife, secure in her role as mother of the son and heir, seemed to have spread her frills and fancies around the whole place. She was a comely woman, plump still with milk fat and with generous breasts whose white skin pressed up above her tightly laced gown, but any attraction she might have held for Baudouin was eradicated by her conversation, which always reverted to the same topic. Baudouin thought to himself that he was not used to women, although—

No. Now was not the time to think about that.

He wanted desperately to be gone but he had to stay. Gilbert was still resolved not to release the crown until he had made what he termed vaguely as further investigations. Neither would he permit the execution of Sibert of Aelf Fen; the course of action he was proposing over that matter was causing Baudouin growing anxiety.

In an attempt to take his mind off his worries, abruptly Baudouin strode out of the hall, leaving Gilbert and his wife lingering over their breakfast and staring up at him with their mouths gaping. He called curtly for his horse to be saddled – he did not agree with Gilbert that servants ought to be spoken to courteously; they were only servants, God damn them – and went out for a long ride.

He had managed to keep abreast of what was happening in the south. There were many rebel lords in the area – even his neighbour at Dunwich had risen up against the king, lost his manor and, like Baudouin, was waiting nervously to hear his fate – and for sheer self-preservation they did their best to pass on to one another what scraps and rat-tails of news they heard.

The rebellion had been a disaster. The man for whom they had risked everything had not even come to fight with them; Duke Robert had not set so much as a foot on English shores. Yes, he sent troops, but almost to a man they had either been drowned or captured. The rumour that he would arrive triumphantly in England in early July never amounted to any more than that. His spies had managed to get word to him of what was happening in Rochester and, wisely, Duke Robert opted to remain safely in Normandy.

Would it have made a difference if he had been with us? Baudouin wondered as, blind to the beauties of the summer day all around him, he cantered across the lush grass. The Norman lords of England had risen to support him, truly believing England would be more secure if she were united with Normandy under Duke Robert's rule. Perhaps, he reflected, the essence of why they had failed lay in that very fact: that Duke Robert had let other men fight his cause for him and only planned to turn up in time to lead the victory march.

They had backed the wrong man.

When Rochester fell, it was said that Odo had sent word to the king suing for peace. Amazingly, it seemed he had proposed that the rebels' forfeited lands should be restored to them, in exchange for which they would promise to serve the king faithfully ever afterwards as their rightful lord. Baudouin could scarcely believe it. Was Odo so secure in his pride that he believed it was going to be as simple as that? He had done the rebels no favours by his high-handed assumption of easy forgiveness. Rumour had it that the king, inclined at first to be lenient, was so incensed by Odo's arrogance that he declared the Rochester rebels must be hanged.

Hanged! The terrible word brought images into Baudouin's head that he would far rather not have seen. Hanged. He saw the noose tightening, the face swelling, the eyes and tongue protruding and the dreadful, shaming loosening of bladder and bowels. Dear God in heaven, it was no fate for a lord, to be strung up like a common criminal for the entertainment of the peasants.

So far, it had not come to that. Aghast at the king's words, powerful friends and relatives had spoken up, bravely facing the king in his fury – it was already well known that a fierce red-hot temper went with the ruddy face and gingery hair – and pleading for the rebels. They had learned a bitter lesson, their friends said. They now freely admitted that King William was the equal of his magnificent forebear and that England was as safe in his hands as it was in those of his illustrious father the Conqueror.

William considered. He kept them waiting, and perhaps he enjoyed making them suffer. Then he declared that he would not enforce the ultimate penalty. The old lords, he announced, would be spared punishment out of the respect they had earned through their long and loyal service to his father. Baudouin allowed himself a wry smile; no doubt, he reflected, the king had reasoned in the privacy of his own thoughts that these old lords would soon be dead anyway and no more threat to him, and it was good for a new king to be able to show leniency that was not likely to cost him anything.

The retribution meted out on others was, however, severe. Odo and the two leaders at Rochester were sent into exile, the king took possession of their estates and their lands, and everything they owned that was not on their persons was removed into the king's keeping.

The rush to make peace with the king began as soon as this news began to spread. All over the country, the rebels changed in the blink of an eye from the king's enemies to his staunchest supporters. It was already being whispered that those with the means to do so were trying to buy their way back into royal favour. The king, they said, was not proving unreasonable...

'I must have my crown!' Baudouin cried aloud. There was nobody to hear. Of all objects to appeal to a king who, not yet a year into his reign, had already had to deal with a rebellion and a possible invasion led by his own brother, the crown must surely top the list. I will tell him all that I know of it, Baudouin thought. I will tell him of its extraordinary powers. The king was reputed to be half-pagan; he had no time for monks and clerics and some went as far as to say that he worshipped the old ways. He was the very man to understand what possession of a power object such as the crown would mean.

Gilbert de Caudebec must swiftly be persuaded to release it, Baudouin vowed, because time is crucial. *I must be one of the first to petition the king for forgiveness, for I cannot rest until I know Drakelow is mine once more.*

Baudouin was caught in a trap, and circling round and round in it was all but driving him to distraction. Gilbert's reasoning for not returning the crown to him straight away was that the place where it had been found – Drakelow – was not actually Baudouin's property at present, but it could not be until Baudouin had won it back: by presenting the king with the crown.

Gilbert had at long last been made to see the irony of this – Baudouin had all but exploded with the effort of keeping his temper – but he was still dithering over whether he would be right to return the crown to the man who claimed so forcefully to be its rightful owner. *Do it!* Baudouin thought fiercely. *Just do it!*

There was another, more serious problem for Baudouin to deal with. When he related to Gilbert and the assembled company of important lords' men the harrowing account of Romain's brutal murder, he had expected to be believed. He was Baudouin de la Flèche, lord of Drakelow; he was one of their own kind and his word should be sufficient. Now Gilbert was dithering over that, too, asking Baudouin if he could possibly bring the witness before him so that he could hear for himself what this person had to say.

The problem was serious, yes. Not insurmountable, at a cost, but still serious. In addition, there was that wretched girl, saying now that she'd been with Sibert all along and he had committed no murder. Fortunately she appeared to have a reputation as a liar. She had already convinced everyone that she had been nowhere near Drakelow and her tale had been backed up by some village healer who he understood to be the girl's aunt. Gilbert, sensibly and reasonably, had dismissed the child out of hand. Despite this, Baudouin had a nasty suspicion that she hadn't given up. There had been something about her; young, skinny and powerless as she was, she had stared him in the eye – something that few dared to do – and he was wary of her, sufficiently so that he had taken the trouble to work out a course of action if she persisted. He smiled grimly. Let her try. He would rather enjoy it if he were forced to do what he had planned. If he was to be denied the spectacle of a hanging – a state of affairs that he persuaded himself was purely temporary – then what he had in mind for the girl would provide some much-needed entertainment...

Reminded, he brought his thoughts back to the most pressing issue. Sibert must be dispatched; there was no other way. Whatever it took, the crown must not return to the boy or his family. They too had a claim on Drakelow; an older and stronger one than Baudouin's, although he would never have admitted that to a living soul. The king was in a strange, unpredictable mood, they said. Because his sympathies were rumoured to lie as much with the old religion as with the priests and the Church, it was just possible that an appeal by the original owners of Drakelow just might tickle his fancy and meet with success.

Then Drakelow, the new house and castle, the land, the outbuildings, would all be lost to him.

That was unimaginable.

*It must not happen.*

With Sibert dead, it was not going to happen.

Sibert will die, Baudouin told himself. The crown will be returned to me, and with it I shall buy back my manor.

The crown...

Apart from its crucial use as a bargaining tool, Baudouin found increasingly that he longed to possess it for its own sake. He had seen it only briefly, held it for an even shorter time when he drew it out of the youth's leather bag and held it up. Nevertheless, it had already taken hold of him and sometimes he woke from uneasy dreams in which it encircled his brow so tightly that his head ached and, when he put up his hands to ease it off, it would not move. And, despite his efforts not to dwell on it, he could not help remembering that terrifying moment when it had seemed to strike him dumb...

The crown.

The crucial aim of making Romain believe that he alone knew about the wonderful treasure hidden at Drakelow had been achieved very well. Romain, indeed, deserved credit for perseverance, for he had encountered that mysterious man, Roger, and, refusing to give up, had finally heard from his own lips the strange tale he had to tell. Romain had been an innocent, Baudouin reflected, and did not seem to have suspected for an instant that his uncle had his own private ways and means of keeping abreast of virtually everything that happened at Drakelow. Much of what happened was at his personal instigation.

Baudouin now suspected – as he was almost sure Romain had not – that Roger deeply regretted having sold his ancient secret to a Norman newcomer. Well, that was too bad. If – *when* – Baudouin regained the crown, then nobody was going to wrest it from him and prevent him using it for his vital purpose. Especially not a turncoat who, in his attempts to ingratiate himself with his new Norman overlords, had even changed his name.

Baudouin let out the breath he had been holding and felt the tension seep out of him. It will be all right, he told himself. Then, calmer, he turned his horse and trotted back along the track towards Lakehall.

I set off with Hrype that night. They'd undoubtedly have stopped me if I'd waited to ask permission and I could think of no excuse to offer to my sister to release me again from her service so, given the great urgency of doing something to help Sibert, overall it seemed simpler just to go. I hoped to be back before anyone became too anxious about me.

I was not worried about my safety at all. I felt secure with Hrype. It's always a sound plan, if you're going into possible danger, to have a sorcerer with you. There was danger; I hadn't forgotten how I'd heard someone in the undergrowth the previous day, when I'd been on my way back to Goda's after my visit to Lord Gilbert. I told Hrype about this and he said nothing, merely nodding briefly.

I had imagined we were going to have to walk all the way back to that clearing where the fat woman had sat by her well. I was very surprised when, a short distance along the track, Hrype dodged in beneath the trees and returned leading two horses. Well, a horse and a pony, actually, but nevertheless I was delighted.

'Are they really for us to ride?' I demanded eagerly. I had put my hand out cautiously to the pony – a bay – and he was snuffling his lips against my skin in a friendly sort of way.

'They are.' Hrype risked a smile.

'But they don't belong to you.' I was pretty sure of that.

'No, I have borrowed them,' Hrype replied shortly.

'*Borrowed* them?' I wondered who, among Hrype's acquaintances, could possibly have offered such largesse.

'Better that you don't know any more.' Hrype's words had a distinct finality about them and I did not dare pursue the matter.

I hoped it was going to be all right. The penalty for horse theft – if we were caught, would anyone believe that the horses had really been lent to us and we were fully intending to return them? – was hanging.

I realized then, if I had not done so before, just how far Hrype was prepared to go to save his nephew's life.

We rode our purloined mounts as hard as we dared. Fortunately they were fresh and frisky, fat on summer grass and, it seemed, more than ready for an outing. We stopped for a couple of brief rests to refresh ourselves and water the horses, and late in the evening of the following day we were on the road east of Diss and I was straining my eyes to find the place where the track up from Dunwich joined it.

I found it at last, but by now it was too late to go on and approach the fat woman we had met by the well. She would doubtless have returned to her tiny hamlet and turned in for the night and we would not increase our chances of success by scaring her in the middle of the night.

Early the next day we were on our way.

We must have missed the place where Romain attacked Sibert and subsequently met his death, for before I knew it we were entering the clearing with the well. There was no one about. We dismounted and tethered the horses, then began searching down the faint tracks leading out of the clearing.

She found us before either Hrype or I managed to locate her cottage. We never did find it and for all I knew she could have been some spirit of the woods, only taking mortal form when people had need of her. That's the sort of fanciful thought you tend to have when you travel with a sorcerer.

She looked at me with a smile of recognition. 'It's the little runaway!' she exclaimed, dumping her empty vessel and reaching out to the chain that held the bucket, deep down inside the well. 'Did you and your young man escape all right?'

I looked at Hrype. He nodded. Taking this as a sign to tell her, I did. 'We reached the safety of our home, yes, but Sibert – that's his name and he's not really my young man – has been arrested for murder.'

Her eyes rounded in horrified fascination. *'Murder!* Who did he murder, then?'

'Nobody,' I said emphatically. 'But someone says he did. This someone says there's a witness to the killing and since it happened not far up the track that leads to the coast road, I – we – wondered if you might have been that witness.'

She was already shaking her head and I knew we had wasted our time. 'I'm sorry, my lass,' she said kindly, 'but I saw nothing. I certainly saw no murder, and I thank the good Lord above for it.' She was still shaking her head, from time to time repeating 'Murder!' softly under her breath, as if she scarcely believed it.

Hrype moved a few paces closer to her and, with a polite bow, said, 'I am Sibert's uncle. His

244

mother is desperate. Is there anything you can tell us that might help?'

She looked at him, her face clenched in sympathy, and after a pause she said, 'I saw this girl here and the young man. Sibert?'

'Yes,' Hrype and I said together.

'Sibert. Yes, the two of them passed through the clearing and they both took a drink, although the young man seemed very nervous, very keen to be on his way. Yes.' She put her hand up to her mouth, frowning in concentration. 'Then a little later another young man came along and I remember I remarked to him that sometimes I don't see a soul from one week's end to another and here we were with three visitors in one day.'

'What did this man look like?' I asked. I could barely breathe.

'He was older than your Sibert, but not much. He was broad-set, with thick, dark bobbed hair, and he wore a fine tunic, although it looked as if he'd been wearing it for days *and* sleeping in it.' Romain. It had to be. I looked at Hrype and guessed he'd had the same thought. 'We had a bit of a chat, and he – *oh!*'

She looked aghast at me and then at Hrype. Clearly she had recalled something else.

'Go on,' Hrype said quietly.

'I described you to him, you and the lad,' she said, turning to me. 'I'm very sorry, I'm sure, if I've done harm by it! Oh, dear me!' She was close to tears.

'You weren't to know,' I said. 'If he was on

this path then he had already picked up our trail and all you did was to confirm that he was right.'

'Oh. Oh, I see.' She did not sound very re-assured. 'And now that poor lad stands accused of murder! Who did he kill?' she asked again.

'He did not kill anyone,' I repeated very firmly.

'No, no, of course not, you said so!' Now she was blushing furiously, the fat red face scarlet with embarrassment. 'Who do they say he's killed?'

I did not think I could bring myself to say it. Hrype gave the answer.

'He is accused of murdering the other young man, the one who was following him and this girl.'

'No!'

'He didn't do it!' I said yet again. The murder had clearly come as a great shock to her so I knew, as Hrype must do too, that she was not Baudouin de la Flèche's witness. She might know who was, however. 'Do others live around here?' I asked.

'Round here? Some, in the little hamlet down the track, although we are very few,' she replied.

'Nevertheless, could one of them have been the witness?' Hrype asked.

The fat woman shrugged. 'Perhaps. I haven't heard anyone speak of it and I dare say I'd have heard tell, by now, of such a thing...' She frown-ed in concentration. 'We do get passers-by too, although, like I said, not many and three in a day's a rarity.'

We appeared to have come to a dead end. She had seen nobody but Sibert, me and then, a little later, Romain. Whoever it was who saw the murder must have waited around until Baudouin came along and then told him what he'd just seen.

Baudouin.

What was it Hrype had said when he came to our house that awful night? *Baudouin was worried for Romain's safety and he set out to look for him.*

I said urgently to the fat woman, 'You're sure you saw nobody else that day?'

'No, dear, no. Just the three of you, like I say.'

For a moment I'd thought I was on to something, but just as swiftly I realized that if Baudouin's intention was to guard Romain because he was concerned for him, then he'd probably make quite sure he wasn't seen, by either Romain or whoever it was that Baudouin feared might wish to harm him.

I remembered what else Hrype had reported that night. The witness said they saw Romain catch up with Sibert, who then doubled back and jumped Romain from behind, hitting him so hard on the back of the head that the bones of the skull shattered.

It made me feel queasy just thinking about it and my heart ached for poor dead Romain. I did not think I could retain my composure any longer and, not wanting to make a scene in front of the fat woman – who, to judge by her face, was quite upset already – I caught Hrype's eye.

He dipped his head in a brief nod. 'Thank you,' he said to the fat woman. 'We must go now and leave you to your water-carrying.'

She was still watching us, her expression sombre. 'I hope your nephew gets off,' she said to Hrype.

'I hope so too,' he replied gravely. 'Farewell.'

'God's speed,' she replied.

Then we loosened the horses' reins and hurried away.

As soon as we were out of sight and sound of the clearing, he said, 'Lassair, we must look closely at the place where the murder happened. It seems likely that it is the spot where Romain and Sibert fought, for you told me that you left Romain there, wounded, and it is very possible that the killer struck while he was down. I am sorry I had to remind you,' he added.

I was sorry he had, too. But I knew he was right and we had to look. 'The place where they fought must be back up this track that leads to the road,' I said, 'since the fight was after we'd stopped at the well.'

We rode on. We had missed the place as we went south towards the well but now I was sure we were on the same track that Sibert and I had followed.

In time, we came to the spot. The events of that day were vivid in my memory and I felt cold at the thought of what had happened after Sibert and I had gone.

Hrype had tossed his horse's reins to me and he was on hands and knees, covering every inch of the ground. I suppose that I should have helped him but for one thing I didn't know exactly what he was searching for and, for another, I was still feeling unwell.

I looped the horses' reins around the branch of a young birch tree and leaned against it, sliding my back down its smooth silvery trunk until my backside rested on the ground. I closed my eyes and immediately saw Romain as he was when Sibert and I left him. Oh, I cried silently, oh, if I hadn't yelled out to Sibert to lift his knee and Romain hadn't been so hurt, perhaps his assailant wouldn't have succeeded in killing him. On his feet and fully alert, Romain would at least have had a fighting chance.

I buried my face in my hands, fingers against my closed eyes in a futile attempt to stem the tears.

I don't know how long the fragment of memory stayed in my mind before I realized its significance. One moment the picture of Romain lying with his knees clutched to his chest was just that, a vividly remembered image. Then the next moment I understood what it was trying to tell me.

*'Hrype!'* I hissed, in a sort of whispered shout; although it was very unlikely that there was anyone about, somehow I felt it was essential that what I believed I had just discovered should only be shared with Hrype.

He was grubbing about in the waist-high

bracken on the far side of the clearing. He straightened up at my call and looked at me, eyebrows raised. I beckoned, getting to my feet as I did so, and in a few strides he was beside me.

'What?' he said softly. There was a light in his eyes; I think he already knew, somehow, that this was something important. I noticed, with a separate part of my mind, that his deep eyes sometimes seemed to shine as if they were lit from within...'*What?*' he repeated impatiently.

'Tell me again how the witness described the murder,' I said, my voice low.

He did not question my request but said, 'Romain caught up with Sibert, who managed to double back and attack him from behind, crushing his skull with a branch.'

'Did anyone see the body' – I hated speaking of poor dead Romain in such detached terms but it was the only way I could begin to cope with this – 'to verify what the witness said?'

'No one that I know of,' Hrype replied. 'Except, of course, Baudouin.'

'And nobody would think to question Baudouin's word,' I said slowly. Then: 'Hrype, if it happened as we think it did, if the assailant attacked Romain when he was already on the ground, then the wound is in the wrong place. When we left him, Romain was curled up on his back, hugging his knees tight to his chest. It would have been impossible for anyone to hit him on the *back* of the head.'

Even as I spoke, my brief moment of certainty broke up and faded. There was no way of telling how long Romain had lain there; he could have rolled over on to his front, or managed to get to his feet, shortly after we had left him. My brilliant idea was nothing of the sort.

Then why, I wondered, was Hrype nodding, smiling even, for all that it was a grim smile?

'It did happen as we envisage,' he said, 'and Romain was not struck on the back of the head.' He hurried back to where he had been searching and held up a piece of branch, jagged at one end where it had been torn off the tree. I prayed that he would not bring it over to me, for I knew what it was, but he did.

He held it up. I could see dried blood on it, as well as some pale matter which I had spotted before I had the sense to look away.

'I am sorry, Lassair,' Hrype said gently. There was a swishing sound. 'There; I've thrown it back in the bracken. It's gone.'

I swallowed back the threatening nausea and said shakily, 'What were you going to show me?'

'When you poleaxe a beast,' he said, still in those soothing, gentle tones, 'the weapon may be stained with blood and sometimes, if the blow breaks the skull, with brains.' *Oh!* 'There are invariably a few hairs, and I would expect to find hairs also on a weapon that struck down a man on the back or the top of his head with sufficient force to shatter bone.'

'Romain had thick hair,' I murmured faintly.

251

'Thick and glossy...'

'There is not a single hair on that branch,' Hrype said. 'If it was what the killer used to murder Romain, then the poor man was hit on the brow, on the front of the face, where hair does not grow.'

'The witness must have been mistaken, then,' I whispered. 'Perhaps he did not get as good a view of the murder as he claims.' I realized something. I said excitedly, 'So how can he be so sure that Sibert was the murderer?'

'How indeed,' muttered Hrype. He was frowning, staring absently out across the clearing.

'We must ride back to Aelf Fen with all speed and tell Lord Gilbert!' I said, already gathering up the horses' reins. He did not move. 'Come on!' I urged.

He turned to me as if about to speak. But then, apparently changing his mind, he nodded and together we set out up the track towards the road.

# SEVENTEEN

Baudouin had located his witness. He was a smallish man with sparse gingery hair and pale skin flecked with scaly patches. He claimed to be a merchant, although his general appearance gave the impression that if indeed he was, then he was not a very successful one. In the company of a sway-backed mule laden with shabby goods that surely only the desperate would wish to buy, he travelled the roads and the tracks of a wide area of East Anglia between the coastal ports and the inland towns, villages and hamlets and his name was Sagar. Brought forward to repeat his tale, he was sweating with nerves and had clearly taken a drink or two.

Baudouin had found lodgings for him with one of Lord Gilbert's men. Lord Gilbert, informed that Sagar had evidence which would condemn Sibert for Romain's murder without any doubt, had instructed his man to present Sagar at the appointed time and meanwhile keep him sober and keep a close eye on him.

The appointed time was the next day.

Tomorrow, Baudouin thought, tense with apprehension. I only have to wait until tomorrow. Sagar's testimony will confirm what I have already said and Sibert will hang. Lord Gilbert will return my crown to me – who else will step forward to claim it with Sibert dangling on the end of a rope? – and I shall present it to the king. Then Drakelow will be mine once more.

One more day of waiting, and then everything would be all right.

Hrype and I covered the return journey to Aelf Fen even more swiftly than we had ridden out. The horse and my pony were sweating and blown by the time we got home and I wanted to rub them down, allow them to cool off and water them, but Hrype would not let me. He was deeply uneasy now and I guessed it was because he feared someone would see us with our borrowed mounts.

'They'll be tended, don't worry,' he said abruptly, almost dragging me off my pony's back.

His face was set in such ferocious lines that I did not dare argue.

I wondered what I ought to do. It was by now twilight, and I did not want to go back to Goda's house, although I knew I should as no doubt she would be yelling for me, furious at my absence and perhaps even a tiny bit worried about me, although that was unlikely. But then was there any point in walking all the way to Icklingham when I was planning to present my evidence to Lord Gilbert in the morning?

Hrype decided for me. 'Go home,' he ordered. 'Make up a reason. Tell your family you're worried about Sibert and your sister has allowed you to come back to try to see him. Something of the sort – anyway, don't tell them you're going to see Lord Gilbert first thing in the morning.'

'No, I won't,' I agreed. That wouldn't be difficult as I was trying very hard not even to think about it, never mind speak of it.

He studied me for a moment. 'You *have* to make him believe you,' he said with sudden passion. 'You must explain how you left Romain lying on his back and—'

'But nobody believes I was even *there!*' I wailed. 'Everyone thinks I was at Edild's house!'

'She will have to say she said that to protect you,' he said curtly.

Poor Edild. A healer's reputation would not be enhanced by the knowledge that she was a liar. And would they believe her any more than they did me? Both of us, after all, were going to have to convince Lord Gilbert that what we had said before was the lie and what we were now saying was the truth. It was not going to be easy.

He took hold of my shoulders, staring into my eyes. For a moment I felt his power, raw and seething within him, then with an almost visible effort he concealed it. 'There will be a way, Lassair,' he said, his voice hypnotic. 'Believe. *Believe.*' He gave me a shake, quite a hard one.

'I believe!' I whimpered. Then he let me go and, leading the horses, strode away.

My family welcomed me with love and sympathy, asking no awkward questions despite the late hour. They obviously hadn't heard that I'd run away from Goda's house without permission – for once I was thankful for my sister's indolence – and accepted without question the excuse that anxiety over Sibert's fate had driven me home.

They settled me comfortably and my mother made me a hot drink and gave me a slab of bread and some slices of dried meat, a luxurious late-night snack. I was very hungry and gulped it down. When I'd finished my father said, 'You've come at the right time, Lassair. We'll know tomorrow.'

I felt a cold shiver down my back. 'What do you mean?'

'They're taking Sibert before Lord Gilbert. There's a witness who says he saw him murder Romain.'

A witness! Oh, dear Lord. I was going to have to stand up and accuse this witness of lying. Or, at least, of not being close enough to detect the details of the murder, such as from what direction the blow fell and who had delivered it. I was trembling at the very thought.

I could not tell my family any of this. If I announced my intentions they would certainly try to stop me and probably succeed. I was a child, they would say, nobody was going to listen to me, and it was far, far better for humble people like us to keep well away from matters that did not concern us.

But this did concern me. I was the only person who knew without any doubt that Sibert did not kill Romain.

I did not sleep much that night.

I slipped out of the house when my family were all bustling about and, in the usual confusion made by seven people and a baby in a very small space, nobody noticed.

I went straight to Lord Gilbert's house and asked to see him. Again, they tried to stop me but this time the man himself was at the door of his hall and he invited me in. From the look on his face, I imagine he thought my antics would amuse him.

'What is it this time?' he asked, smiling indulgently. 'More fanciful tales?'

'No,' I said, standing up very straight and trying to look dignified. 'The same tale, and it is not fanciful. I lied when I said I was at my aunt Edild's house and she backed me up, thinking only to help me. The truth is, as I told you before, that I was with Sibert at the time of the murder and I know that he did not commit it.'

Lord Gilbert studied me for some moments and I grew increasingly uneasy as I watched his expression change from a smile to a scowl. Then he said suddenly, 'Oh, I've had enough of this! You, girl, whatever your name is, you'll get your chance to declare this story of yours before all those concerned.' Greatly alarmed, I took a step back but he was too quick. His arm shot out and he grasped my wrist in a strong hand. 'Wait here,' he commanded. 'Very soon your moment will come.'

He pushed me into the corner of the room and I had to watch as he summoned servants to set out his chair and some benches on the dais at the far end of the hall. The dais, I realized apprehensively, could only be there for one reason, which was to put Lord Gilbert up on high and make the rest of us appreciate to the full our lowly status. Well, as far as I was concerned, he needn't have bothered as I was shaking with fear already and it was taking all my meagre courage not to bolt for home.

He sat down, glared down at me cowering in my corner and then, with an imperious jerk of his chin, beckoned to me to approach. 'Stand there,' he commanded, indicating an area immediately before the dais, on the left side. People were filing into the hall now and several of his men took up their places on the benches beside him. Then a servant slipped out of the hall, to return a few moments later with Baudouin de la Flèche and a thin, gingery man with bad skin and a nervous twitch above his eye. Several of Lord Gilbert's men accompanied them, and they all went to stand opposite me to the right of the dais.

I stood alone.

Then they brought Sibert in.

His appearance shocked me. He looked as if

he had been in some dank, dark cell far below the ground for months, not days, for his face was deadly white and his tunic foul with stains that I did not care to look at too closely. There were shackles around his wrists and ankles and they had made angry red welts in his flesh. Before I could stop myself I opened my mind to him and the force of his terror almost rocked me back on my feet. It was like trying to stop a tempest with a feather but I did my best, battling against his despair and silently shouting out to him, *Have heart, Sibert! I'm here to help! It's not over yet!*

I think he was too far gone in his images of a nightmare – and fairly brief – future even to catch a whisper. He looked up briefly at those arrayed against him. Then, finally, he looked at me. His shoulders slumped in defeat and he hung his head.

I wished I could have gone on trying to give him confidence but, faced with his collapse, my own courage seemed to be rapidly evaporating and I would need what I had left for myself. If only Hrype could have been there, I thought wildly, it would be so much better! He made me believe; or, rather, he had made me believe last night. Now, I felt like giving up and running and running till I was so far away that nobody would ever find me.

I couldn't do that. They'd stop me and besides, I had to try to save my friend. Steeling myself, I tried to blank out the waves of shock and horror coming off Sibert and I turned my full attention to the men who held our future in their hands.

Lord Gilbert opened the proceedings, gabbling quickly and all but incomprehensibly through the formalities and then reminding us, as if we needed it, why we were here and what Sibert stood accused of. He invited Baudouin to speak first and he outlined smoothly and eloquently how, concerned for his nephew and the unspecified but dangerous mission he believed him to be engaged upon, he had gone looking for him. How men had sought him out with the terrible news that Romain had been murdered, taking him immediately to the place where the body of his nephew and heir lay. How he had come across the witness who told him how poor Romain had been so brutally struck down.

All this time, while he told this tale that he so clearly believed to be the truth and that would condemn my friend to the gibbet, Baudouin kept his eyes fixed on Lord Gilbert. It was only when he had finished that he glanced very briefly at me. The gloating look of triumph in his eyes hit me like a fist.

Then he pointed to the gingery man with the twitch and said dramatically, 'Sagar here present is that same witness. Listen now, my lord, to what he has to say.'

Lord Gilbert looked closely at the witness. Then he said, 'Very well. Let him speak.'

Sagar crept forward until he stood immediately before Lord Gilbert's chair on the dais.

Once or twice he glanced back at Baudouin, his eyes sliding away to shoot scared glances up at the plump and imposing figure before him. Then, with an obvious effort, he stood up straight and puffed up his meagre chest. He had the look of a man who was very apprehensive but nevertheless determined to do his duty.

I was quaking.

'Well, man?' Lord Gilbert prompted when we had all been waiting some moments.

'It was just as he says,' said Sagar, jerking his head towards Baudouin. He frowned deeply as if concentrating very hard and went on, 'I was travelling on the track from Dunwich up to the coast road and I came to this clearing, see, and there were these two young men, one following the other, and the second one, he called out to the first, and then the first shot off into the bushes and doubled back, so that he came out behind the other man.' Sagar paused, appearing slightly perplexed, as did quite a few of those listening to him. 'Well, next thing I know, the first man, which is *him*' – the accusing hand pointed straight at Sibert – 'he leaps out at the other one and before he can recover – the other one, that is – *that* one swings this great bit of broke-off branch and catches him full on the back of the head, such a blow as you could hear the skull smash like an egg!'

An awed hush followed his dramatic words. Lord Gilbert leaned over to the man on his right and they conferred for a few moments. Lord Gilbert was looking very serious and once or twice he shot a glance at Sibert.

'There appears to be no doubt in this matter,' he said eventually, 'and we have a witness who has described to us very clearly how Romain de la Flèche met his death at the hand of Sibert here before us. Sibert!' His sudden loud cry made Sibert jump and, with obvious reluctance, he raised his head and stared at his lord.

'Sibert, you are guilty of murder and you will hang,' Lord Gilbert said portentously. 'You—'

I found myself hurrying forward and some-how I seemed to have crossed the floor of the hall and elbowed Sagar quite roughly out of the way, so that now I stood alone before Lord Gilbert.

'He didn't do it!' I cried.

I could hear Lord Gilbert's sigh even from where I stood. Baudouin de la Flèche's intense dark eyes were boring into me as if he wished they were knife points.

'You must explain yourself,' Lord Gilbert said wearily. I think perhaps he thought I'd be so overawed by the proceedings and the company of so many rich and important men that my nerve would fail me. It hadn't.

'Sibert was with me at the time Romain was killed,' I said. My voice was shaking in time with my trembling knees. 'I know I said at first that I didn't go to Drakelow with Sibert and Romain but that was a lie, and I only said it because I'd gone without permission and I was afraid I'd get into trouble, which was why my aunt supported my story that I'd been with her.

262

She was trying to *help*.' The thought of Edild undermined me and I had to bite the insides of my cheeks quite hard to stop myself sobbing.

Baudouin stepped forward. 'How are we to judge which story is the lie and which the truth?' he cried. 'This girl is a well-known liar and nothing she says can be trusted!'

Lord Gilbert was staring hard at me. 'Answer the question,' he ordered.

I was thrown into panic. What question? Mutely I shook my head.

Lord Gilbert shot a glance at Baudouin and then said to me, 'How are we to tell when you are lying and when you are telling the truth?'

'I'm telling the truth *now*!' I cried. 'Oh, you must believe me!'

Again Lord Gilbert turned to the man on his right and I heard them muttering. My aunt's name was mentioned. If I could, I must save Edild from the ignominy of standing in Lord Gilbert's hall and admitting she had lied for me. I said, 'There is something more!'

Lord Gilbert turned his head and stared at me again. So, I am sure, did everyone else in the hall. 'Well?' he said coldly.

Out of all of them, I was most aware – most afraid – of Baudouin and his witness. I made myself turn slightly so that I could not see them. Then I steadied myself and said, 'Sibert and Romain had a fight. That much is true, for Sibert and I had taken – er, Sibert and I had something that Romain badly wanted. Sibert and I left Drakelow – that's on the coast south of Dunwich – ahead of Romain, but very soon he followed after us. He caught up with us in a clearing just south of the road that leads due west from the coast and he attacked Sibert. He had a knife and Sibert was unarmed and he's not much of a fighter at the best of times – sorry, Sibert, but you're not – and so I sort of sided with him – Sibert, I mean – because I thought Romain was going to kill him and I yelled, "Sibert, get your knee up," and he did and he caught Romain between the legs and he went down and that's how we left him, writhing in agony, but you see he was lying on his *back*!' I finished triumphantly, talking a much needed breath.

There was a deadly hush. Then Lord Gilbert said, 'So?'

'Don't you understand?' How could he be so stupid! 'Romain was lying on his back yet that man' – it was my turn to point and I swung my arm round and aimed my forefinger at Baudouin's witness – 'that man claims he saw Sibert strike Romain on the back of his head! Well, he can't have done, because the back of Romain's head was on the ground, so if he says that's what happened then he was too far away to see clearly and so how can he be so sure it was Sibert?'

Now I had their attention. Lord Gilbert was no longer looking at me as if I were something smelly on his shoe and the man on his right was whispering urgently in his ear, his eyes on me. Several of the other men were also murmuring

264

amongst themselves.

Eventually Lord Gilbert held up a hand for silence. 'You have made a valid point,' he began, 'and we—'

Then I was shoved out of the way – so violently that I fell – and Baudouin shouted furiously, 'She cannot possibly know how Romain was positioned, whether he was standing, sitting, lying on his back or his front, *because she wasn't there*! This is another of her fluent, convincing lies, my lord, gentlemen, and you must open your eyes and see it for what it is!'

Several of the men, Lord Gilbert included, clearly did not care for Baudouin's tone, and indeed he had stopped only just short of insulting them. There was more muttering – a great deal more – then at last Lord Gilbert straightened up and addressed the hall.

'We have here a simple case of two conflicting accounts and it is our duty to decide which describes the true version,' he declared. 'Either Baudouin de la Flèche's man is telling the truth, and I must here remind you all that Baudouin himself vouches for the man, or else this girl's account is the true one. What *is* your name?' he demanded impatiently, leaning down towards me.

'Lassair,' I said.

'Lassair,' he repeated. 'So, who are we to believe, the witness Sagar or the girl Lassair? We must now—'

Baudouin spoke up, his voice loud and confident. 'Forgive me, my lord,' he said, 'but there is a method by which this can be decided once and for all.' He shot a glance at me and I felt as if a lump of ice was being run down my back. I knew then that this was what I had foreseen in that awful moment when I had recognized him as my enemy. I did not know what he was about to say but I knew it was going to be terrible.

'What is this method you refer to?' Lord Gilbert asked. 'Speak up, let's hear it!'

I waited, trembling, my heart thumping so high up in my chest that it felt as if it was stopping me from breathing.

Baudouin smiled at me, a cold smile full of malice. Then, turning back to Lord Gilbert, he said smoothly, 'We are faced, as you so eloquently say, my lord, with a choice: which of two people is telling the truth. We are all, I believe, inclined to believe Sagar here, who saw with his own eyes the murder of my poor nephew, a boy I have nurtured and cared for most of his young life and who was to inherit my manor of Drakelow. We have been told the frightful details – I will not repeat them – and Sagar presented himself as witness to this foul deed of his own free will. Against him we have this girl, this *liar*' – he spat the word with sudden fierce venom – 'who would have us believe her falsehoods.'

There was a pause, so full of drama that the air hummed. Then Baudouin cried, 'Let her be tested, my lord! Let the truth of what she says be tried in the old, reliable way!'

266

Nobody spoke for a moment. Then Lord Gilbert cleared his throat and said, 'By – er, by what means would you have us test her, Baudouin?'

'Let her face trial by ordeal,' he answered instantly. He shot me a fierce look. 'If she persists against all reason in making us believe this tale of hers, put her to the test! Build a fire pit, my lord, and challenge her to walk barefoot across the red-hot coals.' He laughed. He actually laughed. '*Then* we shall see who speaks the truth!'

I heard the words – fire pit ... red-hot coals ... barefoot – and at first they made no sense. I shook my head in perplexity.

Then the blessed incomprehension cleared and I knew what he was going to make me do.

The nausea rose up uncontrollably and I threw up my breakfast on the floor of Lord Gilbert's hall.

# EIGHTEEN

I fled. I was aware of shouting. Some of the men were outraged and I heard one of them cry out, 'But she's only a child!' Another protested vehemently, 'He has no right to ask this!' As I raced down the length of the hall Lord Gilbert's voice rose loud above the hubbub, declaring that I had until tomorrow to consider Baudouin's challenge.

He started to say that if I refused, Sibert would be taken out and hanged from the gibbet at the crossroads but I could not bear to listen. Instinctively my hands flew up to cover my ears and I did not hear any more.

There was a small crowd outside the big doors that opened into the hall and suddenly Hrype's face was right in front of me, so taut with tension that I barely recognized him. He too was talking, hurling urgent words at me, but I did not stay to hear them. I shook my head, elbowed the avidly curious villagers out of the way and raced down the steps, across the courtyard and out on to the track.

I didn't know where I was going. I only knew that I had to get away and be quite alone. I had to think. I had to look deep into myself to see if I had the courage to attempt this frightful, ghastly thing that might just possibly save Sibert's life.

I ran and ran until my heaving chest and the crippling stitch in my side caused me at last to stop. I bent over, hands on my knees, panting and gasping for breath. As I began to recover, I straightened up, looked around and saw that I was right out on the far side of the villagers' strips of land, on the edge of a ridge of slightly higher ground where the soil is dryer. There was a band of willows and gratefully I sank down in their welcome shade on to the warm, friendly earth.

For some time I just lay there and after a while I sensed that the sheer solidity of the ground beneath me was giving me reassurance. I breathed deeply several times, then I faced the frightful challenge that Baudouin had laid down.

I blanked everything else out and called to mind everything I knew about trial by ordeal. Normally it was used to sort the innocent from the guilty, because if you were innocent then God came to your aid and protected you from lasting harm. He would make sure that the boiling water in the cauldron did not burn your hand and your arm as you reached down for the pebble on the bottom. He would guard your tender flesh as you carried the red-hot metal in your bare hands. When after three days they removed the bandages and inspected your wounds, if you were innocent then God would already have instigated the healing process and everyone would know you had been wrongly accused.

I had not been accused of any crime but I desperately needed to prove I was telling the truth – difficult, for a habitual liar – and Baudouin had cleverly turned my protestations against me, in effect saying, *Prove it.*

Oh, but what a terrible method he had chosen. Red-hot coals under my bare feet and—

*No.* Don't think about that.

There was a story about Queen Emma, King Cnut's wife and mother of the brutal Hartacnut.

She had another son, Edward, by her marriage to Ethelred and when she became too powerful he plotted against her, accusing her of adultery with her bishop. People whispered behind their hands that to prove her innocence she was made to walk nine feet over red-hot ploughshares, but God must have known the accusations were false and malicious because Queen Emma skipped over the glowing metal, turned to her tormentors and demanded to know when the trial would begin.

It was a good tale. My granny Cordeilla sometimes tells it when she is particularly sad that the days under the Old Kings have gone for ever.

We do not have much land under the plough around Aelf Fen. It's too wet and marshy. I doubt if there are enough ploughshares to cover nine feet of ground, which is presumably why Baudouin opted for a pit of red-hot coals instead.

I took off my shoes and looked at my feet. They are small and narrow, the toes straight and the nails like little shells. I twisted my leg so that I could inspect the sole of my right foot. The skin was hard – unless I was planning on going any distance, I usually went barefoot through the summer – and when I poked it with my fingernail, it felt tough and resilient.

Red-hot coals...

Queen Emma survived unscathed, I reminded myself. Surely I would too? I was, after all, telling the truth...

Supposing I didn't, what then? Frightful, suppurating burns. Infection. Pus and stinking, blackening flesh. The loss, perhaps, of both feet. Life as a cripple, all my dreams of being as fine a healer as Edild come to naught. Could you be a healer sitting down? I did not really see how.

I made myself think about that for some time. So, I thought eventually, I might lose my feet.

Sibert is about to lose his life.

If I lost my feet, I realized, Sibert would lose his life anyway because if I failed to heal, they would judge that God was rejecting me because I was guilty and an evil, worthless liar. I would not be believed when I insisted Sibert had not murdered Romain and my huge sacrifice would have been in vain.

But what if I *did* heal? What if, knowing that for once I was as innocent of lying as Queen Emma had been of adultery, God and all the good spirits put their protection around me and my desperate, hurrying feet and kept me from harm?

I sat there quite a lot longer. Then slowly I stood up. I desperately wanted to go home. I wanted to curl up in my safe little bed and turn my back on the hostile, frightening world. I needed my mother's loving arms, her soothing voice. I wanted my strong, wise father. But both of them would forbid me to take this appalling test. I was their daughter, they cherished me, they did not want to see me suffer ghastly pain. Their reaction would be quite understandable.

They had not been there in the clearing when I yelled out to Sibert to knee Romain in the crotch so that, immobilized by pain, he had been unable to defend himself when his killer came for him.

They did not know that if Sibert was hanged it would be my fault.

If I failed, lost my feet to the fire and Sibert died, at least I would be able to console myself with the fact that I had tried.

I imagined life knowing that I had sat back while they had sent an innocent young man to his death. Then I imagined life without my feet.

I reckoned I knew which would be the harder to bear.

I went to my aunt's house. She loved me too, or I was pretty sure she did, but she was not my parent and I thought she might be better able to distance herself and advise me dispassionately than either my father or my mother.

I nipped round behind the village and approached her neat, tidy and sweet-smelling little cottage from the far side. As I've said, she lives on the very edge of the village, preferring her own company and not being one to gossip at the pump. The bees were busy in the herb beds either side of her door as I hurried up and from the rear of the house I heard the tonk of the bell that hangs round her nanny goat's neck and the soft clucking of her hens.

I tapped perfunctorily on the door and burst in. Edild was sitting on her wooden chair and she looked up and coolly met my eyes. On the low bench on the opposite side of the hearth sat Hrype and Froya.

I guessed, then, that she already knew.

She went on looking at me for a few moments and I had the odd feeling I sometimes get with her, that she's creeping inside my mind to see what's there. Then she said, 'This is not good, Lassair.'

Froya went to say something, but Hrype put a gentle hand on her arm and she subsided. I glanced at her. She is very like Sibert, both of them tall, lightly built and very fair. Her bright sea-green eyes were not as lovely as usual, being red-rimmed and puffy with weeping. She had a dainty linen handkerchief in her hands, surely deeply inadequate for its present purpose, and her fingers worried at it ceaselessly, twisting it this way and that. Also like her son, Froya is one of those people who are just a bit too fragile for life and need looking after. I look after Sibert – or not, in fact, seeing the pass we had come to – and Hrype, I suppose, looks after Froya, as indeed a good man should, especially if his sister-in-law is a widow with a child to bring up.

I could not bear to look into Froya's eyes for very long. There was an expression of anguished hope in them and I knew exactly what it was she was hoping for.

I turned back to Edild. 'Queen Emma managed it!' I burst out. 'She didn't even notice she'd walked over the red-hot metal!'

Edild gave a tut of impatience. 'That's just a story, child,' she said. 'Do you really think anyone would have had the temerity to make someone like Queen Emma do something like that?'

'It was her son that made her,' I mumbled, as if this made it more likely.

Edild did not even bother to answer that.

Then silence extended and they all looked at me. When I could stand it no longer I said, 'I'm going to do it. I've got to, because it's my fault Sibert's in this position and I can't live with my guilt if he's' – I glanced at his poor suffering mother, who had emitted an anguished gasp – 'er, if anything happens to him.' Edild started to protest but I overrode her, briefly explaining my guilt. 'So you see,' I finished, 'really I have no choice. If this is the only way to prove I'm telling the truth and Sibert is no murderer, then I'll have to do what Baudouin demands.'

I could hear the drama in my voice and I'm sure I stood up a little straighter, raising my chin like the brave heroine I was. I fully expected one or all of them to say, *Oh, no, Lassair, you can't possibly do this frightful thing, it is far, far too much to ask of you*, but nobody said a word.

I began to feel very frightened.

Then Hrype said, as calmly as if he were discussing how to cook some new dish, 'I once saw it done. It is quite possible to do it and come to little or no harm.'

I wondered how little was little.

Edild was nodding. 'I too have heard tell of people walking the fire and not suffering hurt.

Tell us, please, Hrype, what you saw.'

He frowned into the distance for a few moments, his light grey eyes unfocused, as if assembling the memory. Then he said, 'It was in the far north, when I was learning with the shamans.' The far north of where? I wondered. And what were shamans? It did not sound like anything that happened or was rumoured to happen in my own land and I realized, with a shiver of wonder, that Hrype must mean the far north of the strange land far away over the sea and he must have travelled back to the place from which his people had once come...

'There was grave trouble in the community,' he was saying, 'for the Sun had withdrawn his strength and the waters of the cold seas were threatening to engulf the lands, so that the reindeer would no longer roam and the people would starve. The shamans held a great ceremony to honour the Sun and his element of fire. They built a vast fire pit and one by one a hundred shamans walked across the live coals. They chanted as they went, mixing their energy with that of the fire, sending their praise into the night sky where the Sun had withdrawn into the darkness. They gave everything they had as they prayed for healing for their community, and their sacrifice was rewarded. The Sun came back, the waters receded and the people grew healthy once more.'

He looked at me, a long look that I could not read. Then he said softly, 'Not one of those hundred men and women suffered lasting harm.

One or two were burned when a coal broke beneath their foot, but healers were standing by to help, giving comfort and relieving pain.'

After some time I tried to speak, but my mouth was dry. I swallowed and tried again. 'How is it done?' I whispered.

Hrype regarded me steadily. 'By courage and by faith. Believe in what you are doing; believe that the task you perform is vital for the general good. Keep in mind that what you do is for the sake of others. Then your guides and helpers will come to your aid and protect you.'

'I can have guides and helpers?' I asked eagerly, then realized, feeling foolish, that he had been referring to the guardian spirits.

'If you elect to do this thing, Lassair,' came my aunt's cool voice, 'Hrype and I will assist you. We will walk alongside you on either side of the pit. We will encourage you.'

She meant it kindly, I knew, but it wasn't their bare feet that were going to be on the coals.

'I don't know...' I murmured. Inside I was crying out desperately, *Help me! Help me!*

My aunt must have heard. Abandoning her detached tone she said with brisk urgency, 'Lassair, you are fire and air. Remember?'

I thought back across the weeks and months to the day when she had explained my web of destiny. 'Ye–es,' I said slowly.

'Fire needs air to burn, and so the two elements that make up your essence are fire's own elements,' she went on. 'The fire will recognize that you are in sympathy with it. You will not be harmed.' A lulling, hypnotic quality had subtly entered her voice. 'You will not be harmed,' she repeated, the words like a soft chant. 'In the instant of your birth' – she was almost singing now – 'the Warrior God was in the fire sign of Aries, and he always acknowledges his own when they demonstrate great courage. He will protect you. *You will not be harmed.*'

Now another, deeper voice blended with hers. Hrype, chanting with her, harmonizing with her, said, 'We will help you. We will support you. We will assist you to raise up your energy until it is at such a peak that it matches that of the fire. The fire will recognize you and you will not be harmed.'

You will not be harmed.

*You will not be harmed.*

Again and again they repeated it until I felt my mind and my voice fall into step with theirs. 'I will not be harmed,' I repeated dreamily.

'Picture your feet, strong like the toughest hide,' said Edild.

'Picture your calm, steady steps across the fire,' said Hrype, 'picture your peaceful, smiling face.'

'See the soles of your feet' – Edild again – 'smooth, unblemished.'

'Imagine your feet in boots of ice,' sang Hrype, 'safe from the fire, cool, protecting. You will not be harmed.'

'You will not be harmed,' they intoned together.

I believed them.

Some time later – I think they put me into a light trance, for afterwards I could not have explained quite how so much time had passed – I was aware of Froya's anxious eyes. I looked at her. I felt full of love for her, Sibert's sweet mother, and I wanted to hug her. I beamed at her, feeling the joyful smile spread to encompass my whole face, my whole being. I dropped to my knees in front of her and took her cold hands in my warm ones. I was fire and air; fire was my element. I would not be harmed. 'Don't worry any more,' I said. I bent to kiss the backs of her hands. 'Sibert won't die.' Another kiss, tiny, the lightest of touches. 'I'll do it.'

# NINETEEN

I would be lying if I said that my mood of serene acceptance lasted until the moment I set my bare feet on to the coals. It didn't. All the rest of that day I suffered dreadful, confidence-sapping periods of doubt, especially when my parents, quietly informed by Edild what I was planning to do, came rushing round to her cottage to dissuade me.

My mother's sobs were hard enough to bear. When I saw tears in my strong, brave father's eyes, I was all but undone.

Edild saw this – of course she would – and took them outside. I heard their voices – my mother's shrill with fear and horror, my father's a quiet background boom – and then Edild spoke, dousing their horrified protests like cool water on the fire.

Fire.

I couldn't stop thinking about fire.

Shortly afterwards Edild came back into the cottage. Her face was set firm as if any leeway that she permitted herself would allow the threatening emotions to take over. She said shortly, 'Your parents have gone home, Lassair. I have explained that you are resolved to do this test and told them why. I have also said that their presence here could distract you and they have agreed to keep away.'

Oh! She was right, I knew she was; I had to fix my thoughts – my whole being – on the trial and, under the instruction of Edild and Hrype, I was working hard on developing a picture in my mind of my feet encased in those imaginary shoes made of thick ice. It was hard enough without having to face my mother's anguished face and my father's desperate need to save me from hurt.

'Will they – will they be there tomorrow?' My voice was little more than a croak.

Edild looked at me dispassionately, almost coldly. She was just then wholly the teacher, and I could detect nothing in her of the affectionate, funny aunt. I knew it had to be that way, but all the same it was hard. 'They will stay inside their cottage,'she said.

Because, she could have added, if they are watching and you know that they are, your concentration will be broken. We were both all too aware of what *that* would lead to.

Hrype went to Lord Gilbert's manor house and informed him that I was prepared to take the test. To my surprise – and Hrype and Edild's too – in the early evening he came to Edild's cottage.

His chubby face was quite pale and he looked at me out of worried eyes. 'You do not have to do this,' he said. 'You are accused of no crime and neither your freedom nor your life is in the balance. It is not too late to change your mind.'

I wondered why he was doing this. 'What does it matter to you?' I demanded. I realized as soon as I had spoken that I sounded rude. 'I am sorry,' I added. 'You have, it seems, my well-being at heart.'

'I have!' he agreed fervently. 'Lassair' – at least he remembered my name now – 'this trial is a fearsome thing! They are constructing the pit as I speak and soon the fires will be lit. You will—'

I sensed Hrype casting round for a courteous but irrevocable way of telling him to be quiet. He knew, as did Edild, that this talk of pits, fires and fearsome things was not good for me.

I spoke first.

'Lord Gilbert,' I interrupted, 'it is kind of you

to take the trouble to explain my position to me.' I knew it perfectly well already, but it was still kind of him. 'However, there is really only one factor to be considered, which is that if I don't do the test and prove that I'm telling the truth, then Sibert will hang.' I tried to hold his eyes but he looked away. 'Is that not so?' I prompted.

'Yes,' he muttered. 'It has to be so,' he added, 'for Baudouin de la Flèche has a witness.'

And Baudouin himself, I thought, is a powerful Norman baron, even if just at present he's a landless one. As Lord Gilbert said, it had to be so.

There was nothing more to be said and after a while he realized it. He gave me a sort of bow – just a slight nod of his head – and it was an extraordinary thing to see, given the huge void between our respective positions in the world. Then he turned and, flinging the door open as if he could not wait to get away from us, hurried away.

I did not think I would be able to sleep that night. The images were far too vivid in my head and the ice boots were having a tough time holding their own against the glowing coals. However, Edild made me an infusion in which I could taste dill and the bitterness of wood lettuce and she made me drink every last drop. Very soon after that, I curled up on the shake-down bed by the hearth that she had prepared for me, drew up the soft lambs' wool blanket and fell into a deep and dreamless sleep.

In the guest chamber of Gilbert de Caudebec's manor house, Baudouin de la Flèche looked out of the small window at the gathering darkness outside and told himself, one more night. Just one more night, and then all this will be over, the crown will be in my hands and I can be off, on my way to plead before the king.

The girl will fail, he thought. He had seen the fire pit and it was good and long. It would take her many paces to get from one end to the other. The coals had been set ready, on top of a bed of kindling and firewood which would be set ablaze at first light. As soon as the coals were red-hot, the girl would be summoned.

She must fail, Baudouin thought. Her feet will suffer terrible burns and no power on earth or in heaven will come to her aid and help her to heal, for she is a well-known liar. This tale she tells will be disproved once and for all and, with nobody left to speak for him, Sibert will hang.

She must fail, he repeated with silent vehemence. She *has* to!

Lord Gilbert's guest bed lay ready to welcome him but his nerves were tight as a snare wire and he could not bear the thought of trying to rest. He paced, leaned against the wall looking down at the fire pit, clearly visible some twenty paces down the track which led from the manor house to the village, then paced some more. Slowly the night passed.

Hrype left Edild and Lassair in the little cottage

on the edge of the village, promising to be back early in the morning. He crossed the village on swift and silent feet to the house he shared with Froya and Sibert. *Sibert!* he thought, anguish searing through him. So much depended on the girl. He and her aunt had worked as hard as they knew how and even greater demands would be made on them in the morning, for he knew, as he was sure Edild did, that they would not leave Lassair's side until it was over. One way or another...

'She will do it,' he said quietly but very firmly.

He opened the door and let himself in, closing and barring it behind him. Froya had gone home some time ago and now was sitting hunched on the floor before the hearth. She was cradling a small square of woollen blanket, smoothing it, stroking it with those restless fingers. He recognized it as the comforter Sibert had treasured as a small child. He'd had no idea she had kept it.

He crouched down beside her and wordlessly she leaned against him. He put his arms round her, reaching up a hand to gently and rhythmically stroke the fair hair away from her high, broad forehead.

'I cannot bear it if he dies,' she said.

Neither can I, he wanted to agree. But instead he said firmly, 'Lassair is strong and brave, Froya. She is full of courage, for she is convinced she can pass the test.'

'And can she?' Froya asked bleakly.

283

'She can.' He reinforced the words by briefly squeezing her shoulder. 'Her aunt and I will be with her. We will not let her falter.'

She nodded and he thought she was reassured, but then her body convulsed in a great sob and she said despairingly, 'He is not strong! I think of him in some horrible, stinking cell, knowing that he may hang in the morning, and I feel that my heart is being torn apart within my breast!'

'I know, I know,' he murmured. He too had been fighting images of Sibert imprisoned, shaking with fear, weeping in the cold darkness.

Would Lassair do it? Or would she burn like a tallow candle and watch from agonized eyes as Sibert was strung up and hanged?

She will succeed, he told himself.

In time Froya's weeping came to an end, although the storm had left her shaky. Gently he got her to her feet and over to her bed on the far side of the cottage, where tenderly he helped her off with her tunic and settled her beneath the covers. He resumed the slow, steady stroking motion across her head. 'Sleep,' he murmured. 'Sleep, dear Froya, and sleep deep.' He spoke more words, incomprehensible syllables, and his low, hypnotic voice seemed to fill the small room, echoing with a forceful, muted boom like the sea in a cave.

The spell worked. Froya slept.

Hrype waited for some time, watching the steady rise and fall of her chest. He tucked the covers more closely around her and then, moving without a sound, let himself out of the cottage.

He made his way to a spot on the fen edge where alders stood close, their trunks wading in the bracken and the low, scrubby bushes. There was a cleared space within the undergrowth where a small circle of hearth stones, carefully chosen and even in size and shape, had been set out. Firewood and kindling lay at hand, protected from the elements by strips of turf. Hrype set a small fire and lit it with his flint, his hands moving with swift efficiency for he had performed these actions many times. It was his secret place, and a mild enchantment lay over it that prevented others from going too close.

When the flames took hold he quickly controlled them so that they rose no higher than was necessary for his purpose. Then he untied the thongs of a small leather pouch that hung from his belt, the leather soft and smooth from long handling, for it had belonged to Hrype's forefathers before it had been his and each successive owner had used it frequently.

He opened the bag and took from it a neatly folded square of fine linen, hemmed with tiny stitches. This object was Hrype's own; it was the first magic tool that he had made and even now he could readily recall the day he had cut the cloth and sewn those careful stitches. He had been eight years old.

He spread the linen square on the earth, smoothing it until there were no bumps or wrinkles. Then, holding the leather bag in both hands, he closed his eyes and murmured a long incantation, calling on the spirits of the place, on the ancestors, on his personal guardians and, pleading and supplication in his chant, on the gods themselves. When he sensed that they were with him, he upended the bag and, as its contents rattled down on to the linen square, opened his eyes.

The rune stones were made of jade, so fine that, held up to the fire, the light of the flame could be seen through them. The jade came from the east; from the vast lands beyond the great inland seas where his ancestors had travelled and traded, pushing onwards, always onwards along the rivers that penetrated the huge, unknown interior. Hrype did not know which of his sorcerer ancestors had cut the raw material and made the rune stones; whoever he was, he – or perhaps she, for women too were sorcerers – had done a skilful job and the rune stones were very beautiful.

They also held prodigious power.

Hrype gazed down at them, lying there in the pattern in which they had fallen. The gold-filled incised marks on their surfaces glittered in the firelight, giving the stones the illusion of movement. Of life. Quickly he read them, his agile mind making connections and forming pictures as he had long ago been taught. He breathed a sigh of relief. Then he looked again, for something had caught his eye.

He stared for a long time then finally sat back, his eyes closed as he pondered. The runes were almost always ambiguous and it took a well-trained mind to penetrate the smokescreen that frequently they threw up. The way in which they had fallen tonight gave one message – the first aspect that Hrype had read – but underlying that there was something else.

Something that both puzzled and, he had to admit, worried him. He was puzzled because, although the question he had framed in his mind had to do with fire and air, the underlying aspect warned of danger from water.

He sat for so long that anyone observing him would have thought he was some stone figure, left from a bygone age. Eventually, barely aware that he was stiff and very cold, he collected up the rune stones, clutched them for a moment in his hands as he uttered his thanks, then put them away in their pouch and fastened it to his belt. He trod out the dying remains of his fire and scuffed at the earth until its small scar barely showed. Then he went home.

I smelt the fire the moment I woke up. I raced to open the door and peered out. Just visible far along the track, at the point where it curved round to approach Lord Gilbert's manor house, I saw a long pit from which flames rose so high that they would have burned off my hair.

I made a whimpering sound in my throat.

Instantly Edild was at my side. 'The flames will have died down before you walk,' she said calmly. 'Now, come and eat your breakfast. You will need your strength today, for deep concentration is draining.'

She might have been referring to a day spent doing nothing more alarming than learning new remedies. Her serenity pulled me back from the brink of hysteria and, to my amazement, I found myself munching a slab of buttered bread spread thickly with honey – Edild was spoiling me – and drinking a sweet and pungent brew which, I was quite sure, was mildly alcoholic.

When I had finished eating she marched me outside to the small, enclosed yard behind her cottage and ordered me to strip. Then she helped me wash all over, from my hair to my toes, rinsing me with fresh, cool water in which rose petals floated. She wrapped me in a length of linen and proceeded to comb the tangles out of my hair. When it was almost dry, she deftly plaited it and coiled it round my head. I struggled into a clean under shift and then she fetched one of her own gowns and helped me put it on over the top, fastening a pretty girdle around my waist.

She stood back and inspected me. Then, at last, she smiled. 'You look fine, Lassair,' she said. She had something in her hand and now she stepped forward and held it out. On a length of leather hung a round disc of fine, smooth wood, into which was etched the sigil for protection. The sigil showed up deep, dark, brownish-red and I knew that it had been coloured with her blood.

She put the leather thong over my head and tucked the amulet inside my under tunic. Then she gave a nod of satisfaction. 'You'll be all right,' she said.

I believed her.

They came for me in the middle of the morning.

There was a sharp rap at the door and as Edild opened it I saw four of Lord Gilbert's men. They did not say anything – they did not need to – and I stepped outside and took my place between them, two in front of me and two behind. I saw Edild walking beyond the guards on my right and Hrype appeared out of nowhere and took up the same place on my left.

Their silent presence was immeasurably reassuring.

Protected by my escorts, we set off up the track. I kept saying under my breath, *Boots of ice. I will not be harmed.* Once or twice I put up a hand and touched the amulet hanging on its thong between my breasts.

So many villagers had gathered, lining the track on either side and milling over it, that I felt the fire pit before I actually saw it. Its heat came at me in waves, beating against my face. Then the people parted and I saw what lay ahead of me.

Edild did not give me any time for the fear to race in. She bent down and, sweeping up the skirts of my gown, twisted them deftly and tucked the end in my belt. I almost laughed then because, amid the vast presence of the fire pit and what I must now do there, I was more worried in that instant that everyone could see my bare legs. Well, I told myself, at least they're not fat and hairy with thick chunky ankles like Goda's...

Lord Gilbert stepped forward, flanked by more of his men. Behind him stood Baudouin de la Flèche, his black eyes fixed on me. Lord Gilbert squared his shoulders and, after one anxious glance at me, stared over my head and said in a booming voice, 'I call on those here present to witness the trial by ordeal of Lassair of Aelf Fen, here before you. She claims that Sibert, accused of the murder of Romain de la Flèche, is innocent of the charge because she was with him at the time of the murder. Baudouin de la Flèche, the dead man's uncle, has brought forth a witness who says he saw Sibert commit the act of murder. Lassair agrees to walk the glowing coals and avows that God will prove that her word is true by protecting her from harm, and the priest here present' – for the first time I noticed the black-clad figure, frowning his disapproval as if he would have liked to stop proceedings there and then – 'will inspect her wounds after three days.'

*Her wounds...*

I quailed. Beside me Hrype hissed, 'Boots of ice! You will suffer no harm!'

There was no more time. Lord Gilbert nodded to the guards and their captain shouted, 'Proceed!'

I stepped forward. Edild walked on my right, Hrype on my left, although they were too far away for me to touch them even with my outstretched fingers.

I do not need to touch them, I told myself. They are with me, their strength and their will supports me.

I closed my eyes for an instant, fiercely bolstering my energy until I sensed it flare up bright-hot, white-hot within me. I am made of fire, I told myself. Fire is my element.

*Fire will not harm me.*

Then I stepped on to the red-hot coals.

Walk quickly but do not run, Hrype had instructed. Keep up a steady pace. Look ahead.

His words echoed loud and strong in my ears. One pace, two, three. The coals were very, very hot and I could feel their threat. But my ice boots protected me. *Your feet are pleasantly cool*, I heard Edild say calmly inside my head. *Take your time for you will not be hurt.*

Four steps. Five.

I was still staring straight ahead but out of the corners of my eyes I could see Hrype and Edild. It was odd because although of course I recognized them, sometimes they did not look like themselves. Or, rather, they did but at the same time they looked quite different and I could have sworn that a silver fox paced on my right and a great brown bear padded on silent paws to my left.

I felt so safe, so secure, that I knew it was going to be all right.

Six steps, seven, eight, then, quickly now, nine, ten, eleven and twelve, then one foot was out of the pit and then the other, the fresh grass cool and welcome.

There was a stunned silence – I had been aware as I walked the fire pit that nobody was making a sound – and then a great roar rose up. Edild and Hrype stood panting either side of me, both of them drenched in sweat; Hrype had bluish cords standing out on his temple and neck. I spun my head this way and that, trying to see what was happening, trying to look in every direction at once, but then suddenly I was dumped down on my bottom on the grass and Edild was plunging my feet into very, very cold water that smelt of lavender.

She must have only recently fetched the water from the well, for the chill bit as the fire had not done and I cried, 'Ouch! That's *cold*!'

She did not hear, or if she did she gave no sign. One by one she raised my feet out of the icy water, closely inspecting each one before plunging it back again. She did this three times and I saw a slow smile of satisfaction spread over her face. I was the only one who could see, however, since she was bent over me, her face hidden. Then Hrype was there too, and wordlessly she lifted up my feet once more and showed him.

His smile was wide and triumphant. They looked at each other for a long moment and almost imperceptibly she nodded.

He stood up.

Lord Gilbert was elbowing his way through the throng, pushing open-mouthed, avid-faced villages out of the way in his fervour. 'Well?' he cried. *'Well? Is* she all right? Is she burned? What has happened?'

He saw Edild's tranquil face and a grin twitched at his mouth.

'See for yourself,' Edild said. She lifted my feet up to show him and I was tipped over inelegantly on to my back, struggling to hold down my skirt to preserve what was left of my modesty.

He stared, shook his head in disbelief and stared again. The grin now splitting his face like a slice out of an apple, he called out, 'There is no need for bandages or priestly inspection after the prescribed three days, for *Lassair has taken no injury*!' The last words were delivered at the top of his voice. Then, in a far more controlled tone, he said, 'I declare that, by virtue of the trial by ordeal, Lassair of Aelf Fen has proved that she tells the truth. God has protected her,' he pronounced gravely.

I felt like throwing back my head and crowing. I felt like getting to my cold but unblemished feet and dancing. I turned to look for Baudouin de la Flèche, already edging his way quickly to the rear of the crowd, and I screamed, *'Yaaaaa!'*

It was pretty meaningless but it seemed to sum up what I was feeling. I saw him scowl at me with furious malice, then he spun round and hurried away.

Lord Gilbert, as if he had suddenly recalled the reason why we were all gathered there, was looking grave. He glanced after Baudouin de la

Flèche, a frown creasing the puffy flesh of his forehead, then looked back at me. 'It has indeed been demonstrated without doubt that you have God's protection, and therefore we know that you speak true when you say Sibert is no murderer,' he said. Then, with a sigh, he added, 'The man Sagar, produced by Baudouin de la Flèche as witness, must be mistaken.' His frown deepened; clearly he was thinking hard. Then he turned to the captain of his guard and said simply, 'Go and release Sibert. The charge against him is dropped.'

The guard hurried away. I looked around for Hrype, a happy smile on my face, for surely he would hasten to go with the guards to welcome Sibert back into the world and I wanted to share the moment with him. He wasn't there; I guessed he had foreseen Sibert's release and had already gone.

The men who had led me out to the pit had all stepped back as if, out of embarrassment, they were distancing themselves from someone who had been treated like a criminal and had just proved, in quite spectacular fashion, that she was nothing of the sort.

I stood alone, for Edild too had melted away. There was no time to wonder where she'd gone because all at once my mother was pushing her way through the awestruck, chattering villagers, my father, my granny and my siblings hard on her heels, and I leapt up and threw myself into her arms.

'I'm all right!' I cried, laughing and crying at

the same time. *'I'm all right!* I proved I was telling the truth and Sibert's going to be freed!'

*'I know!'* she sobbed, her hug fierce and strong. Then, shaking me so hard that my teeth clattered together, she cried, 'Oh, Lassair, Lassair, don't you *ever* do anything like that again!'


# TWENTY

In a joyful, overwhelmingly relieved band, laughing, chattering, we made our way back to our house. I was skipping along hand in hand with Elfritha and Haward, both of them clutching on to me as if I was about to be wrenched away from them to face an even worse ordeal, when Edild caught up with us.

'You feel no pain?' she asked.

'None!' I cried jubilantly. 'I could dance all night!'

She smiled briefly. I realized she looked exhausted. I detached myself from my brother and sister, saying I'd follow along presently, then stopped and faced my aunt.

'Thank you,' I said quietly. 'I don't know exactly what you and Hrype were doing as I walked the coals, but I do understand that I couldn't have done it without you.'

Her smile widened. 'Yes you could, Lassair. You believed in yourself and you did as you were told.'

Slowly I shook my head. 'You did *something*,' I insisted. 'Something that exhausted the pair of you and made you sweat as if you'd just run a mile over rough country. And,' I added, lowering my voice as I remembered, 'it wasn't just you – I thought I saw your guides. Yours was a silver fox and Hrype's was a bear.'

For an instant her eyes widened and she muttered something, then her expression cleared and she said mildly, 'I don't think so, Lassair. It was probably just the excitement and the stress of the challenge.'

I held her eyes and I thought she sent me a silent message. I thought she said, *You are right but these things are not to be spoken of.*

I nodded, just once. Then she took my arm and we hurried after the others.

The next joy was when Hrype and Froya arrived, because walking between them, grinning sheepishly, was Sibert. He was still pale but he looked very different from the last time I'd seen him, in Lord Gilbert's hall. Hrype must have taken him home as soon as he had been released and he'd had a wash – his fair hair was still wet – and changed his clothes. There were neat bandages on his wrists and ankles where the iron shackles had bitten into his flesh.

We all gave him a great welcome. My father had tapped a barrel of the best beer and we were rapidly making our way through it, so that already we were tipsy and loud. Sibert accepted congratulations modestly, his head lowered, and in time he made his way to me.

'I didn't think you'd have the courage to do it,' he said. 'I'm not sure I could have done the same thing for you.'

I felt a little hurt. '*Thank you* wouldn't go amiss,' I remarked.

'Oh, *Lassair*!' Surprising me greatly, for he was usually so distant, especially in a physical sense, he opened his arms and embraced me in a hard hug. Just as quickly he let me go again. 'Thank you,' he said. 'You saved my life.'

Now I felt embarrassed. 'You'll just have to save mine, then,' I said lightly, 'then we'll be even.'

We went on staring at each other. Neither of us seemed to know how to end the awkwardness, but then we heard a commotion and, spinning round, I saw Lord Gilbert standing in the doorway, flanked by several of his men.

We all fell silent. His face was grave and it was obvious he hadn't come to add his congratulations and accept a mug of ale.

'What has happened?' My father's voice was wary.

'The gold crown has gone,' Lord Gilbert said. Somebody gasped. 'While Lassair walked the fire pit, my hall was left all but unguarded, for my wife and my son were tucked safely away in her chamber and everyone else was outside watching the ordeal. When the guards went to release Sibert, one of them noticed that the chest in which I had locked the crown while its ownership is decided had been broken open.'

'I did not take it!' Sibert cried out.

I smiled grimly. It was understandable, I suppose, for him to instantly defend himself, for he had only just been set free from Lord Gilbert's cell and obviously didn't want to be thrown back down there. As a general rule, though, it is unwise to protest your innocence before you've even been accused.

Lord Gilbert had turned to Sibert, and I heard him say, 'No, Sibert, I know that. You could not possibly have done, for you were still under lock and key when the theft was discovered.'

'Whom do you suspect?' my father asked.

I knew. Before Lord Gilbert answered, I knew what he would say. I had seen Baudouin slip away and, although at the time I had been far too full of my triumph to think about where he might be going, now it was obvious.

'Baudouin took it,' I piped up.

'*Hush!*' my mother and my father said together, both turning to glare at me.

'He must have done!' I persisted. 'Now that we all know Sibert didn't kill Romain, the real murderer will have to be found and brought to justice and that could take ages, and meanwhile Baudouin's desperate to get his manor back and he needs the crown to persuade the king to be merciful!'

Nobody spoke. Lord Gilbert and the men with him were staring at me. It was all so obvious to me and I couldn't understand why they were prevaricating. 'He – Baudouin – must have realized that he'd accused the wrong person when he said Sibert was a murderer,' I pressed on eagerly. 'That man Sagar can't have been close enough to see who the killer was, but Baudouin was so desperate to bring someone to account for Romain's death that he picked the obvious person, which was Sibert.'

There was a squawk of protest from Sibert and Lord Gilbert said, 'Why was Sibert the obvious person?'

'*Because he was there!*' Really! 'Well, he wasn't *there*, not in the clearing when the murder was committed, but he'd recently been in the vicinity and Baudouin must have known that. He – Baudouin – was worried about Romain, aware he was planning something reckless to try to help win back Drakelow, and in order to protect him, Baudouin was following him. He probably saw me and Sibert and when Sagar said Sibert killed Romain, there was no reason for Baudouin to disbelieve him.'

'Hmm.' Lord Gilbert looked thoughtful. Then, as if suddenly tired of the whole perplexing matter, he said, 'I do not intend to pursue Baudouin. The crown was, after all, found on his land, or what used to be his land, and I had all but decided to return it to him anyway.' Lord Gilbert quite often showed a tendency to do the easy thing as opposed to the right thing; we had all noticed it. 'My involvement in this sorry business,' he went on grandly, 'only came about because one of my people was accused of murder; wrongly, as it turns out' – he flashed me a smile – 'and now that this has been resolved, I am content to let a matter belonging to the manor of Dunwich find its eventual resolution in Dunwich.'

Did he mean Romain's murder? He must do, but it hadn't taken place at Dunwich.

I watched him, filled with the angry realization that he was far more concerned with his own peaceful, indolent, self-indulgent life than with seeing justice done. But he had been kind to me and I couldn't find it in my heart to hate him for his weakness. Life was so complicated, I thought, quietly fuming, and human beings the most complicated things in it.

Nobody else seemed to find anything to reprove in Lord Gilbert's decision and when a little later two of his servants showed up with another barrel of even finer beer, he was hailed as the finest lord a peasant ever had.

By nightfall we were all far beyond tipsy and I was starting to feel very tired as the drama and the excitement caught up with me. My mother, noticing, began shooing people away and soon just our family were left, wearily settling for the night.

I went outside to the jakes and on my way back in, heard a hiss from the shadows. Sibert stepped forward.

'I thought you'd gone home,' I said.

'I did. Hrype needs to talk to us.'

'Very well, then. I'll just tell my parents where I'm going and—'

'No, you mustn't!' Sibert looked strained. 'Wait till they're all asleep, then slip out and come to our house.'

'But I'm tired and—'

'Lassair, just do it!' He sounded both impatient and scared. 'Please,' he added.

'Oh, all right.' I was excited, despite my protestations. 'I'll be along as soon as I can.'

In fact it was not long at all before I deemed it safe to leave. The beer and the festivities had caught up with my family and soon I could detect the familiar sounds of the adults' snores and my siblings' soft, deep breathing. I got up, slipped off the leather band that secures the door and crept out into the darkness.

I sprinted across the village and, reaching Sibert and his family's house, tapped softly on the door. It was opened immediately by Froya and without a word she wrapped me in her arms. We stood for some moments and then, breaking away, she stared into my eyes and said, 'You saved my son's life. I am in your debt, Lassair, and if ever I may help you, you have but to ask.'

The emotion that pulsed through the little room slowly ebbed and, with a quick nod, she stepped back and sat down on a stool beside the hearth. Bending down – I could see the blush on her pale face and guessed she was as embarrassed as I was – she poked at the embers of the cooking fire and set some small flames dancing along the charred logs. Hrype, seated on a bench with Sibert beside him, watched her and then turned to me. 'So, Lassair,' he said with a smile. 'You survived unscathed.'

'Yes,' I agreed. I realized I had not spoken to him since my ordeal. 'I should have thanked you before, when we were all busy downing the celebratory ale,' I said, 'but I did not see you again after you arrived with Sibert and Froya. Were you with the group outside in the yard?'

'No. I did not stay.'

I remembered his exhausted face, the sweat of great exertion dripping from it and the knotty blue cords that stood out on his temple and snaked up his neck. 'You're not unwell?' I asked anxiously. 'It wasn't too much for you? The ordeal, I mean.'

He laughed, but it was a kindly laugh. 'No, no, I recovered quite quickly.'

'Why did you not stay to join us in the celebration at our house, then?'

He reached down and picked up something from the floor; something that had been hidden by the folds of his long robe. 'Because of this.'

He held it up high and the flames of the fire glinted on the smooth surface of the Drakelow crown.

I could barely believe my eyes. *'You've* got it!' I stared at him. 'How did you manage to take it?'

'As soon as I knew you had survived the fire pit unhurt I left you in Edild's care and slipped away to Lord Gilbert's manor house. There was nobody about; everyone was still standing open-mouthed staring at your pretty feet.'

'How did you know where it was?' I demanded.

'It called to me.'

I did not begin to understand.

'But I thought – I mean,' I stammered, 'when I suggested to Lord Gilbert that Baudouin had taken it, he agreed with me and said he wasn't going to do anything about it because he'd decided Baudouin ought to have it anyway!'

'He has not got it and he must never take possession of it!' Hrype said passionately.

I thought I understood. 'It's yours, isn't it?' I said eagerly. 'Your ancestor made it – Sibert said so.' I looked at Sibert to back me up but he said nothing. 'You're going to keep it, which is right as it surely belongs to your family, and—'

'I will not keep it.' Hrype's almost savage hiss cut across my words. He said something else; it sounded like, 'I do not dare.'

Without my volition I found that my gaze had slid from Hrype's impassioned face to the crown that he still held up. I became aware of its power. It was humming quietly and the sound was waxing steadily stronger.

I was suddenly very afraid.

I said in a whisper, *'What is it?'*

And Hrype told me.

This is the story he told.

'My ancestors were men of importance in our

303

homeland,' he began, 'for among our number runs a strain of magic-workers, and the kings of old trusted us and depended on us. So it was that when the waters rose and our lands were flooded, the king who led us here to England took the precaution of surrounding himself with protective magic. My forefather Creoda was his close adviser, ever at hand to warn him of unsuspected perils and provide the means of dealing with them. Thanks to him, the king and the people settled safely in their new homes on the coast. The king built his great hall, the people settled nearby in their round houses and the land proved fruitful, so that the people prospered and the children grew healthy and strong. Creoda, whose invaluable place at the king's side had won him both favour and wealth, asked for a parcel of land on which to build his own hall and when the king readily agreed, Creoda selected Drakelow, for he knew it was a place where the power that is in the land and the sea manifested itself with unusual force.'

'That's why they built the sea sanctuary there!' I whispered.

'Creoda did not build it,' Hrype replied. 'It was there years, centuries, ages before Creoda's time.'

'Yes, I know. I meant that the ancient people who built the sanctuary recognized the power.'

Hrype stared at me. 'Yes,' he said. He went on staring at me and then, as if coming out of some inner place of contemplation, picked up his tale.

'The king and the people lived in peace and contentment,' he said, 'but then came the dread threat from the east, and in helpless horror our people heard tell of how the dragon-prowed Viking ships advanced out of the dawn light, grinding on to our shores and discharging their cargoes of ruthless fighting men. Settlement after settlement fell, the people cut down, the dwellings and the long halls burned, the wealth of the people plundered. Our king, fearing for the very existence of the new realm he had carved out for his people, called on Creoda and asked him what should be done. Creoda said there was a way to defend the king's realm, but it involved great peril. "Do it," said the king. "Whatever it takes, do it," and he gave Creoda free rein, offering gold, offering men, offering a secluded place in which to work the magic.

'Creoda did not need the men and he took only what gold he needed for his purpose. He went quite alone to his secret place and there he built a fire so hot that it turned solid metal into molten liquid. He put the king's gold on to the fire and watched as slowly it melted. Then he used his magic arts and out of it he formed three crowns, putting into them the essence of his soul so that they turned into objects of power, each one bursting with strong enchantment. As he weakened – for he had used almost all of his strength and was now little more than a shadow – he spoke the words of the spell. Then, laying aside the crowns while they cooled, he wrapped his burned hands in clean cloth and lay down to sleep.

'When he was partially recovered – and he never regained more than a small portion of his former vigour, having poured it into his creation – he rose up and returned to the king, seeking a private audience. "Behold what I have made for you," he said, and as he unwrapped the crowns from their protective linen, for the first and only time their magical voices were heard in the king's hall. The king covered his ears in abject fear and quickly Creoda replaced the linen wrappings.

'Slowly the king recovered from his terror and asked, "What must I do with these dread objects?" "You must bury them on the shores of your land," replied Creoda, "where their power will blend and combine to form a defensive shield that will repel those who would invade and rob you of what you have won."

'The king and his sorcerer talked long into the night as they pondered the best locations for the crowns, and at last the king made his decision. "One shall I bury here at Rendlesham," he declared, "for here is my hall and my high seat, the heart and the centre of my realm. One you, Creoda, shall take with you to Drakelow, for your power is in these objects and it is fitting that one part of what you have freely given should remain close to you, hidden where its force shall guard my port of Dunwich. The third we will take north and bury at Bran's Head, so that the northern shore of our realm shall also be defended from the men who come out of the east."

'It was done as the king decreed. Creoda and his king took a strong bodyguard and they went secretly and by night. Keeping to the ancient tracks along which run the lines of power, they went first to Bran's Head, where with solemn ceremony and deep magic Creoda called upon the old gods and buried the first crown on the margins of the realm, where the land meets the sea and the forces are strong. Then they proceeded to Drakelow, and Creoda buried the second crown on his own land. Finally they returned to the king's hall and on the long shore below Rendlesham, Creoda donned the horned headdress and, in the light of the crescent moon, buried the third crown. Then he took the fly-agaric potion and, with a winged horse and a goose to guard him, set out on his last and greatest spirit journey, using what was left of his magic power to spark the three crowns into everlasting life. Creoda, greatest of all sorcerers, had interred the crowns and it is not for any man to undo what he did.'

It was some time before I realized that Hrype had stopped talking. My eyes were closed and my mind was alive with images. I saw a magical flying horse with a woman on its back and she whispered her name to me: *Andrasta*. And there beside her was Epona riding her giant goose; my granny Cordeilla flashed across my inner eye and I recalled how she always called on Epona and her goose when she embarked on a tale, for Epona is the mother and patron of all storytellers. I saw the Goddess of the Sacred Grove, and she was holding out her sword arm straight and true as with the tip of her great weapon she blessed all those who accepted the challenge and fought, in whatever way was their particular talent, to protect the sacred homelands of the people.

Creoda had done that, and he was Hrype's ancestor.

I opened my eyes and stared at him.

It was as if he had been waiting for me. Sibert sat immobile as stone and his eyes were still fast shut. Froya was hunched on her stool, her back bent as if under a heavy load.

I could have believed that Hrype and I were alone.

I felt his thought. It came at me like an arrow and as soon as I understood, it seemed to me that the awareness had been there all along.

'The crown must go back,' I whispered, my voice hardly more than a breath.

'Yes.'

I hesitated, for I was tired and afraid. But he was relentless and I knew I must speak. 'Must I take it?'

'You must, and Sibert must go with you.'

'Why?' I asked. I sounded like a wheedling child.

'Because it was you and Sibert who took it,' he answered.

And all at once it made perfect sense.

# TWENTY-ONE

Sibert and I set out while it was still dark and for the third time I embarked on a long journey far from the safety of my home.

Hrype promised to reassure my parents but I knew they would be so very worried about me. They must have hoped that I'd had enough of excitement for the time being, as indeed I had. Returning to Drakelow was the last thing I wanted to do and, glancing at Sibert as the dawn light steadily grew stronger, I thought he probably felt the same.

We were lucky this time in that we got a lift from a garrulous carter eager for somebody – anybody – to talk to, and he picked us up just south of St Edmundsbury and took us all the way to the place where our track branched off the road south-east to the coast at Dunwich. Despite the nervous tension and the underlying fear, both of us managed to sleep, although I don't suppose even that stopped the carter's chatter.

Rested and well-fed as we were – the carter had shared his food with us and, thanks to Hrype, who it became clear was much better at putting together travelling rations than Sibert, we were provided with a generous pack – we made good time on the last leg of our journey. We arrived at Drakelow in the late afternoon and stood side by side on the top of the low cliff staring out at the crumbling timbers of the sea sanctuary, just becoming visible above the out-going tide.

'I think,' Sibert said thoughtfully, 'it's even more damaged than it was last time we were here.'

I agreed. 'The sea is reclaiming it.' I felt strange; sort of dreamy. 'Soon it'll all be gone and there will be nothing left to mark where it was.'

'Then we'd better hurry up and put the crown back,' Sibert replied. 'It'll be safe then.'

He was right. Although I'd have given any-thing not to have to do this task, I realized that we could only be free to go home once we'd steeled ourselves and completed it.

We decided to wait until twilight. It did not seem likely that there was anyone around to see us but you never knew. We settled in a hollow on the top of the cliff and ate quite a lot of Hrype's supplies. Then Sibert had a doze and I sat watching the waves. The tide had turned and was coming in again but I reckoned we still had plenty of time to get out to the sea sanctuary and bury the crown.

When it was growing dark I packed up our belongings and roused Sibert. We clambered down the cliff and struck out across the pebbly sand.

There were puddles on the foreshore and as we splashed along they struck chilly on my skin. The air, too, felt colder than it ought to have done for a summer's night. I looked up and saw a bank of cloud blowing up out of the dark eastern sky, slowly and inexorably blanking out the bright stars. A mist was rolling in on the silvery surface of the sea. I felt suddenly afraid and instinctively I moved closer to Sibert. He glanced at me and I saw my apprehension reflected in his face. He clutched at the crown in its bag at his waist and said gruffly, 'Come on. The sooner we've done it, the sooner we can be safely back on dry land.'

Back on dry land. Yes, how much I wanted that. How alien, by comparison, was this mysteriously threatening watery world whose margins we trod.

We were holding hands. I don't know which of us made the move, but all at once Sibert's strong, warm hand was clutching mine and I was so glad. The mist had crept up to our feet now. It was as if some element of the sea were stealthily extending its reach to draw us in, grasping for us with thin, silver fingers. I glanced down at the strange sight of my legs appearing to end just above my ankles.

All at once the wrecked posts of the sea sanctuary rose up right in front of us.

We stopped. Then Sibert squared his shoulders and said, 'We must put it back exactly where we found it. Can you recall the place?'

I could. Even in the growing darkness, with

the mist blotting out all firm outlines, my instincts were leading me right to the spot. It was as if the crown's power had left a trace of itself down there in the sand beneath the ancient wood. For someone like me it was as easy to read as a candle in a window on a moonless night.

'This way.'

Confidently I stepped forward into the circle. Then, crouching down, my skirt flapping into a pool of sea water, I started to scoop out the sand. Sibert placed the crown carefully down beside one of the timbers and then began to help me and quite soon we had made a significant hollow. Sibert sat back on his heels, brushed his hair off his sweaty forehead – it was hot work digging the hard, wet sand – and said, 'It's not deep enough yet. I think we ought to—'

Something big and black rushed up out of the darkness and buffeted into him, knocking him over. I screamed, for in that first horrified shock I thought it was some nightmare creature out of the sea. Then I heard the sound of fists on flesh. Someone grunted. Someone cried out in pain.

Struggling, locked together, the two shadowy shapes were now out on the far side of the sanctuary and I could hear their feet splashing about in the water. I rushed after them, panicking, trying to make out which one was Sibert, and as I watched, my thoughts flying wildly from one rescue plan to the next, each of them equally futile, I saw the shorter, stockier shadow raise its arm and with a sickening crack, land a heavy punch right on the point of the tall, slim shadow's chin.

Sibert went down.

He stayed down, for the other shadow was sitting on his head and his head was under the water.

I leapt on to the man's back, pummelling at him with both hands, then when that failed, trying to reach round to stick my fingers in his eyes, up his nostrils or into the corners of his mouth. His broad shoulders felt like iron and he brushed me off, taking no more notice of me than a bull does of a gnat. He was gasping, groaning with effort, for Sibert must have sensed death coming for him and he was thrashing about like a landed fish.

I gathered myself and leapt on him again, punching harder, screaming, shouting. Sibert was dying right before my eyes and I had to save him.

Then two things happened. Sibert stopped struggling, then the man threw himself backwards and I was flung off him into the deepening water.

I leapt up again, hampered by my soaking-wet skirts, and flew at the inert shape that was Sibert. I tried to raise his head up out of the waves that were now running powerfully up the shore, but savagely the man kicked me away. I fell again, and this time I hit my forehead very hard on one of the timbers of the sanctuary. I shook my head, stunned, and bursts of brilliant light exploded behind my eyes.

The man pushed Sibert deep under the water and held him there. Then he splashed across the sea sanctuary until he stood over the crown, still lying on the sand where Sibert had put it.

Even as he spun round to face me, triumph written all over him, I knew who he was. Baudouin de la Flèche cried out in a voice that was hardly human, 'This treasure is not going back under the waves! I claim it, and with it I shall win back Drakelow!'

'You've killed Sibert!' I sobbed. 'You've taken a young man's life, purely for your own selfish reason!'

He laughed. 'His life means nothing! I have killed before and I shall do so again.'

In an instant of shock and horror I thought I knew what he meant. No. *No.* I shook my head in denial, for if I was right it was a dreadful, abnormal act. I must be wrong – I *must* be...

Now Sibert was dead too – I dared not think about that – and I knew I was going have to fight his killer.

He stood quite still and I heard him laugh again. It was as if he were daring me to speak, to tell him what I was thinking. He actually said, 'Go on, then!' and I knew my horrified conclusion was the right one.

I've never been one to turn down a challenge.

'You killed Romain,' I said. 'There was no murderer other than you, and you bribed Sagar to say it was Sibert.' I shook my head. 'Romain was your nephew and your heir. *Why?*'

'Romain was a hot-headed fool.' He spat out

314

the words. 'I went to such trouble to make him think he had found out about the crown by himself, when all along it was I who had arranged it so that he just happened to meet the one man who had the necessary information.'

'Why didn't you take it yourself?' I cried. 'Were you scared of it?' I knew it was foolhardy but I could not resist the jibe.

He made a sort of growling sound and raised his fist, so that for a moment I thought he was going to hit me. I flinched.

He regained control. He said very coldly, 'You forget, girl. That madman Roger might have been able to provide a rough location for the crown but nobody was going to find it without help. Sibert's help, and yours.'

'Then why did you not seek us out as Romain did?' I flashed back.

Something in him seemed to snap. *'Because I could not approach it!'* he screamed. Then, his struggle for calm very evident, 'Even if you and Sibert had led me right up to it, I could not have taken it from its hiding place.' He glanced down at the crown, lying at his feet, and I thought I saw a long shudder go through him. 'It all but overwhelms me when I am close to it,' he added, half to himself, 'and here, where its power is far, far stronger and when, before you came, no human hand had touched it for centuries, I knew it would be reluctant to let me near.' He breathed deeply for a few moments. Watching him intently, I saw some fierce struggle within him, as if even now, with his prize at his feet, a part of him was desperate simply to run away.

With a visible effort, he stood his ground.

'I let Romain think he was acting alone but I was watching him all along,' he said. 'I saw the three of you, splashing around out here and letting yourselves get caught by the incoming tide. I saw you *fail*, curse you. Then I slipped away.' He spat into the small waves running over his feet.

'When I returned in the early morning, you and the boy had gone and you had taken the crown, and Romain had set off after you. I followed him. He had let you get away and I had to find him. But both of us failed. He managed to catch you up and he attacked that pale, spindly boy, but somehow you and he managed to fight back and you laid Romain on his back, writhing in agony.' I shut my eyes tightly for a moment. It was an image I could not bear to dwell on. 'Sibert still had the crown,' Baudouin said bitterly. 'I had to think of another way of getting it back.'

'So you killed your nephew and made out that Sibert was a thief and a murderer.' How callous and cold-hearted he was!

'I did,' he agreed. 'Nobody was meant to doubt my word, and when that fat fool Gilbert insisted on hearing what my *witness* had to say, I had to pay Sagar to provide the information.'

I was still having trouble accepting that Baudouin had killed his own nephew. 'But Romain was your heir!' I said. 'You were going to all this trouble to win back Drakelow, but what was the point if nobody would come after you to inherit it?'

'Oh, don't you worry, somebody will,' he said roughly. 'Congratulate me, girl, for I am to be married. For some time I have my eye on the plump and comely daughter of my neighbouring lord, and she has consented to be my wife. She comes from a line of wide-hipped and fertile sisters who all have families of their own, so she will undoubtedly start filling Drakelow's nursery within nine months of our wedding.'

Was this true? Or was it the product of a mind slowly being pressured to implosion? I did not know.

The sea was sucking and pushing at my feet and I was very cold. I was cold on the inside, too, for I kept hearing the echo of his words: *I have killed before and I shall do so again.*

He had just confessed to me that he was a murderer. He had killed Romain and I had just seen him drown Sibert. Oh, Sibert!

I knew that he would not allow me to live.

Without thinking I flung myself sideways out of the circle of crumbling timber posts. I had some idea of running around the perimeter and turning for the shore, where if I outran Baudouin I might be able to hide. I was small and light on my feet and I really thought I had a chance. It was better, anyway, than standing there dumbly and waiting for him to kill me.

I flew round the circle. One post, two posts, then a big wave came galloping in behind me and launched itself at my legs. I stumbled and almost fell, but recovered and ran on, my lungs on fire and the muscles in my legs crying out their pain as I forced a way through the water swirling around the sanctuary. I could see the shore line ahead of me – it looked so far away – and I leapt forward towards it.

He caught me around the knees, launching himself at me so that we both fell into the water. Then he was on top of me, his boot or his fist on the back of my head. My face was under the water and I summoned what was left of my strength to try to jerk it up.

I twisted and wriggled and managed to get my nose above the surface. I sniffed in air but the waves were stronger now, sending up a lot of spray, and I felt the cold bite of sea water as it invaded my nostrils and slid down the back of my throat. I choked and coughed but I was under the water again and it was not the life-saving air that I took in but the swirling, savage water.

I held my breath. I could feel my desperate heart hammering in my chest and blackness was gathering on the edge of my vision. I'm dying, I thought. My mother and father will be so sad...

Suddenly the murderous pressure was off me.

My head shot up out of the water and I took in a huge gulp of air. There was water in my nose, my mouth, my throat, and I coughed, gagged and coughed some more, then I vomited up a great gout of frothy brine. I was on fire. I

318

had never known that salt water burns like flame.

I was on hands and knees, the tide now racing up the shore and threatening to push me back under the water. You have to stand up, I told myself.

Very shakily and unsteadily I did.

Sibert was standing beside the upturned tree stump. Well, he wasn't exactly standing, he was sort of hunched over it.

I splashed over to him.

'Are you alive?' I asked. It was a stupid question, but then I had just seen him drowned.

He neither answered nor turned. He was, I noticed, peculiarly intent and the muscles of his slim back bulged out under his soaking wet tunic...

The water around his knees thrashed and boiled. Then it was still, then it splashed up again.

The next time the movement ceased it did not start again.

After what seemed a very long time, Sibert said, 'He's dead.'

I nodded. 'Yes.' I felt strangely unreal, as if this were a dream.

'He would have killed you,' Sibert went on. 'I had to stop him.'

'Yes,' I said again. Then, belatedly, 'Thank you.'

'That's all right. You saved me, now I've saved you.'

'Yes.' I was puzzled. For one thing, I'd

thought Sibert was dead. For another, how had he managed to overcome a fierce, strong man like Baudouin? 'What happened, Sibert?'

'I took him by surprise,' Sibert said proudly. 'He wasn't expecting an attack.'

'No, you were dead,' I agreed.

'I was lucky,' he went on modestly. 'When I leapt on him he fell against the buried tree bole and, as you'll no doubt have noticed, there are several places on it where branches were once cut off, leaving downward-pointing stumps. I managed to hook his belt on to one of them and after that I just had to push down on him to make sure he didn't manage to release himself.'

'What are we going to do?' I whispered. Shock was affecting me badly. I was shivering so hard that my teeth rattled and I very much wanted to cry.

Sibert took one last look at the dark shape under the water and then left it. He came over to me and put his arm round me. 'We're going ashore to dry off and rest. We'll wait till the tide turns and then we'll come back here, unhook Baudouin's body and let the sea take it. Then we'll go home.'

It sounded wonderful. But we had come here to do a job and if we didn't succeed, Hrype would send us straight back again. The very idea made me weep. 'What about the crown?'

He hugged me. Reaching out for my hand, he put it against the bag that was once more hanging at his waist. 'The crown is safe,' he said. 'When we've dealt with Baudouin, we'll put

320

it back.'

I hardly recognized this new and masterful Sibert. Perhaps saving my life and killing my would-be murderer had at long last changed him from a boy into a man. It was going to take some getting used to but, I thought as, cold and weary, we waded ashore, I thought I might grow to like it.

# TWENTY-TWO

It was a strange ceremony that Sibert and I performed soon after dawn the next morning. Looking back, it seems more like a dream than reality, although I am pretty sure that it did happen...

We were soaked to the skin when we came ashore. Sibert lit a small fire and insisted that we both take off our clothes and dry ourselves. It was very odd, sitting here naked before the welcoming heat, and I don't think I could have done it if it hadn't been for the concealing darkness. Well, and the fact that I'd probably have died of cold otherwise. Sibert made me eat some dried meat and bread, then he held a mug to my mouth and forced me to take all of the hot drink he had prepared. I tasted honey in it and soon I was feeling better.

We slept, or at least I did, curled up in my still-damp clothes but warm in the heat from the fire, which Sibert must have tended all night. I had a very vivid dream in which I opened my eyes to see him, standing on the other side of the fire, with the light of the flames reflecting off something that lay on the ground between us. Something that was circular and made of gold. Sibert looked different – taller, stronger – and the naked man I saw in my dream was utterly different from the pale, cowed and shrivelled boy who had stood in Aelf Fen before his accusers. I thought I saw a sheen of power rising up from the crown, surrounding Sibert in its aura as if bestowing a blessing, and my dreaming self said, 'Your ancestor made it, Sibert. He wants you to have some of its strength. He's trying to help you because he's proud of you for what you've done.'

Sibert did not answer.

He woke me at dawn. The memory of my dream was still too fresh to allow me to look him in the eye and, to my surprise, he seemed similarly affected. I did wonder briefly if it had really been a dream.

He had already kicked out the fire. Now we stood up, left our boots in the sleeping place, descended the low cliff and walked across the foreshore to the sea sanctuary.

The sea was receding but still, as we approached the sanctuary, we were ankle-deep in water. I carefully twisted up my skirt and tied it round my waist; it was so good to be in dry clothes again that I did not want to risk another soaking. Sibert paused to roll up his breeches. Then we went into the sanctuary.

Baudouin was on his side, his stout leather belt still hooked over the stump of branch. Sibert bent down to release him. Together we pushed and dragged the body to the far side of the sanctuary. Soon we were wading in deeper water and the corpse was floating. With a shove, Sibert gave it up to the tide.

We returned to the sanctuary.

We waited until the water had cleared the sands and then, as we had tried to do the previous night, we buried the crown. I found the right place; it was easy, for in my heightened emotional state it seemed to me that a soft purplish-blue light was guiding me, as if the crown were sending out a message to let us know without doubt where it wanted to be. Even after five hundred years, some of the magic of Creoda, greatest of all sorcerers, still lingered.

We dug deep, for, without either of us saying so, it seemed that we both felt the need to do the job really well. It took a long time.

At last we were ready.

Sibert took the crown out of its bag one last time. We both stared at it, wanting to imprint its beauty on our eyes for ever. Then Sibert wrapped it up again and, each of us holding one side, we put it in the deep, dark space beneath the tree stump. Painstakingly we filled in the hole, piling on the sand and tamping it down. We left signs of our activity – we couldn't help it – but we knew we were safe; they would be gone with the next tide, washed clean again so that the crown's location was secure.

Then for the last time we turned our backs on the sea sanctuary and its precious secret and headed for the shore. I looked up into the soft blue sky of very early morning. There was scarcely a breeze and not a cloud to be seen.

It was going to be a lovely day.

Our return to Aelf Fen went without incident except that I developed a blister on the ball of my foot. What irony, I thought; I walked across red-hot coals without taking hurt and yet a long walk, which was really nothing out of the ordinary for someone like me, gives me a blister that burns like hellfire.

We were both apprehensive as we neared our home; Sibert because he would have to confess to Hrype that he had killed Baudouin and I because I knew that, despite whatever Hrype had cooked up to explain my absence, my parents would have been beside themselves with worry.

As it turned out, neither of us need have been so anxious. Hrype accepted Sibert's account of how he had slain a man with a brief nod, the suspicion of a proud smile and the calm words, 'You had no choice, Sibert.' Sibert told me later that Hrype had also seemed satisfied with how we'd reburied the crown. He had said little, according to Sibert, except a brief and mystifying, 'Time will tell.' Nobody I know is nearly as enigmatic as Hrype.

My parents had barely listened to Hrype explaining that I'd gone off with Edild because the morning after Sibert and I slipped out of Aelf Fen on our way to Drakelow, my sister had her baby.

I hurried over to Icklingham as soon as I could to find Goda sitting on the bench by the hearth, Cerdic beside her, with several of her neighbours circling around and satisfying her whims as if she were a queen and they her handmaidens. Honestly, you'd think no woman had ever given birth before! All the same, I had to admire my sister for her sheer cheek and, catching her eye, I gave her a smile that came from the heart.

'Well done,' I said, pushing a way through the chattering women to get to her. 'I'm sorry I wasn't here for the birth and to help you afterwards. Was it...? Did you...?' I felt embarrassed suddenly at the thought of my sister giving birth and I was angry with myself for my foolish prudery. Fine healer *I* was going to make.

Goda confounded me totally by smiling back. 'It was all right,' she said quietly. 'It hurt but it didn't take too long.' Then – for this was the woman who only a short while ago had routinely cursed her husband and thrown clogs at him – she gave the man beside her a loving glance and added, 'I didn't need you afterwards. Cerdic's been looking after me.'

Just at that moment I couldn't think of a

single thing to say. Cerdic, perhaps understanding better than anyone, said gently, 'Go and have a look.' He pointed.

I stood up, walked to the far corner of the little room and found my mother, pink in the face with delight, nursing her first grandchild.

I looked down into the beautiful little face – the baby was a girl – and her eyes opened and stared back. She did not resemble Cerdic – which wouldn't have been too bad as he's a nice-looking man – but, more to the point, she was nothing like Goda.

She looked like Edild.

My mother, watching me study her, smiled. 'Can you see it too?' she asked softly, her finger clutched in the baby's tiny fist.

'Yes. She looks like Edild.'

My mother laughed. 'Yes, I suppose so. But she looks far more like someone else. Someone I nursed as a tiny baby, just as I'm nursing Gelges here.'

Gelges. It meant white swan. What a lovely name...

My mother was still watching me, waiting for me to say something.

I didn't.

Just then Gelges gave a small sound rather like a tired sigh and it was so sweet, so endearing, that involuntarily I held out my arms and my mother put the soft, solid little bundle into them.

Gelges and I considered each other.

My mother said, 'She looks just like you.'

My mother and I stayed with Goda and her little family for another couple of days and then we went home to Aelf Fen. As my mother wisely said, before long Goda was going to have to get used to looking after her house, her husband and her baby by herself, just like any other woman, and the sooner she started, the better.

Life settled down again and resumed its usual pattern. Straight away I went back to my regular sessions with Edild and the joy with which I took up her steadily more challenging lessons was an indication of how much I'd missed them – and her – all the time I was looking after Goda.

I waited, at first nervously, to see if anything would happen. I'm not sure what I was expecting: retribution, I suppose, for Sibert and I had stolen the crown and killed a man. Because of us, Romain de la Flèche as well as his uncle both were dead. We had put the crown back, it seemed successfully, and as time went by and no one came to accuse us, I started to wonder if the crown might be protecting us, just as its long-ago maker made it to protect this land. We had stolen it in the first place, but we had returned it, at considerable risk to ourselves – I still had nightmares about Sibert's drowned body and that awful moment when I tried to gulp air and sniffed in sea water instead – and surely that must count for something.

I kept my eyes and my ears open and in time I learned that many of the great East Anglian lords who had risen against King William had had their lands and their manors restored. I wondered if any one of them had bought his way back into royal favour with anything as extraordinary as the Drakelow crown. I suspected not.

I had no idea what would happen to Drakelow. Baudouin and his heir were both dead and, although he had claimed to be betrothed to his comely heiress, he had not yet wed her or, as far as I knew, impregnated her. No de la Flèche would ever live at Drakelow again.

I pictured the brash, coarse Norman buildings. I made an image in my mind of the long hall that Sibert's ancestors built. Then I saw the cliff fall away into the sea, taking the hall with it. It did not look as if any of Sibert's clan would live there again either.

I supposed that, lacking any other claimant, Drakelow remained the property of the king. Well, all of England belonged to him; that was the Norman way. We just had to accept it.

I have found it a fact of life that if something you really dread goes on not happening, in the end it loses its hold over you and finally you forget about it. I threw myself heart and soul into my work with Edild – she seemed to think that now I had risked death and handled a magical crown I was ready to go up a level in my studies – and I loved almost every moment of my time with her in her fragrant little cottage. Quite often Hrype came to join us and I learned from him, too, as he revealed just a very little of the mysterious heart, soul and spirit that made him what he was.

I grieved for Romain. I knew there had never been any chance of my sweet fantasies ever turning into reality, but all the same he was very often in my mind and I recognized that I truly had loved him, a little.

I thought about what Edild had told me of my web of destiny, in particular what she had said concerning my relationship with my lovers (the thought still made me blush, even when I was quite alone). She'd been right about my being fire and air, and my triumph in the fire pit supported her. Was she also right when she said my friends and my lovers would never feel close to me?

Time would tell.

In the absence of lovers I worked hard on my friendships and especially hard on my closeness to my family. Goda's sunny mood on the day I first went to see her after she had borne her child did not last, I'm sorry to say, although we all agreed that her temperament had improved very slightly with motherhood and I tried to convince myself that the improvement would continue. For now, she tended little Gelges with haphazard but effective care – her vast breasts could have fed five babies and Gelges thrived – and on rare occasions even managed a pleasant word for Cerdic.

My little niece and I saw as much of each other as my busy life allowed. Until she was weaned she had to stay close to her mother, but already I looked forward to the day when I might be allowed to take her off with me while I went about my daily round. If Goda had another child, I thought, then she might well ask – no, *demand* – that I help her by taking Gelges off her hands. It was something to look forward to.

I discovered an unexpected side-effect from my fire-walking: people had started to whisper about me and it seemed that quite a few believed I was a sorceress. I had imagined, if I'd thought about it at all, that they would accept the official verdict, which was that my unburned feet meant that God had protected me in my innocence. I had reckoned without village superstition; we were, after all, very close to our pagan origins and many secretly prayed to the Old Gods. I rather liked this new image of myself.

I saw Sibert often. What we had gone through together had forged a link between us and although he could not compete with the shadowy memory of Romain as far as my romantic interest went, nevertheless he was my friend. I had saved his life and he had saved mine. It's not something you share with many people.

I never heard anyone mention the Drakelow crown.

I thought afterwards that, just before Sibert and I stole it, it had performed the task for which its maker had designed it, for Duke

Robert of Normandy had not invaded but stayed safely on the other side of the narrow seas. It had not had the same success twenty-two years earlier, when the Conqueror had come, but perhaps he had been a truly unstoppable force, beyond even the power of a magic crown.

Such mysteries were not for me; I was far too green an apprentice in my craft to understand them. All the same, it was a comforting thought, as I went tiredly to my bed at the end of a long, hard day, to think of the Drakelow crown deep beneath the sea sanctuary. Others would come roaring up in the dawn light with the aim of taking our land, of that there was no doubt. It was good to think that there was something there to stand in their path.

The fact that I had played a part in ensuring that it was there in its special place, where it was meant to be, felt even better.

# HISTORICAL NOTE

The Norman Conquest of 1066 changed England drastically, although the mass of ordinary people living at subsistence level in the countryside would have been less affected than the men of power and their rich tenants. The reign of William the Conqueror, the first of the Norman kings, was marked by a phase of fortification as the new king made sure of hanging on to his hard-won territory; where before the Anglo-Saxon lords had lived in their long houses in sympathy with their surroundings, now the new men of power built and inhabited military strongholds designed with only one purpose: to remind a conquered people who was now in charge.

The Norman lords and lawmakers brought a new and harsher way of thinking and with them, marching in step, came the priests, the monks and the cathedral-builders. England had long been nominally Christian but now, under the tough new regime, the country entered into the long twilight of the old ways. History was in the main written by men of the Church, the least likely people to describe how the old customs, superstitions, spells and magic lingered on. Their enduring existence can only be guessed at from the other side of the coin: the laws which, in what was meant to be a totally Christian country, went on being passed to suppress the old ways.